"Beware of the writer who says, 'I beyond love. It's knowledge. That what George Eliot had and so, I'm pleased to report, does Elizabeth Tallent. It doesn't matter if she's a good person, or even a nice one. . . . When a writer can tell a story as beautifully, as thoroughly, and with as much knowledge as Elizabeth Tallent possesses, no one should care." —Valerie Martin, *New York Times Book Review*

"Driving, furious, erotic, gilded, the sentences flying at you like arrows. . . . Her book is a meditation on the state of marriage." —*Tin House*

"Tallent's characters are most nearly themselves, because of or in spite of love, and that is the rich truth of this book." —*Oregonian*

"This collection of stories in the American realist tradition has an adventurous, untethered feeling, with wide-ranging locales and points of view. . . . Tallent's assured voice is a pleasure to follow through this book. . . . An ambitious and wide-ranging set of stories that creates empathy for most of its characters due to Tallent's generous imagination." —*Kirkus Reviews*

"Elizabeth Tallent is, and always has been, a vivid, meticulous, and astutely inviting writer. These new stories vitally tell us how things are for us, in the most acute and memorable ways. Her ear is perfect; her gaze searing and unmistakable." —Richard Ford

"All I can say is, it's about time. It's about time for Elizabeth Tallent's work to return to bookstores so that a larger audience can know about the world she's been building, or discovering, in Mendocino. Of course the first pleasure here is the glitter and darkness of the prose only Tallent can produce; but the profounder gift in these stories is the author's empathy, a tireless empathy, her knowledge of her characters' peculiar entitlements and pangs and assumptions. Readers will find themselves inhabiting fully, in 3-D, because Ms. Tallent's prose is like a virtual-reality machine—the lives of a dozen or so human beings they'd never imagined themselves knowing, let alone loving."

—Louis B. Jones, author of *Innocence* and *Ordinary Money*

"Elizabeth Tallent's style is so distinctive, and it's the kind of writing I so enjoy—never obvious, full of complex thought and perception, so boldly ambitious."

—Tessa Hadley, author of *Clever Girl*

"In her fourth collection, Tallent explores the spaces between people through ten expertly crafted stories. . . . Tallent's collection offers a smart, thought-provoking study of desire and disappointment." —*Publishers Weekly*

"The characters in these stories have been around the block a few times. They are often exes. Their sexuality has settled into one column or another, their bad childhoods have been surmounted, even their ghosts have evaporated behind them. But they are no match for Tallent, who, in a finely articulated style, shows herself to be quite deft at throwing monkey wrenches into the machinery of complacence."

—Carol Anshaw, author of *Carry the One*

Mendocino Fire

Mendocino
Fire

STORIES

ELIZABETH TALLENT

HARPER ● PERENNIAL

NEW YORK ● LONDON ● TORONTO ● SYDNEY ● NEW DELHI ● AUCKLAND

HARPER ● PERENNIAL

Grateful acknowledgment is made to the editors of the publications
where the following stories appeared:
"The Wrong Son" appeared in *The Threepenny Review*, Summer 2009.
"Tabriz" appeared in *The Threepenny Review*, Summer 2007,
and in *The Pushcart Prize: Best of the Small Presses* (2008).
"Mystery Caller" appeared in *The Threepenny Review*, Fall 2001.
"Eros 101" appeared in *Tin House*, Summer 2004,
and in *Best of Tin House: Stories* (2006).
A different version of "Nobody You Know" appeared in *Boulevard*, 2001,
as "Woman Weighing Pearls."
"The Wilderness" appeared in *The Threepenny
Review*, Spring 2012, and in *The Best American Short Stories 2013*.
"Never Come Back" appeared in *The Threepenny Review*, Spring 2010,
and in *The PEN/O. Henry Prize Stories 2011*.
"Mendocino Fire" appeared in *ZYZZYVA*, July 2014.
"Narrator" appeared in *The Threepenny Review*, Winter 2015.

A hardcover edition of this book was published by HarperCollins Publishers in 2015.

HarperCollins books may be purchased for educational, business,
or sales promotional use. For information please e-mail the
Special Markets Department at SPsales@harpercollins.com.

FIRST HARPER PERENNIAL EDITION PUBLISHED 2016.

Designed by Jo Anne Metsch

Library of Congress Cataloging-in-Publication Data has been applied for.

ISBN 978-0-06-241035-1 (pbk.)

16 17 18 19 20   OV/RRD   10 9 8 7 6 5 4 3 2 1

for GLORIA

Contents

Mendocino
Fire

The Wrong Son

Among the son's *bright fucking ideas*, that last summer they worked together, was the notion that since there was good money in sportfishing they ought to start taking out parties of tourists. Shug could savor a rank cigar, resting up his bad shoulder while doctors and lawyers baited hooks, and when a senator failed to reel in a big Chinook Shug could grin around the last skunky inch and salt the wound with "Wave bye-bye to your wallhanger, son." Nate figured guys like that would secretly dig the condescension and come back for more, because no matter what he said or how he treated people Shug was indulged, a dispensation Nate had not inherited. He did get his share of the Dawe looks—lank black hair that came to a widow's peak in front, large homely ears, definite jaw—but the mix could go different ways, in Nate a semicomic near miss, in his father strong-boned, remorseless beauty that misleadingly suggested great depth of character. Women, sure—the beauty of women was supposed to cause trouble, but Nate would not have believed such havoc could be wreaked by a man if he hadn't witnessed the consequences firsthand. He was sometimes asked by unsmiling women how his dad was doing these days and had figured out that the right, if fallacious, answer was "Not so good." Once as a kid Nate was given a packet of red licorice by a high-heeled out-of-town-looking woman who said earnestly, "I know he's your father but he's a liar." And then: "You know better than to tell your mom where you got that, right? Yeah, I can see you do."

Fishing guide was a comedown, and Shug surely viewed it as such, but Nate's plan held out the promise of redeeming pleasures. The same stories that caused Nate to grind his teeth lightly together—the freighter lit up like a nighttime skyscraper bearing down on Shug through fog, the mast clustered with barnacles that flaked upward as a whirlwind of monarch butterflies, the shark in whose sliced-open belly Shug found a seagull— would be taken for gospel by tourists eager to experience the real Mendocino. If there were wives along, Shug could charm them—saying this, Nate suffered a familiar pang. Shug did more than charm. He would grin back at the big black sunglasses hiding the wives' curiosity, and at some point he and one of the wives would rendezvous in a fifty-dollar room with a factory seascape over the creaky bed, but Nate could handle this if it meant saving the boat, and whether Shug acknowledged it or not they were in dire straits along with every other fisherman they knew, government regulations hemming them in on every side. This last was a good point to make to Shug, who hated the federal government worse than Vietnamese abalone poachers, worse even than bankers. Reborn as a party boat, the *Louise* would be consistently booked, and they could rely, day by day, on the money coming in, a certainty no Dawe had ever before possessed, and worth a try, Dad, right?

"Over my dead body."

Which phrase caused Nate to tread guiltily, eyes averted, past that dead body cast up on the pebbled beach of consciousness.

Like most who count on intuition Shug had his ritual, resting scarred knuckles against the bone over his dark eye and waiting. His green eye was ordinary, but the tortoiseshell one saw down through the world's surfaces to its deep, shifting currents of luck, and even when other boats came home empty the *Louise* was nearly always in the fish. When, seven years old, Nate first said he wished *he* had a weird eye, the confession met with the rebuke, mild for Shug, that he was imagining things.

This was on the *Louise*, a diamond afternoon shattering across the ocean, waves hurrying at the pace of a fire-drawn crowd, Nate captive in childhood, in an old life jacket, arms dangling like a fat boy's, meaning his tall graceful father was even more likely to lash out than usual because he was irked by awkwardness as a cat is by wet paws. The dirty, mildewy, sunwarmed hug of the life jacket braced Nate for confrontation. He was seven and alone. This was life then, this bravery, this scaredness, this love of the truth in your possession, the thing you had seen that set you apart and somehow *was* you. You and no one else. That morning when his mother had squatted to fasten the buckles of his life jacket, Nate had studied the center parting in her red hair and seen the jog the parting made to accommodate a pink mole, and this revelation, that his mother had flaws previously undisclosed to him, drove home the extent of her vulnerability, and he would have given anything to protect her from his father's hectoring, his father saying *Don't fucking teach him that, no real fisherman wears one, fall overboard and you're dead so you don't fucking fall.* His mother said *He's a kid, kids have accidents.* As if Nate was not listening she said *Say he falls.* Nate tried to get in *I won't fall*, but already (and it was not like her: she was not an insister) she was saying again *Say he falls, Shug, tell me what would you do then*, a protest, a demand, a bargain because she was letting his father take him, entrusting his life to his father and his father did not say what she wanted him to say, *I would find him, of course I would find him*, but then Shug never said what she wanted him to, and it was dismaying that she still nursed reckless hopes. Now, on the boat, Nate reasoned that if Shug was wrong about his own eyes, as he plainly was, he could be wrong about other things, and that in the gap between what his father insisted was true and what *was* true Nate's private perceptions could take root and thrive. He stood there in his sissy life jacket confronting this prospect, with scarcely time to rejoice before the big rough hand cupped his head and his dad said *All right now? Back to work*, as if Nate worked as hard as he did, as if they were together all day long. As they ended up being.

Another memory, harder to account for, in which there was no life jacket: Once when he had made some mistake his dad had picked him up under the arms and swung him back and forth over the edge of the boat, out over the dazzling drop. Below the half-moons of white rubber capping his Keds an abyss reeled past, scintillae shuttling back and forth at the speed of panic. Nate hung there, legs dangling, hating with such concentration that he feared his father would sense it and, as punishment, let go. Instead his feet thumped down on the deck and Shug said *There you are*, as if this were a natural initiation into terror and

Nate should have expected it. And as if he, the father, had performed it ably and even with a measure of affection. And Nate stood there, and among the things he felt was love, as if what had happened had been pure rescue.

Nate's friends didn't like when he started in on Shug, first because they believed in keeping family shit in the family, second because Shug took them out on the boat for their birthdays and asked *How's it going* and if there was a problem with some girl he told them what to do with an authority Nate alone understood was totally bogus, since Shug hadn't ever stayed around for problems but simply disappeared until the woman, whoever she was, concluded it was over. Still, when things got rough for him at home Nate's best friend, Petey Crews, would say he wished Shug was his father. His screwed-up longing caused Nate to glance away: not his job to set anybody straight. Stoned the night of senior prom, Petey said it was mutual and Shug had told him he got the wrong son. What the fuck did that mean, the wrong son? Petey tried to wriggle out of it. *Shug likes a good time, right? You gotta admit you're not a lot of laughs.* Maybe that had something to do with working for a living and maybe Petey should try it, Nate said, and then report back about the laughs. Petey said *Nate, man, you're too hard on your old man, you need to—.* It could have been Nate's look that caused him to break off, or the quicksand shame of condescension going awry, but whatever it was Petey said *It's just we're more alike, him and me.* Nate thought *Both motherfuckers.* If he had said that aloud the friendship would have ended then and there, and not because he had called Petey a motherfucker, but because he had called Shug one. But it was Petey who couldn't leave it alone. *You hate fishing, while me, I*

would fucking love it, that's all Shug wants, a son to love what he loves,
out on the ocean every single day, who gets to live like that, only you,
right, the last of the last? On your own, live or die, make it or don't
make it, it's down to you and your dad and how hard you work and
whether your luck holds and, man, I would fucking love that.

For months afterward they didn't talk, but it was only when
Rafe told him about Petey's enlistment that Nate understood
how wrong things had gone. He got emails from Iraq that
sounded as if they were still best friends, but it seemed cruel to
write back about his wife and his baby, and besides, thinking
of Petey aroused an obscure and guilty sense of finality. He just
didn't want any more to do with the guy, and he let the emails
accumulate unanswered.

But before that, while they were in high school, the best times
were Nate and Petey Crews jammed into the cab of Rafe
Figueredo's truck, talking about driving down to the city or
farther, LA, Baja, Austin, *If we want to we can just take off,* ending
up at the little beach they thought of as their own, the brothers
Owen and Jeff Jennings and Boone Salazar there already along
with Boone's girl, brown-eyed Annie Brown leaning back on
one arm in the damp sand, tossing mussel shells into the drift-
wood bonfire for the glassy *tink* of breakage, Nate liking that,
not sure why, standing there nursing his longneck, another Saturday burning down to embers, wind from the west pasting
his shirt to his skin, his abs impressive, he'd gone too long between haircuts but he thought he looked pretty good, he liked
brown eyes and it would be nice having a girlfriend, telling his
mom they were thinking about getting married, his troubles
recounted to somebody who cared, who would argue it wasn't

right that Nate *worked for* his dad when he should be an equal partner, with an equal say in business decisions, if you could call the *Louise* a business.

Nate turned nineteen, then twenty, and when somebody wanted to talk about him in town they said *You know—Shug Dawe's boy, that's out on the boat with Shug. Thought he might go away to college but he never did.* In the Smoke River fashion the *thought* was unattributed, detached from any particular thinker. In Smoke River a thought was scarcely conceived before it was presented as common knowledge. That way if the thought turned out to be wrong nobody could be held responsible; that way the basis for an assertion was clouded. Nate *had* wanted to get out, had imagined the friendly anonymity of crowded lectures, secondhand textbooks, girls with ponytails bending over laptops, calls where he explained he couldn't come home over the weekend because there was this big paper due Monday. If he went home he would be asked to help, spend the day on the boat maybe, and the old life would take hold and insist that it alone was real and nothing out there, certainly no other means of making a living, would ever come close, and the fantasized Nate, the Nate who had gotten away, would have to stay gone long enough to build up immunity, and how long would that take? Shug swept an arm toward the horizon, dove gray below slate gray, mother-of-pearl cloud scrolling toward a waning sun made of naked pink light, and said *Another rough day at the office.*

As close as he ever came to saying *beautiful.*

Even as fishermen went bankrupt the tourist trade flourished. From the wide spectrum of out-of-towners to hate, Shug singled

out for particular venom the abalone divers who flocked to
Smoke River each August and stood around their SUVs hoisting
beers, wetsuits unzipped to display big white bellies. Inevitably
one or more of their photos would appear in the Smoke River
Sentry in their new guise, as drowned men.

More skillful were the Vietnamese poachers whose fine-
boned clever faces never made the front page, though sometimes
one of their vans with the tinted windows figured in a photo
with Fish and Game guys swarming over it, and their names, Lu
and Tran and Vinh and Ng, chimed through the court report,
which detailed the number of abalone taken and the fines and
jail sentences assessed, but as Shug said, for every thieving Tran
they caught, a hundred drove home to San Francisco or Sac
with a fortune in abalone. They sold to Chinese dealers who,
with abalone increasingly scarce, paid not by the pound but by
the gram. The poachers ran calculated risks for serious money,
five, ten, twenty grand worth of abalone in the coolers inside the
black vans parked at night near remote coves. Within, the funk
of unwashed maleness, neatly stashed diving gear, glossy black
heads protruding from cheap sleeping bags—so said Boone Salazar, a classmate whose boastfulness Nate had always distrusted.
Boone was hired by Fish and Game when Shug put a word in for
him, and had fallen into the habit of stopping by the house for
a beer with Shug, which seemed funny at first, a guy Nate's age
hanging out with Nate's old man. But they were two of a kind,
Boone and Shug, inclined when drunk to taunt each other in
the glottal stops and high-pitched whines of made-up Vietnamese. Maybe it was reassuring, having another person echo your
racist ignorance: Nate didn't want to think too hard about it.

Nobody had been doing well this summer, but this morning the salmon had started biting so hard before dawn that they

didn't have time *to shit, shower, or shave*, Shug said, and when Nate poured the last of the coffee from the thermos and handed the cup to his dad, Shug said, "Kept up with me pretty good." Under its mask of salt spray Nate's face warmed at the praise; relief swept in, as if he had at last been recognized as the right son. As if they could go from here, and disappointment in him would never again cloud Shug's expression or turn him sarcastic. Money worries were eating at Shug, and on a boat there is no escaping somebody else's foul mood. Late at night when Shug was topside, bullshitting on the radio, Nate sought comfort by imagining different girls from high school straddling him, their hair swinging forward, palms on his chest, the fantasy heightened if he didn't summon a particular girl but passively awaited a face or a voice. That the face, when it appeared, belonged more and more often to a girl named Ollie surprised him. He had never gone out of his way to talk to Ollie, nobody did, but sometimes they had ended up together on the graffitied boulder jutting from the weedy slope descending to the football field, the boulder the designated site for pairings permitted nowhere else, the refuge where she set about dismantling his naïveté. What had gone wrong in Newfoundland was going wrong all over and within fifty years every fishery on the planet would collapse, did he *get* that? Or: the tsunami that was destined for the coast would roll right over the cliffs and plunge across the field below with its bright scatter of seven-year-old soccer players jogging into the wind. They sat on their boulder smoking and picturing drowning second graders. Ollie was their school's oddball star, the kind of student teachers wanted too much from: flashes suited her, intuitions, but not structure, not obligation or rules or any voice urging responsibility or *goals in life*. Boundaries offended her, a fact that partly explained why she systematically violated his, pinching the cigarette without asking, tipping her head back to exhale, comically vamping. He could not overcome his sense that she was a disaster, but this was not entirely off-putting. Ollie clasped her knees in her arms and rocked, or she tinkered with her hair, fooling with this project on her head, tatty homegrown security blanket. Faithful as she seemed in her obscure devotion to him, she was rumored to sleep around, and Petey Crews added her name to the boys' john's tally of girls who gave head, but Nate didn't believe it, not this girl who wanted to crew on a Greenpeace boat, whose T-shirt claimed *Fur Is Murder*, who believed the world needed saving, starting with him, Nate. He remembers asking about her dreads once. *Why do you want to look like you don't give a shit?* Had she been hurt by the question, had she cared what he thought? He was pretty sure she had, even if the realization was late—more than a year late—in coming. After graduation she must have left town. She had never talked about what things were like at home, and he can't remember any mother or other family showing up at high school events. Her dad had died when she was nine, and another girl would have incorporated the tragedy into her persona, but Ollie told him no details. Nate conjured her expert theft of his cigarette, her chin tilted up, the crawl of smoke from her parted lips, but this version was too accurate, friendly, failing to mine the erotic potential of her vehemence, and fuck this, he was too old to live in such close quarters with his dad, two berths angled toward each other in the V of the bow, the iron woodstove crowding the space even more and smelling sickeningly of the boot polish Shug had dabbed on its scratches. *Jesus, get a fucking life*, he imagined a good friend telling him, but what friend? Petey Crews was in Iraq, Rafe worked for Aboriginal Lumber. Nights off, when Nate made it to the inn at the crossroads south of town, its gingerbread eaves laced with Christmas-tree lights nobody ever bothered to take down and its marquee promising live music, he had that feeling of waiting for someone, but it wasn't clear who until, one night, Rafe slid onto the next bar stool saying, "N Dawg," Petey's old greeting. After they had gone over what they knew about Petey and how he was doing, Nate asked Rafe if he remembered a girl named Ollie something.

"Who had a thing for you."

"She had a thing?"

Rafe smiled down at his beer.

Nate made sure he could be heard over the music: "I was thinking she might of left town, right? Nothing to keep her here. I mean, why're *we* still around?"

The crease at the corner of his mouth deepened as Rafe appreciated his beer. "'Member Annie Brown? A year behind us? Teaches second grade now."

"Sure. Annie. Went out with Boone Salazar."

"Not anymore," Rafe said, and his left hand did a stiff-fingered hula till Nate identified the gleam and said, keeping his tone warm, "What the fuck."

Rafe said, "At the county courthouse over in Ukiah. Spur of the moment or I would've called." In high school they had vowed to be there for each other, to work it out so they each got a shot at best-man-dom, Rafe and Nate and Petey Crews, but Nate didn't hear any real apology in Rafe's tone, and his embarrassed sense of exclusion, disguised by rapping the bar for another couple of beers, drove home the sadness of their having gone separate ways. Petey had been the glue, Petey had seemed to have the most at stake in their comradeship and had gone to great lengths to keep them entertained, or as entertained as they could be in Smoke River.

This luminous afternoon when their luck turned for the better, Nate said, "I guess we ought to get back to it." The hard morning had left Shug's face sweaty and sunburned, his pulse tripping where a vein swelled in his temple, this visibly hardworking vein striking Nate as dangerous. But the veins that were really troublesome were deep in the brain, he told himself, not right out there in the open. "Dad?" "Give me a minute"—not an answer Shug had ever voiced before. "My damn shoulder hurts. You go ahead"—two more things Shug had never said. What it came down to was that time was taking its toll, and at least for this one radiant day he couldn't keep up with his son.

Past midnight now, and Nate hoped Shug had done the smart thing and gone to bed instead of staying up swapping lies on the radio. In the ice hold's echoing chill, his two or three different and overlapping shadows flaring in the corners as the fluorescence quickened, Nate's boots imprinted a melting black meander as he crossed back and forth, slinging fish into the silver dune, tired enough that the prospect of sleep made him want to sink to his knees in the ice like one of those climbers yielding to death on Everest. He clicked off the light before climbing to the deck for a last look around. They were far enough from shore to drift for the night and the *Louise* had settled into near silence. Below in the fo'c'sle he found Shug asleep, longish black hair fanned across the ticking of the pillow, tattered and filthy, that he refused to part with or let Louise wash because he believed it was lucky. Disgusting, Nate said, but his mother laughed and said it could be worse, what if he had lucky Jockey shorts? The shushing of the sea against the hull turned the space chapel-like, and the need to keep quiet as he undressed made Nate feel like a good child, respectful, or as if he was in the presence of his dead father, feeling what he was supposed to feel.

Not that night but the next, Nate woke to the awareness that Shug's bunk was empty. "Hey, Dad? Where'd you get to?" The deck gleamed back at the moon, the day's blood sluiced away, Shug working while Nate slept: walk barefoot the length of the boat and your feet would stay clean as a newborn babe's. Nate retrieved the toilet seat and clapped it on the bucket, the seat an old wooden one, paint rubbed away in a bottom-shaped arc, his dad's arse and his, any other son would have conceded no more than a postcard, Santa Fe, Sydney, some lawless postmark north of the Arctic Circle. Nate emptied the bucket over the side.

"Dad?"

An arm extended from the door of the cabin, the hand resistless as a dead thing when Nate gathered it up, when he crouched saying, "No, no," his fingers against the inside of the wrist finding nothing, hoping, finding nothing. Nate let shock carry him a short way into death after his father by neither moving nor blinking, concentrating on the death in his father's face but not knowing what it was like or how to go deeper, to take part in this death that intolerably excluded you and left you hanging. Then stupefaction as the pulse flailed against your fingertips and the need to make sure you weren't deceived by the force of longing. The sea slid past, the moon poured down, and Shug sat up sick and disheveled with a glare that held Nate responsible.

"I think you fell, Dad. Fell and banged your head. Hold on, hold on, don't be thrashing or you could hurt yourself worse."

In trying to get him to lie back Nate was reminded that Shug was a big man, his back broader across than his son's and showing a distinct slide and play when he worked shirtless, a bunching and cording along his forearm when he threaded the hook into the herring and trimmed its tail till the glint of metal was perceptible, baitfish and hook coequal, no excess for salmon to snatch unscathed. On first demonstrating the technique to Nate, he had said *This is sex. Nothing to spare, no little bit to nibble off. The beauty of it: it's all hook.* Nate had been what, nine? Shocked. Hiding it.

"You got to lie back down, Dad."

Nate's boots squeaking against the deck, the two men struggled in moonlight strong enough to contract the pupils in Shug's devastated glare. The core of bright mind he had left refused to trust his son.

Even now: refused.

Under his dirty T-shirt, Shug's collarbones were set against him like bull's horns. Gaining secure footing at last, Nate levered his weight into his dad's bad shoulder, and when he yielded his fury was terrifying, Shug gaping up from the deck with his hair strewn across his sweat-polished temples and crazy disbelief in his eyes at having been handled thus. This wrong somehow whistled up more wrong and Nate bent close to say savagely, "You're fucked up, Dad. Now let me do what I need to."

Nate called from the hospital in Eureka to tell Louise that she should come as soon as she could. Absolutely, the doctor was the best. Yeah, a bypass, kind of thing they do all the time, they said it takes four or five hours and Shug's chances were good but they don't tell you more than that cause they don't want to be liable.

He had resolved not to lie for the sake of reassurance, though the impulse was strong. Nate rested his knuckles against his brow, then recognized his father's gesture for summoning the right answer and dropped his hand, as embarrassed as if he'd stolen something small and personal from Shug. He wasn't sure what to do and whether he should hang around here in the hospital or get back to the harbor where he had left the *Louise*. Nate thought of her as knowing nothing about the boat, but his mother answered that he should stay where he was, the catch could wait until tomorrow, there were plenty of buyers in Eureka and it would all work out. He had expected her to fall apart but she calmly went on. Night driving was hard for her and she wasn't going to rush out the door. Nate heard her light a cigarette, and then she said it was ironic that it wasn't her heart attack, she was the smoker. Nate knocked his forehead against the wall, needing to bump up against something that behaved exactly as expected, and she said she would leave early and get there by ten or eleven. When there was no reply she said, "Are you crying, honey? You did fine. You got the boat in to the nearest harbor, you got to the hospital. Nothing to blame yourself for." At her saying this, he discovered he'd feared she would hold him responsible for Shug's overexertion. Without meaning to, he had absorbed his father's sense that she could not handle things, but now he got it: she had always handled things, she had seen and understood and had been dealing with god knows how much truth they believed they had kept from her. The thought that came to him was *All that fucking work*. Whose? Theirs. Theirs as a family. He was astonished to the point of tears—more tears. Whatever he confessed would be absorbed and answered in this same intimate, practical tone that wanted only to figure out what they should do next. Treasure was within reach, the treasure of being listened to and honestly forgiven, but what he came up with was "Mom, I'm so dirty. Right from the boat. I stink," and she answered that he should find the men's and wash as best he could because he had a long night ahead of him. He should wash his face in cold water. He'd see, that would help.

He told her goodbye and was tapped on the shoulder. Nate could go in for a couple minutes before they put Shug under. He was led through a series of hallways into the room where his father lay on a gurney, his black hair hidden, his large ears jutting from a crinkled shower cap. Against the crisp gown Shug's windburned forearms, the backs of his hands scribbled with fishhook scars, looked more beat-up than ever. He was not sure how he had come to be here; he was balking at the notion of surgery and would have walked out if he could have gotten to his feet, but they had doped him with something that left him subdued and lost. The heart attack and Nate's rough handling had vanished. Apprehensively Nate took Shug's hand and said *You're gonna do fine, Dad*, shocked by the grateful response, Shug's big-knuckled fingers interlacing with his, their hands clasping, tightening, holding fast. Their sustained silence made the nurse frown when she returned, as if they should have been using this time to say last things. In the waiting room Nate found, in a corner, a shabby wing chair, upholstery already so far gone he didn't worry about the stench on his clothes rubbing off. It must be destined for replacement soon, this chair. Hospitals didn't usually tolerate the threadbare companionability of long use. Throughout the murmuring public night people came and went, speaking the cryptic language of anguished uncertainty and, once or twice, breaking down and crying, for which Nate pitied them in his sleep.

"Good news," a male nurse said, waking Nate. "Your dad

did great! He did fantastic! You can go in and visit. Frankly some people seem a little taken aback but I told them there's a lot of mileage left in that handsome old man. But who listens to me."

With Shug housebound, Nate was able to take out a couple of persuasive Sacramento lobbyists for several illicit jaunts, and the lobbyists let some friends in on the secret, and those friends told others. Getting caught with scuba gear and abalone would mean a steep fine, suspended fishing license, even jail time, but the lobbyists basked in the risk like it was sunshine. When they went back to Sacramento, Nate figured, he'd better do a couple days' hard fishing to account for the cash in case the IRS or Shug ever ran a cold eye over the books. He was alone, leaning to toss a bucket of refuse, when a wave lolloped into the bow and the *Louise* shrugged him into the sea. Opening his eyes underwater, he had a vision of fish guts unknitting in a bumbling cloud. He slid down as if he had let go of a rope and the speed of his descent scared him into kicking. He surfaced in breathable light, scales gumming his hair and lashes. He spat and gagged. Ten minutes to hypothermia, the cold already searing, and how far had he been carried, and take a breath, take a big breath, here it comes. Concentrating underwater, he scraped his toes down his heel, shedding one sluggish boot, then the other. He surfaced and the shadow of a gull rumpled interestedly across his head, followed by another wave. He strove against the cataract and lost, borne backward into a trough rolling with echoes, and despite this setback he felt his body coming back after long years' absence, gathered and intent and smoothly useful, his soul right here too, brilliantly distinct, a thing that could be torn from him, and he wished to cradle and save it, his soul, and to do that he had only to swim, he was for once wholly aligned with necessity, rejoicing in the clear, clear light of live or die, taking pleasure in his strength, given a stinging outline by the cold, *stroke, breathe, stroke*, narrowing in on what he needed to do next, which was to swim around and take hold of the rungs and climb. A Jacob's ladder, wooden rungs on sturdy ropes. There she was, a neat small craft, handsomely white in the early radiance, illumined from behind so that he noted the opalescence of spindrift within her shadow, the changeable, suddenly darkened, redoubled green of a wave sliding through the tent of the boat's shadow and casting a shattered pearliness up through the shadow into the bright air, where it floated in a brief-lived haze. No boat used for trawling salmon had a ladder. Potbellied, arrogant, the lobbyists had been in such bad shape it was hard to believe they wanted to dive, and it wasn't a pretty sight watching them clamber up that ladder, but now they were about to save his ass. Without the ladder he would have been treading water between the swells, keeping the *Louise* in sight though she was no use to him, staring at her as long as he could because she was the one known thing, the last human thing out there with him.

In the cabin, whose disorder proved it was no longer Shug's domain, Nate found a change of clothes, his dad's, and washed his face and rinsed his mouth clean of brine with bottled water, rubbing his hair dry with a rag saturated with engine oil. To his scoured senses the world was a glittering, reeling heaven of sensation: he would forever after associate the smell of engine oil with the shock of being alive. Elation like this wouldn't last long—he knew even a minor setback could confound it, by introducing reality—but once the *Louise* was docked, the gladness was still there, and in hopes of sustaining it he stopped in at the Harbor Cafe on the wharf. Leaning back in his booth, he greeted the approach of the waitress with a smile inspired more by his own exhilaration than by her familiarity, and this smile, which wasn't about her, which suggested a rowdy, causeless pleasure in being alive, caught her off guard. Her hair was a blond ponytail falling not down her back but across her shoulder, as if she'd drawn it forward to show off its length. She had something in her left eye, and the compulsive blinking made her feel ridiculous. In her distraction she lost his name and sought it in a quick inner stammer of guesses. Blinking, she poured coffee into the cup he nudged forward, and he beat her to it. "Ollie."

Then he said something she was never to understand. He said, "There you are."

It wasn't Shug's heart that gave out, it was Louise's, in her sleep. *Peaceful*, people said, and *Such luck she lived long enough to hold the baby.*

Nate and Ollie and the baby lived in a trailer set on cinderblocks behind the house that was now Shug's alone, in a yard knee-deep in thistles and sorrel and wild radish that Ollie resolved every spring to turn into an organic garden, but before they knew it it was midsummer and that plan, like their others, withered into bemused postponement. Sometimes it was Ollie who said wearily *Look at this place*, sometimes it was Nate, coming home exhausted and hoping for some gesture from her that would compensate for his frustration and the weirdness of having to pay rent to his own father and his fear that he would never get them out of this trailer into a real house. Where had it gone, the scruffy dreadlocked rebelliousness of that girl on the boulder? If she was tamed, was she even the same girl? They were trapped; the future was closing down fast and soon would shut them out altogether. Up to her to convince him otherwise, to reason with, comfort, and inspire him, but how? He said (and regretted it during the saying) that there must have been a time when the prospect of giving him a blow job didn't turn her stomach. At that, the girl on the boulder would have turned on him the Medusa glare of murderous feminism, but she was gone. In a clearing in the trailer's mess the baby sat and blinked and sucked, muzzled by his binkie. It got so the only time they heard each other laugh was when they hunkered down to baby level and adopted funny voices, playing roles they had somehow assigned each other, Nate a talking bear with a hankering for pie, Ollie a vain, dim-witted fairy. Before long their friends with kids started to shake their heads. *Indulge that baby's every wish, let him think your lives revolve around him, and you're creating a monster:* such was the advice directed at Nate and Ollie, who shrugged and smiled. *I pity you two guys,* Rafe announced one stoned midnight when Ollie and Nate both jumped up at a bad-dream whimper from the bedroom, *if it ever comes to working out joint custody.* Rafe didn't have a big mouth usually, but Nate kicked him out for that remark and volunteered, because Ollie was crying, that Rafe was an asshole and jealous besides, and what had happened to Rafe and Annie was never going to happen to them. Which only made Ollie set her two fists against her face, her elbows poked out as if she wanted to punch her own eyes.

He pried her wet fists away, but she wouldn't talk.

Fourteen-hour days for days on end, he worked. Let *her* work, now. Let her pick away at the crazy knot of resistance to him that had tied itself in secret. He didn't know why it had, but it had.

Left over from the brief spellbound time that had followed

his finding her in the café, she had one trick, and when their drought had gone on long enough—almost too long to permit backtracking—she used it, turning to Nate and saying, "What if it was the last time we were ever going to see each other and you knew it, how would you fuck me, what would you do?"

She had taken a chance. He rested rough hands—almost as gnarly as his dad's—on either side of her jaw, and gazing past her everyday self to the deep-down soul-shelter where betrayal stirred—they both knew she was not entirely pretending—he said "I would kill you" with something like the ferocity she needed.

Petey Crews was back from Iraq, and Rafe said they needed to celebrate, the three of them, hit the beach, that little cove where they used to hang out, make a bonfire and get high and drink some beer.

Petey and Nate got an early start and were already drunk, so Rafe drove Nate's truck, hauling hard at the wheel as if caught off guard by each curve. Jammed together in the cab they were not as easy as they had once been—they had lost the hang of shoulder-to-shoulder intimacy. Rafe kept wanting to know if he should turn now—was this the road to the cove?—and they all three squinted at the road snaking out of the dusk, their disorientation a fall from grace, each separately determined to ignore this failure and do what he could to regain the high school sense of rightness, because without it who were they, what had they become? This had been their kingdom—this crescent of nondescript beach, streamers of foam borne toward them, flung high, disintegrating, drained away in pebble-glittering rills. The moon. The companionable shapes of dunes embracing the dead end that served for a parking lot. Where there was, gradually looming into visibility, another vehicle, a black van with opaque windows and mud-obscured license plate. "Don't fucking tell me," Rafe said.

They got out and prowled around the van.

"Nobody in there now," Nate said.

"How do you know?" Petey drank and wiped his mouth, drank again and flung the bottle away, but that was a good thing, not at the van, away into the dark.

"Tracks and scuff marks going away but none coming back," Nate said.

"Tonto."

"Let's just leave it," Rafe said. "Go further down the beach. Make our fire."

Once the fire was sending seething mares' tails of sparks upward, Petey said, "Isn't it too dark for them to be out there?"

"Using lights, maybe," Rafe said.

"If they were using lights, wouldn't we see them?"

"Or they saw us, driving up."

"Shug wants to go out early. I am so screwed. I haven't been this drunk in forever," Nate said.

They couldn't help watching the surf while they drank.

"Here he comes," Rafe said.

Ushered onto the beach by a gentle wave, the slender figure advanced with a hampered frog-footed delicacy, his raft rasping and hissing across the sand. Pausing, he slid his mask onto the top of his head, revealing a pale oval face rimmed in sleek black and aimed in their direction. When he moved, points and glimmers from their fire skidded across his oily wetsuit. He set down a bag whose clatter they could hear from where they sat.

Petey said, "Too heavy to carry, the greedy fuck."

"Gonna be more than one of them," Rafe said, but they waited and no others emerged from the surf.

"He's alone," Nate said.

"Dangerous diving alone," Petey observed.

"You know, Fish and Game really messes with these guys," Rafe said. "Hits them with these ridiculous fines, basically ruins their families. Bankrupts 'em. Five or more over the limit means they go to jail, and, Jesus, it's not like they're dealing heroin. They're just trying to get by."

"All I know is, Shug really hates them," Nate said.

Petey ground his cigarette out in the sand and got to his feet. "This is for Shug."

Rafe said, "Petey. Come on—who is he hurting."

But Petey was already halfway to the black figure, who tried to run, tripping on his fins, curling up with his arms wrapped around his black bulb of a skull when Petey drove the toe of his boot once, twice, again into the small of his back, then moved around to the head clasped in slender arms, Rafe and Nate pounding across the sand, Rafe screaming, "Not his head," Nate screaming too, unsure in the end whether the diver had made any sound at all, and when Petey backed off and Nate knelt with a flash of déjà vu, he believed that upward gaze was the one he had been waiting for all along, the dark gaze that had seen to the end and had nothing to report.

But the limp black frog-footed figure was hoarsely breathing, and it became a question of what to do. Petey stood off to one side while they tried to figure out whether they had to take him somewhere or whether he could be left right there in the sand. "Where he bleeds to death from internal injuries," Rafe said.

"I dunno," Petey said quietly. "It could be worse to move

him. His back took some pretty hard hits. Maybe his spine." As if he had nothing to do with it.

"We're taking him," Nate decided. "Count of three, we all lift. Petey, you get his hands."

"This is how we get caught." Adamant, but throwing down his cigarette.

"You get his hands."

"I'm telling you, this is the mistake, not what I did. And fuck you pussies, I can carry him myself."

Staggering over the sand with the diver cradled in his arms, Petey went down on one knee but didn't drop the guy.

Rafe said, sliding his fingers down inside the black cowl, finding a pulse in the throat, "Still with us."

"Now what do we do?"

"Drop him off in front of the emergency room. In that grass in front of the hospital," Nate said. "Being careful not to get seen."

They settled the unconscious figure on a sleeping bag in the camper—Nate remembered just in time that he should be arranged on his side so that if he vomited he wouldn't choke on it—and were climbing into the cab when Petey said, "Wait, man. The goodie bag."

"Leave it."

Petey slogged back across the sand toward the raft and came back, listing comically to demonstrate the bag's weight. "More money than any of us've made this year. Who wants it?"

"Put it in the back."

Within a quarter mile Rafe had to pull over to permit another vehicle, a huge SUV none of them recognized, to buck and lunge past them with inches to spare, Nate swearing at the other driver for almost scratching his paint job, Rafe saying, "What the fuck, nobody used to come here but us."

Before light, the phone rang, and Nate reached from the futon to answer, knocking it from the wine-crate nightstand and having to search across the carpet—sandy rumpled topography of his discarded jeans, the ringing chiming through the trailer, rabbit's tail tuft of a balled baby sock, the ringing, slick foil of a condom package, when was that, ringing, constellation of glowing buttons that he held to his ear, scared, remembering, sick, life as he knew it over, a last importuning ring before he hit the right button.

"N Dawg. I fucked up."

Nate said the first thing that came to him: "It's gonna be all right."

"Who was he hurting?" Petey was crying.

Ollie sat up, the T-shirt she slept in whiter than her nakedness would have been. "Who is it?"

"Listen to me," Nate said. "It will all be all right."

Back jammed against the wall, arms around her knees, Ollie said, "Is it Shug?"

"I've called the hospital like five times and they won't tell me alive or dead. I said I was his brother. I made up some Vietnamese name but they laughed—the nurse laughed. That has to mean he was awake and told them his name. If he was dead nobody would laugh, right?"

Aware of Ollie listening with her back to the wall, Nate said, "Yeah, that's a good sign. Now listen to me."

"One of your famous plans, N? I got a plan. Mexico. Tell

Rafe so long and he was right, but then you had to go and say
that thing about Shug, and Shug, man, Shug is like a father to
me." He coughed.

No longer caring that Ollie could hear, Nate said, "Shug's
not like a father to anybody."

Ollie uncrossed her arms. *Fur Is Murder.* Crossed her arms again.

"Why didn't you two fuckers hold me down?"

Nate didn't answer.

"My big mouth, shit, I'm sorry, man. That was unjust. You
would've stopped me if you could, I know that rationally. I got
to get going. Hey, I left the bag in your backyard."

"What bag?"

Petey was gone.

In the five A.M. kitchen Shug was dabbling together a breakfast
heavy on salt and lard, whisking eggs and *amen*ing the cadences
of his favorite talk show host. When Nate came through the
door Shug dialed down the volume—the jackal voice hectored
from a dollhouse—and shook his big head in sullen wonder.
"Left it right out there where anybody could come across it.
Boone's been after me about buying the old truck and he could
have come by. Then where would we be? Well, you. You would
of still been in bed. But me, Boone trips over that bag and I'm
looking at jail time. Fish and Game," Shug added, in case Nate
had forgotten who Boone worked for.

Nate barely managed not to say *Jesus, Dad, put your shirt on.*
It didn't matter how used to each other they were on the boat,
here in Louise's kitchen he was bothered by Shug's ribby, potent,
belly-hanging nakedness, and especially by the scar between the
old man's slabby breasts, the gleaming millipede that should

have been decently covered by the shirt hanging on the chair. Curious, that Shug had brought the shirt downstairs but not tugged it on over his shaggy head. Or had he taken it off when he started cooking? Though this time it was a trivial matter, Nate tried once more to figure out why Shug did what he did.

"If it was just you running the risk, I would almost agree you have the right to screw up your own life, but when your lying cheating deviousness threatens this family I can't turn a blind eye. You think I don't mean it, or that I can't handle the *Louise* on my own, or that I'll never draw the line because I'm your father, but you fucked up for good, and Ollie and the baby can stay but you've got to go. Now. Today. I don't want you spending another night under my roof."

Nate's mind, groping, discovered not a single word of protest, and this was too bad—later he would understand that the one way he could have salvaged the situation was to get right into the old man's face. That might have worked. It might have meant their lives could go on. Much, much too late, he was to grasp the consequences of his silence and wonder why, when so much depended on it, he had not been able to come up with the straightforward *Fuck you* of a blameless man. Instead, as he had too many times before, Nate placed his faith in explanation. The problem was, his dad did not under*stand*. Look how quickly he could clear this up! "Somebody left the abalone in the yard while I was sleeping. Left them without my knowing."

"Ah, now. Like I don't know how this world works. Like anybody would leave that bag if you weren't in on the deal. You think I never wanted to break the rules? Cheat some? But did you *ever* see me? How much do you think is in that bag? Did you count? I'm guessing—fifteen, twenty grand? You think I don't know you take divers out? A blind man could tell from the mess you leave behind. You got your cut, and if you hadn't been drunk you wouldn't have left the bag out where I would find it. But part of you wants to screw up. Part of you always has."

"No, Dad, this is about you. What you've been waiting for," Nate said. "And here it is, your chance to end this, because now that Mom is gone there's nothing to keep me from hating you."

He ducked, but then stood shaking his head, aware that nothing more would happen, now that Shug had tried to hit him. The words had come out wrong and he would have liked to explain that piece of it. He wasn't the hater. In his confusion it had come out backward. What he meant was: *Nothing to keep you from hating me.*

He was almost through town, Highway 1 running between steep old false-front buildings housing four antiques stores and a used bookstore and a shoe store and an art gallery and a hardware store doomed to another day of almost no sales, when he noticed the star sparkling in the rearview, twinkling from red to blue, sharpening, fading, falling behind, his truck running good though he'd neglected to get the oil changed—well, he hadn't been contemplating any long trips, and even now he wasn't sure where he was going, except that he had an aunt he had liked when he was a kid, and she lived in a little town in Washington, Wenatchee, and that might work for a while, long enough for his dad to calm down. They could use a cooling-off period. Shug was right, Nate couldn't see him handling the *Louise* on his own, not for long, and if Nate chose a lucky evening to call, Shug would answer the phone as if there had been no fight and Nate had inexplicably taken off, leaving him shorthanded. That was exactly how Shug would play it, as if Nate was in the wrong, and this forgiving, exasperating recognition of his dad's ability to put him endlessly in the wrong was complicated by the realization that the ricocheting red-blue twinkle was *for him*, and then as clearly as he had ever seen anything in his life he saw Shug rest his knuckles over his dark eye, recollecting the numbers of Nate's license and reciting them to the officer on the other end of the phone, and as it gained on Nate that scurrying to-and-fro light show would burn brighter and brighter and more righteously, its anger justified when Boone Salazar or whoever swung down the tailgate and dug under the tarps in the pickup bed until, aha, the goodie bag was hefted and swung before Nate's believing, disbelieving eyes, the shells within chattering like stones poured down a well except these would not be poured anywhere but held as evidence, and it didn't matter what he said or didn't say, they had the proof in the Vietnamese diver's bag, and if Petey was wrong and the man had in fact died this could get very, very bad and Nate could be gone for years, and there would be Ollie alone with their little boy in the trailer in the yard knee-deep in thistles and bindweed, and nothing Nate could do about it when Shug crossed that yard, and he would cross that yard, he'd already been crossing that yard, and with this recognition Nate was alone in icy water and it was time for him to go down and he really didn't care. It was just too bad that the end was on him before he understood his life. The end had been coming forever and now that it was here he saw no reason to object. He downshifted and pulled onto the shoulder without worrying about it because he was cradled in the shadow of his destined wave, heaping itself, its high rim a spitting, flinging banner of foam, and Nate rolled the window down and rested his face in his crossed arms on the steering wheel and waited.

"Nate."

"Yeah."

Boone said into the open window, "I'm gonna need to see in the camper," and Nate said, "Yeah, okay," but before he could get out of the truck Boone said, "Did you know that diver was a kid when you-all broke his ribs?" and Nate said, shocked, "It was not a kid," and then, "How old?" Boone said, "Seventeen," and then, "Well, now things get more problematic, because he's hurt pretty bad," and Nate figured he might as well ask, "How bad?"

"He'll live."

"That's good."

"Well, yes it is," Boone said, "yes it is and I'm surprised you're so damn calm in the face of important good news like this, but maybe you called to check on the kid during the night."

"I didn't know it was a kid and I didn't call."

"Been a night of interesting phone calls. A couple to the hospital during the night and an anonymous tip to my office a half hour ago. Christ, Nate, how could you get into shit like this, break your old man's heart?" And then: "Look, I'm gonna do something I'm bound to regret, so don't say anything and don't give me any fucking reason to think twice. Just drive." He slapped the roof of the cab. "Just drive away." He stepped back. "This is for Shug. Now you tell him that the next time you talk."

In the rearview mirror Boone Salazar was backlit by alternating flashes of crimson and blue, his hand lifted in a wave, but it took an hour of dark highway, winding through the woods with no lights whatsoever in his rearview, before Nate could believe that he was free, and more miles passed before, remembering what he was supposed to tell Shug, he began to laugh, seeing the beauty of it.

Tabriz

David Merson, heartsore in the way of old activists, a stooped, unkempt forty-eight, leafs through his so-called love life for precedent and finds none. (Waiting in a parked car overlooking an arroyo induces introspection.) The other guys in EPIC share the leanness of long outrage, frequent marathons, and enduring luck with women, but obsession has not been good to David's relationships, his days spent tracking the toxins that bleed through watersheds, questioning children in hospital gowns printed with teddy bears, inking cancer clusters onto topo maps, bringing his peculiar skill set to bear, his milky mildness, what his second ex calls his anti-charisma, the hang-dog air of bewilderment that makes even dying children strive to enlighten him, the harmlessness that glints through his wire-rimmed specs when he shakes hands with some CEO or other, except that mostly they know better, now, than to let a bigwig

sit down with David. Don't so much as nod when you pass him
in the courthouse hall, they're told. Despite his scruffiness—one
judge told him to get a haircut—he is sleek in pursuit, righteous,
relentless, a scorner of compromise, a true believer.

Whose own luck with women was flawed, leaving him
grateful for joint custody. David loves his two sons with the
appalled passion of a dad whose work acquaints him with small
coffins. From his right hand to the hollow of a kid's well-worn
glove runs a taut thread of inevitability, the ball held aloft and
displayed—*Dad, look!* In the making of a boy psyche this is the
key phrase. It's David's job to arrange plenty of occasions for its
happy proclamation: *Dad, look!* His rendition of *Goodnight Moon*
is famous for the oinks, whistles, and cheek pops enhancing the
line *Goodnight noises everywhere.* He's fed trembling white mice
Coca-Cola from an eyedropper for the sake of fourth grade science, though his coworkers' connections in the Animal Lib-
eration Front would rip his heart out and nail it to the front
door—*Environmental Protection Information Center*—if they found
out.

His abuse of white mice—with their teeny old-lady hands!
their suffering docility!—is an unusual departure from the party
line. Though they have long since abandoned ecotage, the five
members of EPIC hew to the rituals of brotherhood, to their
affinity-group habit of staying up until two or three, baring their
souls, though they do so now under the harassing buzz of fluorescence, tipped back in ergonomic chairs, ties loosened, feet
up on desks variously avalanched or anal (David's: anal) when
in the old days it was shirts printed with raised fists, army surplus sleeping bags, a high-desert campfire sucked toward the
moon, shooting sparks. Ice may be melting out from under polar
bears, breast milk brims with mutagens, but change hasn't ever

before touched EPIC, not deeply, not at the level where they are
bonded. At David's wedding last Saturday they slouched in at-
titudes of conscientious celebration. They kissed the bride, they
told her when she was done with this loser to give them a call,
they stuck orchids behind their ears, and David alone understood they were holding back, and why. Of the five of them, he
was the reliable loser in matters of the heart, and the phenom-
enon of Jade, the fearful symmetry of teeth and cheekbones, plus
the fact that she's on the other side, the sexiness of her being,
basically, the enemy, can be neither assimilated nor forgiven.

The wedding's meticulously repressed question: *What does
she see in him?* In his rented tux, David had shrugged, reading
minds he'd been reading half his life. They could have had a
little more faith, though. For a profoundly good man to find
love shouldn't strain credulity. David caught himself thinking
profoundly good and palmed his thinning fair hair in a manner
Jade recognized as embarrassed or sad. She'd lifted her brows:
What's wrong? He'd slung her over his arm, leaned in as if kissing were drinking, held her practically horizontal until people
said *Aww.*

But it was a moment's uncensored private felicity to have
meant it: *profoundly good.*

He's earned it.

What he regrets now is not that thought but the ruefulness
of his gesture, palming his hair—the mild, contrite, revisionist
embarrassment—so that she'd had to lift her brows, to wonder
what was wrong when nothing was.

In the arroyo a couple of wrecked trucks sail past a rusted
washing machine, a listing, doorless refrigerator, tires of various
sizes and degrees of rottenness, a cathedral window's worth of
shattered glass and the jutting wing of a small plane. The boys

love coming here because nowhere else are they permitted such
an array of dangers—prickly pear, anonymous stained underpants, rusty nails, rattlers. Actually, the altitude's too high for
rattlers, but the boys reject this fact. Before he lets them out of
the car, David lectures. Careful, careful, careful, the poisoned
echo of small white coffins. Down in the arroyo, out of his sight,
they look out for each other, a good thing for brothers to learn.
They are step-mothered now, in fairy-tale jeopardy, though in
taking them on Jade has shown an easy, can-do confidence. She
read up on step-parenting, and it turns out that beauty figures
even here, in the reconfigured family calculus, the boys defense-
less as their father. Regarding love, David has always been a
doubter, a holder-back, the lukewarm opposite of his passionate work self. As a husband he was often described as *just not
there*, and he had accepted as deserved the amicable breakups
of marriages one and two. Along came Jade: they had gazed,
eaten, drunk, fucked, the usual plot, but then fucking took over,
the great power of fucking had been awakened and they fucked
themselves mutually transparent, fucked their way into a dazed
adoration, discovering there this clandestine status in being the
two of them, this insolent sexual satisfaction coexisting with
the improvisational restlessness of genius, this safety, this bliss
exempt from inhibition and nagging history, neither one bothering, neither needing to explain their *hasty* marriage, because it
was natural to want to seal such transcendent fucking with that
cultural kiss of approval, dubious though you were, otherwise,
about that culture.

Crossing to the arroyo's edge, he can make out the boys'
voices, and guesses they're intent on intergalactic slaughter.
Lasers, viruses, dirty bombs—their games incorporate everything there is to fear. This is good for them, David believes.

"Hey Shane.

"Edmund."

He calls the ill-assorted names—ranch hand, dandy—chosen by two of the three women he's loved and, from the hush that follows, figures he's been heard. A scrap blows by, and David stomps. This is the usual lawlessness, the regular Joe's cost-effective contempt for the environment. People find this waste-land irresistible: free dumping! Showing a perverse initiative, somebody has carted an oil drum out to the tip of this stony spur where the road dead-ends. The human love of shortcuts accounts for a lot of devastation, David thinks. The ADHD species, distracted from the story unfolding down at the level of chromosomes or up in the ozone. He releases his scrap to the wind, and it's whisked away. As if a signal has been given, more bits and pieces swirl past, the dervish blowing by, revealing that an object he had mistaken for a plank or beam sticking out of the oil drum is in fact a furled rug. It seems undamaged, and as David puts an arm around it and levers it out, a kamikaze egg carton rears up and crunches into his shoulder. He studies the oil drum's seethe: tin cans, a partially melted telephone, a doll's head trailing singed acrylic hair, a coil of filthy rope, a shirt stippled with blood, a clock, rain-fattened paperbacks, egg-shells, ashes, a melee of electrical wire, a high-heeled shoe. As he works it loose, the rug dislodges a cascade of junk that tumbles along the ground, light bits scattering, heavier things rolling this way and that. Something, an envelope, wings past, nicking the corner of his eyebrow.

"—wouldn't *be* anybody." Panting. "Left to. Operate. Lasers."

"Wrong! Somebody lived! Cause they hid in—"

They come clambering up the slope.

"—caves—"

"—that, like, connect, a whole underground—"

"—*city*—"

Reaching the arroyo's rim, the half brothers come to a halt and stare.

Squatting, David peels back a corner of the rug. With only a few square inches revealed, the workmanship is unmistakably fine.

"Hey guys," he says. "Look what I found."

For a breezy minute they ponder the scene, litter skittering and dodging past. The moon catches their eye-whites. Two hours' reckless play brings out the brother in them.

"So?"

One brother's cool slides its knife blade through the bonds of pairdom.

"Show some fucking interest in what Dad found, whycantcha."

Ordinarily, and despite the unfairness of enforcing rules in this male wilderness, David would have to deal with *fucking*. He does a quick check. Edmund does not appear hurt, only newly severed from his older brother. His eye-whites glitter. Not with boredom, either. Freshly relieved of intimacy, both boys are radiant. David gives the rug a good yank, and it thumpingly unrolls.

"Wow."

"Wow."

David sits back on his heels, trying and failing to understand, to account for the intrusion of marvelousness, the rug's fanatically executed geometry interrupted just at the point of frigidity by winding, organic movement, delicate leaves, impish involutions, this diversion, this near escape from paralysis part of its tale, its secret proffered with the bristling incomprehensible vitality of bees dancing within a hive, vision inspired by the challenge but the mind's movements tentative, repeatedly stubbed out, this agitating impenetrable beauty the work of how many nights and days, its blood reds and ominous crimsons contending with, outnumbered by, a choir of blues, azure, lapis, jay feather, baby blanket, forget-me-not, but to number them like that, to try to say what they're like, that's merely a poor, doomed attempt to domesticate them. They are gorgeous blues, and they assail peace of mind. In the center there is an oval where nothing happens, visually, and this is the indeterminate dun of animal camouflage, of a doe fading into underbrush, and what appears to be peaceful is really another wild evasion.

Edmund, at nine still sometimes playing the baby, hangs an arm around his neck. "You pulled that out of the garbage, Dad?"

"It shouldn't have been in there."

Shane leans into David from the other side. "Why was it, then?"

"I really have no idea." No taint of yeast or compost, no halitosis of souring milk carton, no oil-drum dankness mars the rug's dry, antique compound of *grass*, *twine*, *stone floor*.

Edmund says, "I want to see in the can."

"Honey, there's nothing else in there, and we've talked about syringes and dangerous sharp things and how the guys handling garbage wear gloves."

"You didn't have gloves."

He tries a technicality and some italics, an old parenting tactic. "I wasn't reaching *down* into the garbage, the rug was right on *top*, and I carefully carefully *carefully* pulled it out."

"Dad I really really need to see."

Father and son go over and peer down into the oil drum: garbage. "Okay?" David says.

Behind them Shane wings stones at the drum until David says, "Cut that out." Shane pitches a last defiant stone and the drum gives off the resonant *gong* of a bull's-eye. Edmund runs back to try to match this feat, and David decides to let them have at it, because what can they hurt? He rolls the rug up tight and improvises a kind of fireman's carry. The metal whines when the stones whang against it. The brothers have refined their aim, and as David grapples with the rug, shoving it into the car, he takes pleasure in his boys' prowess. Hunters. He's the father of a pair of slender, moonlit, stone-throwing boys: there may be no deeper pleasure on earth. He pauses to admire them. They sense this. It throws their aim off. They want to be fatherless, motherless, outcast, a savage tribe of two, their terrible prey—black, squat, stinking like a bear—moaning when it's dinged. Before they can leave this place, the spirit of the bear that the oil drum mysteriously incarnates must be stoned back to the underworld. If there were no boys throwing stones, that spirit would never have emerged from the underworld in the first place, but put a stone in a boy's fist and the old world breathes out reeky ghosts. The Pleistocene lives on in the heads of boys. In fact, three-fifths of EPIC believes that we're headed back that way: when weather chaos descends big-time and the center cannot hold, humans will regroup as hunter-gatherers. That's the optimistic view. What the other fraction of EPIC believes cannot be spoken aloud, since (David is one) they are fathers, and certain thoughts are forbidden to fathers. *Annihilation. Universal extinction.* Nestled, still tightly rolled, in the rear of the station wagon, the rug's strangeness is muted: it could be rightfully his, bought and paid for. David calls to the boys to *get into the car* but finally has to start the engine—David's own dad's long-ago threat—before the boys climb in. They're overextended, he figures, long past the hour when they should have been freed of the intensity of their love for each other by the bleating electronic triviality of Game Boy.

"It's skanking up our car," Edmund complains, and Shane chimes in, "It smells all old."

"Hey, does everything have to be new? Plastic? Old's not such a bad smell, is it?"

Pleading, always a wrong move.

"It's not ours." Edmund, doing a good imitation of Jade. She's new enough that they shouldn't be able to mimic her this well, and the boys' appropriation of Jade's voice and style when they want to drive home a point slightly worries David, and feels unfair, as if he's being ganged up on.

"It's ours now, sweetie."

Sweetie is fatal, registered in jolting silence. Jolting because the next thirty miles are so bad, the road seeming as lost as a road can get, running aimlessly along and then madly swerving, barely managing to avoid outcrops of rock or steep drop-offs.

"You mean you can just take anything out of the garbage, whoever left it there, and if they want it back you can say no, it's yours?" Shane, bent, at eleven, on discovering the moral workings of the world.

A hard curve, and as he slows the car, David tries his mostly successful good-father voice. "Look, I don't want you going through *any* garbage *ever*. You never find anything good."

"*You* did."

"*You* did."

Jade says, "It must be worth a fortune. Twenty or thirty thousand dollars, even, depending on how old it is. Really, somebody's going to want it back. Because how could it have been left in a garbage can? I've never seen anything like this except in a museum. And why didn't I know that you go for these drives? Was this a thing you did before?" Before her. "Were you just having a really bad day? Is something going on?" *Do we have secrets now?* "The rug is a problem, David. There's been some kind of mistake, because this is not the sort of thing that gets thrown away, not ever. You took it? What made you think you could just walk off with it?"

"Which question do you want me to answer? It clearly *had* been thrown away. At the end of a dirt road in the middle of nowhere. Nobody was coming back for it. It was getting dark."

"I just think you were a little hasty," she says, "impetuous," and he shouldn't be flattered, but he is. "Draw me a map of how you get there?"

Her love of proof, documents, evidence, is very like his, and on the back of an envelope he sketches a map, the journey's last leg a squiggle meant to indicate arduousness, culminating in a cartoon oil drum.

"This is your secret guy place? There's nothing there."

"That's what's good about it."

He wants to explain further, to point out the sadness of there not being many unowned places left, but she's already asking, "How do you know nobody was coming back? Maybe the real owner is there now, looking, and it's gone."

Cross-legged on their bed, husband and wife consider the rug unfurled across the tiles of their bedroom floor, and he watches, under the lowered lids of her downward gaze, the REM-like movements of her eyes as she follows, or tries to, the rug's branching and turning and dead-ending intricacy, its profusion of leaves and petals or the geometric figures that might be leaves and petals, which the gaze barely discerns before relinquishing them back into abstraction. Jade, leaning forward, her elbows on her knees, frowning, her right breast indented by her right arm, her shadow thrown across him because her reading light's on, her backlit profile showing the radiant lint of her upper lip, the angle of her jaw, the length of her throat, and below that the contour of the heavy breast, the nipple's surprising drab brown color, the unaroused, modest softness of its stem, its wreath of kinked hairs. Best of all, in love, in what he's experienced of love, are those moments when you can watch the other's self-forgetful delight.

She says, "I have to tell you something."

In his work, he's a good listener. More than that, he solicits the truth, asks the unasked, waits out the heartsick or intimidated silences every significant environmental lawsuit must transcend. Someone has to ask what has gone wrong, and if the thing that's gone wrong has destroyed the marrow of a five-year-old's bones, someone has to *need* that truth or it will never emerge from the haze of obfuscation. Of lying. But this isn't work. This is his wife.

"I'm a little afraid," she says. "I know that's not like me. This is hard."

"Whatever it is, you can tell me."

"Whatever it is?"

"You can tell me."

"Whatever?"

"You can tell me."

"I'm a Republican."

He's been blind to the syllogism chalked on the board: X is a corporate lawyer. All corporate lawyers are Republicans. X is a Republican. The outrage that blazes through him makes the leap to her. When she says, "I knew you couldn't handle it," her tone is prosecutorial.

"You waited until we were married."

"Until I thought you could deal."

Dismay is cranked so high his pulse ticks in his temples. "I'm having trouble believing this."

"Calm down, calm down a little, try seeing it's love, my telling you, it's wanting no secrets between us."

"The deception," he says. "The hiding who you really are. When you know how I feel about lying."

"I hated it too, every minute of it, but I couldn't lose you."

"This makes us like everyone else. Lying. Being lied to."

"It doesn't. We aren't." She catches hold of his wrist. "Are you all right?"

He waits until she lets go before saying, "Blind, wasn't I. You must have thought *He's incredibly easy to fool.*"

She changes tactics. "David. Let's deal with the other issue first. Say the rug was in the office of some Los Alamos scientist, and one day somebody ran a Geiger counter over it, a random check, a sweep, cause they're human, accidents happen, and despite the most thorough precautions—"

"They're not thorough enough," he says, and he knows.

"—traces of uranium stick to the soles of somebody's shoes and get tracked across the rug, and out of fear for their jobs they decide to dispose of the rug in this furtive undocumented way, the sort of thing you're always telling me about. You, the expert on how contaminants get into the air and the water and into people's houses, you bring it *home*, into our *house*, with no clue why it was left in a trash can. This just isn't wise."

"I love you as the expert on wise decisions."

"My politics are my own, and I could've gone on keeping

them to myself. Ultimately I chose not to, because you and I tell each other everything."

"One of us does."

"So okay, right, you're the honesty prince, but this is new territory for me. You're the first person I've ever even wanted to tell everything to. I needed to work up to it. Is that a crime, to have needed time?"

"There's nothing wrong with this rug," he says. "You're being paranoid."

"There is something," she says. "I can feel it."

"For the first time," he says, "how you feel doesn't interest me at all."

He's let down when, without another word, Jade clicks off the light. If they were both wolves they'd be lying just like this, their senses on alert, their fur on end. How about a little red-in-tooth-and-claw sex? He wants her. But who is she? She may intend to amend the constitution to rule out gay marriage, or drill for oil in the Arctic National Wildlife Refuge. How can he fuck someone who wants to drill for oil in the Arctic National Wildlife Refuge? All the same, he's hard. Postcoitally, he can convince her that caribou have rights to their ancient migratory routes. He's not sure where she is in her progress toward sleep, and when he bends over her, the intense repose of her body on the bed tells him she's wide awake. This treachery—another in her string of deceptions—exhausts him, and he gives up. He's asleep.

Before dawn he's startled by her cry. He can't make sense of her naked, placatory stance in front of his computer, or his own accusation: "What did you do?" His voice is rough, his body recollecting their fight before his brain does.

"I walked across your rug and must've picked up some static

electricity, because when I touched the computer, I got a shock, and—"

He scrambles from the bed, the rug's nap pricking the soles of his feet.

"—it crashed. It made this little match-strike sound, and the screen went black. David. I wasn't going to look."

Well, then, what was she doing there? He never confides in her about his work. He's tediously ethical that way. She could end up representing a corporation he's going after.

"I wasn't going to look."

The repetition really scares him.

Her fingertips patter across the keyboard. Panic tenses her shoulders as she leans over his laptop, and her hair sticks up in tufts, dirty with yesterday's gel—for the first time, he finds her unattractive. "Leave it," he says; she says, "Let me just—" His chest hurts: Is this a problem, should he be paying attention? No, it's okay, his heart. It's only that his chest has constricted with frustration and another emotion, uglier, more imperative, pounding away. Fury.

"This weird thing happened."

Sunday afternoons the boys and their belongings trek back to the house of Shane's mother, Susannah, according to an agreement hashed out with Nina, Edmund's mother, an academic on a year's sabbatical in Paris. Nina trusts Susannah, but then so does almost everyone, including David. He sits with Susannah on her back steps, the boys dodging through the neglected garden whose sunflowers are ten feet high, yellow petals tattered and their brown, saucer-sized centers under attack by sparrows.

"—never make it out alive unless—"

"—we find a way to neutralize—"

Just hours ago Jade walked across the rug, acquiring a crackling charge of electrons that flew from her fingertips to his keyboard, cases compromised, the irreplaceable interviews, the painstaking documentation zapped, and yeah, he has some of it on disks, but not all, an uncharacteristic lapse, one he's going to have a hard time forgiving himself for.

"When I finally got it to the guy I've always relied on, he said it's permanently fried," David tells Susannah. "Which is bound to cause problems in a number of cases. But the worst part is, I don't know what she was doing with my computer. She has no business touching it."

"Maybe she was looking for incriminating email. That's the usual reason for fooling around with the other person's computer. She must want to find out about your life before."

"It's not like that."

"She could be looking for email from a previous relationship. Like with me. She could want to know how things stand between us."

"I don't think so. She hasn't wanted the lowdown. She sees us more as a clean-slate kind of thing." Or a lightning strike. An angel's wing passing over their upturned faces.

From the shoes ranged on the wooden step—shoes with neon glyphs, striped shoes, shoes with soles thick as antelope hooves, shoes bristling with spikes—Susannah chooses one whose laces are a gray snarl and begins, with her dirty nails, to pick the knot. She says, "You do barely know her."

Angry at her superbly divorced reasonableness, the very quality he loved a moment ago, he says, "The rug is evil."

"Oh, David. Things aren't evil. People are. And not that many of them, though I can see why your line of work leads you to think otherwise."

Evil: he had continued pecking at the keyboard as if lucky ineptitude could conjure, from the dark portal, the blip of returning consciousness. Jade—exasperated by his manic persistence, in which she rightly detected anger meant for her—left for work. In the fugue state of technological thwartedness, he heard the *scream*, shock blazing down every dad-nerve, and danced backward to see out the French doors: Edmund hanging from a branch of the apricot tree, shrieking at his own daring. With this shriek ringing in his ears David lost his footing, and in a slow-motion trance of remorse went over backward. Falling, he seemed to view himself from above, and if he was helpless, his arms flung out and his mouth gaping, the back of his head about to connect with the floor, he was also suspended in a peaceable realm that had detached itself from terror. David had time to marvel at this double consciousness before the impact slammed it out of his skull.

"My god," Susannah says. "You could have been really hurt"—and her palm on his nape radiates solicitude, but this kind of comforting costs her nothing, really: she can do it in her sleep. With the broad Norwegian planes of her wide-open face she's so different from Jade, so *accessible*. "But you're okay," she says.

"Well, my back sort of—"

She turns his wrist to read his watch, and the kitchen telephone rings. The screen door bangs behind her sturdy freckled legs.

"Hi.

"You can't?

"You can't?

"I know but why does that have to—

"I know it is but why—

"I know.

"I know.

"I said I *do* know.

"Yes.

"I will.

"I won't.

"Me too.

"Me too. Bye."

She's high enough from this abortive exchange to sit down beside David and confess, "I think I'm in love. After all this time. I mean, you've been through two wives since me. My turn, I guess." The smile she gives him is expectant, but he's having trouble reconciling the two realities, the reality before she vanished into her kitchen and this new version, because weren't they still, until this confession, still, really, in spite of everything, *married*? She has eluded him, slipped away taking her critical possessive practical generous irreplaceable and beautifully *accessible* love with her, and David says miserably, "Oh."

"*Oh?* After I listen to the wonders of your love life for *six* years? *Oh?* That's not trying, David. That's not even—nice. *Oh?* That's cold."

"I need to ask you about something."

Such a transparent grab at her vanished attention: she grimaces, exaggerating the expression but truly pissed off. "Were you even listening?"

"You're in love. And it's, from your side of the conversation, kind of complicated."

"When isn't it complicated?"

He *uh-huh*s prevaricatingly.

She says, "Oh, of course! Marrying somebody you barely know. That keeps everything nice and simple."

"I'm in trouble, Suse."

"You do know you are completely selfish." But she's curious. "What kind of trouble?"

"This is a hypothetical. What if someone you were in love with turned out to be a Republican. How bad would that be? Would it be a thing you'd leave them over?"

"That couldn't happen."

"Sure it could."

"Nope. Because when you're talking to a Republican, you can't talk long before you hear something, some opinion, that makes your blood run cold. Like what Emily Dickinson said about poetry? It's poetry if it makes you feel like the top of your head's coming off? That's how you know it's a Republican." As she's been talking, she's been processing. "*Jade's* a Republican. David? She would be! But you're an activist, you can't possibly— whoa. Whoa! This *changes* things."

"Of course it changes things." But he's confused. "What things?"

"How does she discipline, David? Are there bedtime prayers? I can't believe how trusting I've been. How naive. Intimidated! I was intimidated by her. I never really believed she liked the boys. She was probably pretending to be into them out of some kind of phony family-values baloney. Or to get you."

"Hey, you've seen her with the boys, you know she's—" Well, wasn't Jade a little detached, really? Confident, but maybe too offhand? He'd chalked it up to her heavy workload and to never having spent much time with kids before. "Suse, Suse, please. Come to the house. Because I don't know whether I'm crazy to think the rug might be—" He can't say *evil* twice in one conversation.

"It makes no sense to blame the *rug*. Blame Jade! That's what you're trying to avoid with this obsession. You're resisting taking a hard look at a relationship that was flawed from its very inception."

"If you see it and say *There's nothing wrong with this rug*, that's all I need to hear."

"Is that how obsessions work, really?" She snaps her fingers. "*Snap out of it, guy*? That works?"

In her twice-weekly trips to this house to retrieve or deliver the boys, she has waited, eyes averted, outside the front door, and now, entering this bedroom, his and Jade's, Susannah appears struck by emotions David could probably have predicted: jealousy, confusion, vengefulness. She gives the rug a perfunctory once-over, but the unmade bed gets her complete attention, and then, oh shit, an actual, daunting bra of Jade's, silky cups upturned, and Susannah sits down on the rug and begins to cry. David rubs at his ill-shaven chin, weathering the storm, riding it out on his end of the rug. At last her crying peters out in breath-catches and little cries. He tears a tissue from a box on the nightstand and offers it.

"Thanks." She blows her nose and shudders.

"Want to tell me what's going on?"

"It wouldn't help."

"Want to try?"

"You *tricked me*. You went ahead and made this other life, and you're hopeful. I was used to you being more or less despairing. It wasn't like I wanted you to despair. But I was used to things going wrong for you. With women."

He doesn't intend to sit down beside her. On his feet he has some distance from the rug's malign influence, which she's succumbed to. At the same time, it's kind of sexy, standing over Susannah like this, her head at crotch level. He quashes the thought.

"If you were your old self, you'd never trust her again. She lied! But I don't understand how she got you in the first place. She might be able to get you back. How would I know how much you can forgive?"

"Suse, can you just—"

"See, I always thought that in life there was one person you got to know everything about. You get your one person, and it doesn't really matter whether you end up living with them or not, because the way you know that person, nothing can undo or diminish it. There's one single person out of everyone on earth who is your own private safe person, who you can talk to in your head and know what they'll say. After we broke up, you were still my one safe person. You know? But if *you* can turn out to have a Republican wife and blame a run of bad luck on an evil rug, I guess I don't know anything about anyone, not really. I'm in love and now you've made it so I have to distrust him. Will you tell me something, David? Tell me. Did I *know* you? Was I your person?"

Because if he answered her honestly the answer would be *no*, because he can't bear to hurt her, from reckless solicitude, he rubs a palm down his fly. "Suse. Do you want to do something?"

"I want to do something," she says, standing. "I want"—and, optimistically unzipping, he's staggered by her swift backhanded blow, by the moan of protest that is neither his nor hers, causing them to turn, the ex-husband and -wife, to find their child standing in the doorway in his pajama bottoms. "Honey," David says, "Shane," but after a long and disbelieving gaze that pivots from mother to father and father to mother, Shane bolts. David touches his jaw and says, "He saw that. He was right there."

"Did he see what was before? The zipper?"

"I don't think so." But he's not sure.

"David. Let me take him home. I need to talk to him. Let me get this."

He lets her get this. Edmund, discovered in the boys' room, turns piously cooperative, as if to preserve what's left of his family's sanity. Jackets are tugged on, backpacks snatched up, as if the house is on fire, and Susannah is hustling both boys out the front door when they encounter Jade. The women's voices spar in a little ecstasy of mutual dislike. David stands there, apprehensively feeling his jaw, holding his own, if barely, against an onslaught of guilt. Before it can drag him under, he sits down. Here is the rug. He straightens glasses knocked cockeyed by Susannah's blow and trails a hand over its nap. Threads ran one way, a warp, and another, a woof. Jade slams the front door. "Okay, what's going on?" she calls. "Why was Susannah so weird? She goes, 'Make him put some ice on it.'" He closes his eyes to postpone her interrogation, meanwhile attending to the throbbing in his jaw.

"Shit!"

Jade does the instinctive hopping step that keeps one foot from touching down, and in the second before he understands she's in pain he thinks she is goofily performing her fear of radioactive contamination.

"What's wrong?"

"I stepped on something. Was there glass in this rug? Oh, why didn't we vacuum?"

The trash can: the toxic seethe of its debris. David is half sick with guilt, driving her to the emergency room, because some shard from that roiling cauldron has driven itself into her darling foot, because he brought the thing home in order to impress her, to prove he is not merely a dutiful soldier slogging through muddy depositions but a hero capable of wresting beauty from chaos. The doctor is a sleekly handsome Indian with a tranquilizing lilt, but Jade won't melt, and when the doctor leaves the cubicle and David explains in a low voice that the rug is behind everything that has happened, she shivers and commands, "Shut up." The handsome doctor returns, bestowing on David a discreet frown of sympathy, an acknowledgment that Jade is not the only person suffering in this harshly illumined, far-from-soundproof cell. To explain that he's fine, David touches his swollen jaw with two fingers, *This?*, and shrugs, *This is nothing*, and now, when the doctor frowns, there is no sympathy in it: *Submit to spousal abuse if you will*. A blush creeps up Jade's throat and tints her ears, her shame exacerbated by the doctor's indifference, for he, assuming she is a highly troubled individual, ably ignores her, bending to his task. Extracted from her heel, brandished under the hooded medical lamp, is a sliver of rusted metal. No, she can't remember when she had her last tetanus shot. Hatred figures in the look she gives David when the needle goes in.

"We need to talk."

"I have to get to the office."

"With that foot?"

Left foot in a steep high heel, the injured right mummified in stretchy bandages and jammed into an old moccasin, she faces him asymmetrically. "Do you know why they do this? Make the bandages this sick *beige*? It's the shade of cadaverous Caucasian flesh. It's an intimation of mortality. It's so you wrap your rotting foot in your own future dead skin." In frustration, she kicks off the high heel and tries a flat. "I did hear what you said, and yes of course we'll talk, but I seriously have no time, this morning's the Kelsis thing."

"Kelsis?" he calls. "Kelsis?"

"The thing," she calls over her shoulder. "The thing I told you about."

The thing she didn't tell him about.

He needs to collect his wits, to shave skittishly around the swollen hinge of his jaw, to negotiate rush hour traffic with Zen serenity, to sit down at his desk and chart the decline of the black-footed ferret. He needs the escapism inherent in any ordinarily bad day. After lunch, he opens a fat packet that informs him he's been hit with a SLAPP suit. Nobody else in EPIC is named in the suit, only him. He is married to a lawyer, and would solicit her ultracompetent advice except that, this morning, she said Kelsis, and Kelsis is a small mining operation near the Arizona border whose radioactive runoff has been turning up in wells in the next county. Even worse, his records for the prospective Kelsis suit, like all the files on his computer, have vanished. He goes through his desk drawers hoping to find penciled notes or a backup disk holding some pertinent trace, but no, there's nothing, and in trying to reconstruct the basic outlines of the case, he loses track of time, and it's well after midnight when he turns the key in his front door. As was his habit on certain dire nights in his previous two marriages, he eats a bowl of children's cereal over the kitchen sink, then swallows a couple of aspirin to mute the ache in his jaw and the pain in his back, which has bothered him more in the last twenty-four hours than it has since he fell. When he glances into their room, Jade is sitting up in bed, a legal pad against her knees, spectacles on her nose, and though she knows he's there, she doesn't stop writing. This means either that she's hot after an idea or that last night's grievance—the belief that he was responsible for the needle's piercing her foot— has festered during ten professionally hostile hours at her firm. The rug has disappeared from the floor, he notes, and notes, in himself, the absence of any reaction to the loss, for which Jade will manufacture some credible explanation, but why does she get to preside over what goes, what stays? The rug was *his* catastrophe, *he* should say how it ends. The door to the boys' room is ajar, their nightlight on, Shane's bed a mess, because Shane is a poor sleeper, rousing and turning at the slightest of sounds—the back of his mother's hand connecting with his father's jaw, say. Neither boy is there, of course. There's no telling when Susannah will entrust them to this household again. The nightlight is a nautilus shell shielding a miniature bulb, and by its glow, David sits in the corner, wishing he could get the boys back. If he only had his boys here, asleep in their beds, he would know how to begin to set the rest of his world right. He would start with the sleep of his children and work outward.

When he comes back into the bedroom, Jade continues to scrawl her legal pad with corporate-attorney trickery, reasons radioactive well water is good for you, maybe, and if not that, then some other bullshit David or someone like him will have to contest, and with nothing left to lose, he lets his anger show. "What did you do with it?"

She takes off her glasses, folds them, sets them on the nightstand. He might be some witness she's treating to this stilted performance whose essence is her offended disbelief. "How did we get here?" When he doesn't answer she says, "You wanted it gone. You told Susannah things started going wrong when it came into the house."

"When did you talk to Susannah?"

"I called her to ask what was up last night. Why she rushed off. How your face got hurt."

"What did she say?"

He's invested this question with telltale anxiety, and she frowns. "She said to ask you."

"Tossing the ball around, and Shane threw a wild one. It looks worse than it is."

She regards him gravely. "Also she wanted you to know Nina called. From Paris. She's flying home and she intends to take Edmund back with her. Evidently I'm not to be trusted with either child."

"But the boys have never been apart."

"It looks like they will be, now. Because I'll make them say bedtime prayers for the health of Dick Cheney. I'll knit them little American flag sweaters, and mock Darwin." She shakes her head. "When you didn't come home, and you didn't call, and your cell went right to voicemail, I couldn't just sit here stewing, could I? I followed your map. That road is awful, it took me an hour each way, but I thought things would calm down if you knew the rug had gone back where it came from. 'Evil.' Susannah said you said, 'Evil.' You've been so irrational about the rug."

What he wants to say: *The whole world could have gone on lying. Gone on fucking up weather and watersheds and the marrow of little kids' bones, and I could have stayed steady, I would have been able to bear it, day after day, as long as there was you, here in our house, you to come home to, you whole and sane and beautiful and telling me the truth.* What he says, keeping his tone even: "Can you see why that bothers me? You should have waited to talk to me, we could have decided together how to deal with the rug. That's how people who trust each other behave."

"No, something needed to be *done*. You can trust me to see things as they are, and to act. You were used to such com*pliance*, with Susannah. After her, Nina, Shmina, who from everything you say and despite her supposed feminist credentials was basically this *mouse*. Now there's me, and, right, you and I don't know everything about each other, and we never will, and what matters is how—you're leaving? David?"

The road unwinds before him in moonlight, rough as ever, and he takes its curves too fast, absorbing the adrenaline hit whenever a clump of cholla looms in the headlights, or a redoubt of sandstone. Once a coyote ghosts across the road, and the station wagon fishtails to a halt, swallowed in its own dust. The wipers squeal, clearing the haze, dirty rivulets rippling horizontally as David picks up speed, the desert laid out for him in luminous swipes, loss a particular taste in his mouth, a rising bitterness he can't swallow away, his heartbeat manic, though it had been calm enough while he stood listening to Jade. There are no boys in the car to heed the warning, but David lectures. *Careful, careful. You'll get there. You'll find it. It was there once, it will be there again. Have a little faith.*

But the oil drum perched on the spur of rock is empty, turned over on its side, rocking when he nudges it with a toe, its trash blown over the rim, he supposes, scattered across the floor of the arroyo, rags fluttering from prickly pear, shards variously glinting. She left the rug here, she said. That must have been around sunset. It's unlikely that anyone has driven the road since then. The wind has been hard at work, lashing and moaning: Could the rug have been lifted and sailed over the rim? Here is the trail, wide enough to suit deer or two small boys but tricky for a grown man, stones kicked loose by his missteps, preceding him in clattering showers, his descent entirely audible, if there was anyone to hear. The interior of that listing refrigerator is pierced by spokes of moonlight: bullet holes. Paperbacks cartwheel past, shedding pages. When he picks his way among the wreckage, he meets another moon, hanging in the unsmashed headlight of a wrecked truck, the starry refraction of light coming from some earthly source. David makes for that glow eking out from under the tilted wing of an airplane. The throb in his jaw is worse, the pain in his back nagging, but apart from that, he feels good, looser, a little winded but freer, defiant, trying to recall the last time he pursued something, some aim or intention, under the night sky. *Twenty years ago.* With the other four, his brothers, prowling a mesa in the dark, tossing survey stakes over the rim after pouring sugar in a backhoe's gas tank. Nothing he does now can compare with the satisfaction of that sabotage, with its clean, unequivocal high. He's grown old, tame as office air. Jade had revived him, for a time. *Ow.* When a chip of stone grazes his chest, its sting—and the primal weirdness of being struck by a flying object in the dark—brings David entirely awake, but when he squints around, there's only the gusting sand, cholla rearing up spookily to his left, his shadow dipping and lengthening as he hikes toward the glow—a campfire, maybe. Something pelts his chest again, then his arm, and before he can shield his eyes he's assailed by a whirlwind of grit and twigs. Bewildered, he walks right into it, grazed, poked, showered with debris, leaves, twigs, and flying sand. If she were with him, Jade would hide her face against his chest, and he'd shelter her as best he could, her ferocious lawyer-hair lashing his face, and even with the wind whipping and scouring they could protect each other. David reels along blindly, and from the way his lungs strain he understands he must be shouting, though he can't hear himself over the wind. This is what he has seen happen to small bald-headed children: death blows you away while you struggle, the truth, the outrage, dying in your throat. Flinging a last handful of grit, the blast relents. David has passed among the cholla unscathed, and here is the shelter under the airplane's wing, from which a lantern is suspended, shining down on a boy and a girl, entwined on his rug, its arabesques dimmed, its choir of blues bleached to lunar grays and faint violet. The boy is fast asleep, but not the girl. The girl is awake. She tightens her arms around her boyfriend, and lifts her chin defiantly. She's got the inky hair favored by punked-out runaways, a fright wig trailing sharp fangs over her forehead, the pinched-together brows and eyeholes whose expression can't be deciphered. When he takes another step toward his rug, she flashes a palm. Stop. He takes another step, and gets both palms. She wants nothing more than to stop him, and he stops. It all stops, moon, love, breath, heartbeat. David sprawls there, feeling the hardness of the ground, the nerve-revival of panic, the terror that she won't know what to do, that she's stoned and can't help. The wind dies down and the moonlight blinks and he doesn't know what comes next on earth. No one knows. But there are footsteps coming toward him, and if there is any chance of saving a life through the sheer force of one's love for it, he is already saved.

Mystery Caller

 Ten years later, this can happen to her: someone can set his coffee cup down on the counter instead of in its saucer, and she can, for that, love him. Who is he? No one, a colleague she likes but who isn't important or especially close to her—no one she has ever imagined herself *with*. Office politics tend to sweep them, if not into collusion, at least into a nicely practical kind of empathy. There is relief for each of them in understanding the other, when they understand so few people around them, and he has supported her at key moments, strategically, in a manner that prevents his seeming too much her *friend*. That would be resented, as friendships are in offices—someone would set out to sabotage it. So they meet in amiable secret: it means nothing. He would say—it's one of his phrases—it's not *hugely significant*. She likes and admires him, but would be careful about saying she knows him, careful about asserting any kind of claim to his attention.

He rarely drinks coffee. He's doing so now, he's explained, because of insomnia the night before. Until this morning she hasn't known that he resists setting the cup in the saucer just as, ten years ago, her first husband did. She relied on it: really, she waited for him to set his cup down on counters or tables rather than in saucers, and this sense of *waiting for* this or for some other gesture or inflection unique to him *was* her sense of what it was to love. It was a thing she loved, his resisting the convention by which the presence of the saucer compels the placement of the cup, a thing he did that no one else did, and she hadn't expected to encounter that habit again, or, encountering it ten years later, to feel love. To have a fraction of an instant's love exacted from her for someone she does *not* love: What does it prove about love, about *this* love (she means not love for the man sitting next to her, but love for her ex-husband), about what you can know about what you feel? You think you are aware. You perceive that you are drawn to the angle of your father's cheekbone in an otherwise unknown face, you understand that the presumptuous way your wrist is taken hold of and a thumb is run across your palm (she is thinking of meeting her second husband) works on you because in your family intimacy had had so much distance to cross it had needed the power of presumption, there had had to be something intractable about it, really, or it couldn't have existed at all. You believe, in short, that you are informed about what you feel. An intelligent consumer, a diligent recycler, a woman who, the second time, married wisely and well. You allow for contradictions and gaps because it is wise to. You have never before hit a wall like this—never run into some way in which you are truly, blindingly wrong about yourself. Because a man sets his coffee cup down alongside his saucer, you can conceivably love him. It would be no less love than what you feel for your husband, yet this can't, in any reasonable, enlightened view of things, be true. She wants to gape in her companion's face, or to shout, to offend or alienate him so that he, dismayed, will assume responsibility for maintaining distance.

He gets it. Something's gone awry, and his voice is unsure, fractured by hesitation, when he says, "Okay, what?"

"Nothing."

He says with a plain kind of gentleness, no wiles, no manipulation, only a rightful affection for her in his voice, "Come on."

"You could be my first husband."

"Oh? Would I want to be?"

"I just realized." Aware he needs more to go on, she withholds; she lets him wait, she wants him to; it is the first consciously *unequal* moment they've experienced, her inflicting this brief interval of suspense upon him. This is the answer to the rightful affection in his voice: for her part, no affection, none, and the absence of reciprocal affection lets in sex. "I don't know why I didn't see it before."

He says, with the satisfaction of someone too intelligent to be flattered (who is nonetheless pleased), "We look alike?"

She's not going to tell him what it is. She wants no self-consciousness to intrude in his way of setting his coffee cup down or she'll never get to see it again. She says, "There's something."

"Is that good?"

"I'm surprised."

"Good surprised?"

"I can't tell." She considers. "Good, I think. I haven't thought about him for a long time. *Can* you go years without thinking of someone you once loved? It makes a life seem very long."

"What?"

"That you could love someone for years. Then forget them for *years*."

"Then remember them? I've felt that. There was this girl—my first wife." He'd like her not to have caught *girl*, a word potentially problematic: his status in the office has much to do with his being deemed progressive. "We were married three weeks."

"That long?"

"No one takes this story seriously when I say three. It was a mistake, but at the same time, we were serious, we were in deep. And I guess I haven't done that that many times."

In his voice, the sudden amplitude of truth telling, the sense of language widening out, of constraints loosening. This, the shift to self-delighting spontaneity, is what she's always hoping for in her dealings with others: she sees that now, even as she recognizes her inward wish to end this conversation before the rapport between them twists toward franker, sexier seriousness. When she prods her empty torte plate across the counter, it's so that the scrape of china across Formica will stand in for her voice, so that he will be interrupted by something other than her protest, and also so that, theatrically, she can read her watch. "God! I've got to run."

He says ruefully, "You stopped it."

She's shrugging into her coat. There's a cottonwood leaf on the coat's shoulder, and he picks it off. He rubs his palms together, the stem between them, and the leaf twirls. Says, "Okay. Something happened. I understand something happened, but not what. You're not going to tell me what, are you?"

"No."

"At least you don't lie. At least you don't say, 'Nothing happened.'" He shakes his head. "I'm lost."

She smiles. "You know when to leave things alone."

"But I don't know. It's you who's decided to leave. There's only one of us who understands what just happened. But okay. I guess you know what you need to do."

She smiles again, not as pleased with him as she was a moment before, not as pleased as she was with herself. "I'm still learning."

But it's not true—or, rather, it's so newly true that she can't accept it. Sitting down with him, fifteen minutes ago, she would have said with perfect conviction that she knew all she needed to know about herself. It's odd to think that her sense of herself has ruptured, that she must now conceive of herself as *still learning*, as unfinished and anxious, necessarily vulnerable to surprises and intrusions, because it's only by the narrowest of margins that her decision to get out the café door triumphed over her desire to lean nearer, to prolong her smile until its very duration transformed it into proof of willingness.

Outside, the high-altitude October radiance causes a darker blue to melt across the photosensitive lenses of her sunglasses. Her reflection skates across a plate glass window. One mannequin appears to have thrust a hand through the glass. That is, on her side of the glass, her wrist meets the pane; on the exterior, positioned to match her wrist, her upturned hand is fastened in place. Someone, probably a child, has dropped five bright blue gumballs in that hand. The other mannequins sport garter belts and laddered silk stockings, and seem to have just roused themselves from a tumultuous, sexy group sleep, like a gang of puppies. A horse wanders down the street: it takes her a moment to understand that there is a rider, and the rider is a police officer. The parking garage smells of oil-stained cement and deep shade; the way shade smells in the desert, even in an industrial setting, is one of the pleasures of her western state.

The cruising cars are tourists, but it's late enough in the year that traffic across town is light. She feels as if she's been waiting all day to drive. Sometimes driving is like this, a kind of consolation that's taken your measure and suits you exquisitely. She realizes also that she likes being alone. She has no idea how long she has wanted to be alone, because it's not a desire that can easily be teased apart from the mix of calculation and confusion, misgiving and worry and relief, that makes up her workday, yet now it's an available luxury: when she gets home neither her husband nor the boys will be there. Her husband has taken the twins to soccer practice. She wants them gone, and they will be—rarely does domestic life offer such a happy intersection of desire and circumstance. There is an early-evening vacancy to the suburbs, a kind of careful otherworldliness, and she's aware she is about to laugh as she bends to retrieve one of the twins' baseball gloves from the lawn. She holds the glove to her face and breathes in grass, leather, sun, little boy. She thinks if any neighbor came up and she turned her brilliant eyes on him he'd be frightened, he'd have to think it was something bad. Facing this imaginary neighbor, the glove still tipped against her face, she does laugh. She laughs into the leather palm hollowed so that the flying ball can lodge there, perfectly clasped. That rush, the exhilarated momentum of attraction, the assurance of sexy *fit* between two bodies, could have become the decisive factor. It had wanted to dominate, it had wanted to divert and disrupt, and it had felt wonderful. *She could have done anything.* It's a realization she has to hate if she is not to hate her life. In her husband she loves calm, wit, sanity, even a certain resistance to her. If she said of the marriage, "We understand each other," she would mean something far more like "We have a deal" than "We know everything about each other," but "We have a deal" is cold and can be dismissed, and her marriage is neither cold nor dismissible. A child in a yellow slicker passes by on the sidewalk, kicking leaves, and for a moment everything seems set right, all dangers safely behind her.

The first thing she does, on entering the house, is start to undress. Her husband likes to tease her because she always stands just inside the closed front door and eases one black heel off, then the other, always heels, always black, then tilts her pelvis forward to unzip herself behind. Sometimes she hangs her jacket over a dining room chair on her way through, and her earrings chime down into the delft dish where her husband leaves his car keys and change. Once she's in their room she gets into the clothes that feel like her, his oldest sweatshirt, her black leggings, her feet bare as she crosses the room, and, without thinking at all, sits on the edge of the bed and dials.

Because it's not true that she hasn't thought of her first husband in years. She thinks of him. She forgets thinking of him, she forgets doing this, she forgets all of this, yet it happens. She knows his number. He still lives in the midwestern town where they had lived together. The very first time, she had only to call directory information and say his name. There had been two listings under that name, she was told—which was the strangest part, for her, of what she was doing. An improbable coincidence, another person bearing his unusual name in such a small town; it had seemed to diminish him. Of course she hadn't known his address, and the first number wasn't his. He had answered on the second number's fifth ring. She's not sure how many rings it takes to be truly importuning, and his voice had in fact sounded impatient, bothered by something happening elsewhere in the house, his attention only nominally with whoever was on the phone. He'd had to ask, "Who is it?" He'd waited. He'd asked again, "Who is it?" She could not say who it was. She couldn't answer him, and she couldn't hang up. She hadn't wanted to trouble him, but she had acted just like someone who wishes to cause that curious kind of trouble, the suspensefulness and uneasiness of not knowing who's called your house and then refused to say anything.

When he'd hung up, that first time, she'd tapped his number out again, an electromagnetic refrain she already liked the way she'd always liked his name. She meant to say, "It's me, that was me before, I was just so surprised by your voice that I couldn't speak," she'd meant to apologize, to embark on some sort of conversation, to tell him something of her life, to ask about his, but when he answered, she was silent again. Haplessly, helplessly, yet with some sense of this act as—bizarrely—expected by him, she was silent, and then he'd done an odd thing himself: he'd left the receiver off the hook and, it seemed, walked away.

After a minute or two she could hear his children's voices, muted as if they were running through a hallway, and then his wife had come into the room. A refrigerator door opened and closed. She could hear something—milk?—poured, and then his wife said, with that gaiety peculiar to women talking to themselves, "What's this doing lying here?" and after two tentative and unanswered "Anyone there?"s hung up the receiver.

Another thing, stranger still: she had called him from the hospital room after the twins were born. She'd let the phone ring longer than ever before, seventeen or eighteen times. During labor her chapped lips had begun to split open in tiny cuts; she'd panted and blown her way through the night, only to end, that morning, gazing into the anesthesiologist's neutral downward gaze. Her left arm rattled inside the webbing that bound it at a rigid right angle to her body. Her hand quaked and convulsed, and her teeth chattered. She'd asked, "Am I supposed to shake like this?" He'd said, "Some do." She told him, "My *body's* scared," meaning that she, herself, down in the deepest core of self, was somehow fearlessly calm and lucid, however she appeared to him. He gazed down, masked, feelingly or un-feelingly, it was impossible to tell. Her husband was let into the room, and he too was wearing a mask, and each boy in turn was lifted in the doctor's hands, squalling. There was a feeling of its having nothing to do with her, of her being pushed aside or neglected during this turn of events, in which the babies were hauled into the newborn world. This feeling had gone away when she nursed the twins, one after the other. Once they were in the nursery, and her husband had gone home to sleep, she had dialed the rare, familiar number. It was another instance of not knowing what she was doing, of dissociating, because again, *again*, she hadn't been able to speak. It was his voice, though: she'd needed his voice. And, that time, after his voice left, a dog was barking. She remembers the pain of smiling with cut lips to hear a dog barking like mad in what was surely his backyard.

This evening she crosses her legs, upright on the edge of the bed, listening to his phone ring. Today, today, she will say, "It was me, all those times," and he will say, "I was sure it was; but why?" She won't answer directly, but instead will tell him, "Someone reminded me of you today. God, so *much*."

He answers. This is probably more than luck: maybe, un-consciously, she structures it a little, calling at times when he's likely to be at home. Well, assuming he's continued freelancing journalism, his job during their marriage, he works at home, and probably most calls *are* for him. Not counting that time his wife picked up after he'd abandoned the receiver, and however much the odds are against it, she's never gotten his wife or one of his kids, only him. Now he says "Hello" twice to be sure of what's happening. He's never said, "I know who you are." He's never said, "Don't call here again." He's never, out of curiosity or the need to assert his authority over events, hit star sixty-nine, which would cause his phone to dial her number, and if some digital readout on his phone informs him of her number and its area code, if he's fairly sure his caller is her, he's never tested this conclusion by saying her name, he's never sought to resolve the mystery. Though weeks separate the calls, it takes him only few seconds to understand something like "This is *this* again." He never hangs up, just lays the receiver on the counter. When he does so now, she thinks *Good.* Today, if he had demanded to know who it was, she really would have told him. His laying the receiver down on the counter means they get to go on like this a while longer. The room he's in is the kitchen, of course. She listens. Water runs from a tap.

A pot or kettle clicks down on a stove burner. *Do you still make terrible coffee?* she thinks. *Or has she taught you how to get it right?* Probably barefoot, he crosses and recrosses the kitchen. But how long can this last? What is in it for him? Distantly, his wife calls for one of the kids—that particular rising, questioning inflection is maternal, and the voice is irked in a way that's also maternal. She knows this intonation well. She knows it's tenderness in yet another disguise. If the voice calls for him, she knows, or if his wife approaches the kitchen, if there's any chance of her spotting the receiver left lying on the counter, he will hang up the phone before he can be caught. This is, somehow, their agreement. As long as it hurts nothing, she can listen all she wants. Whoever she is, he lets her have this piece of his life.

Eros 101

Q: *Examine the proposition that for each of us, however despairing over past erotic experience, there exists a soul mate.*

A: Soul? In some fluorescent lab an egg's embryonic smear cradles a lozenge of silicon, the vampiric chip electromagnetically quickened by a heartbeat, faux-alive, while in a Bauhaus bunker on the far side of campus, a researcher coaxes Chopin from a virtual violin, concluding with a bow to her audience of venture capitalists, but for true despair, please turn to Prof. Clio Mitsak, at a dinner party in her honor, lasting late this rainy winter night, nine other women at the table, women only, for the evening's covert (and mistaken: you'll see) premise is that the newly hired Woolf scholar will, from her angelic professional height and as homage to VW, scheme to advance all female futures, and the prevailing mood has

been one of preemptive gratitude, gratitude as yet unencum-
bered by actual debt and therefore flirtatious, unirksome
even to Clio, its object. Clio who, hours ago, hit the button
for auto-charm, absenting her soul (*there*) from the ordeal of
civility. Gone, virtually, until dessert. Set down before her,
the wedge of cake, black as creek-bed mud parting under
the tines of the fork, brings her to her senses, but then she's
sorry, because the whipped cream is an airy petrochemical
quotation of real cream, and the licked-tire-tread aftertaste
provokes an abrupt tumble into depression. It is an attribute
of the profoundest despair not to realize it *is* despair. Kierk-
egaard. Mitsak. She's vanished down that rabbit hole known
as California, and her cell never cries *Text me*. Her past has
gone dead quiet; her exes have adopted Chinese infants
abandoned in train stations. This candlelit table, strewn with
cigarettes ashed in saucers and wineglasses kissed in retro
red, makes her want to cry out a warning. Nine hopefuls
embarked on the long romance with academia's rejections:
she has everything they long for, and look at her! Old! Old!
Old! Old! Old! Alone! Alone! Alone! Alone!

It's not really there, is it, such stupidity, on the tip of her
tongue? Yes it is—(she's drunk)—but wait, she's saved, struck
dumb by a voice.

The voice can't be described as *honeyed*. It doesn't intend
to flatter. Neither gratitude nor the least career-driven taint
of ingratiation figures in its tone. It belongs to the woman
at Clio's left, whom Clio has managed, since seating was re-
shuffled for dessert, not to notice. Such gaps or rifts in social
obligation are the prerogative of charisma, with its sexy,
butterfly-alighting attentiveness, its abrupt, invigorating

rudeness, the masochistically satisfying cold shoulder turned toward any less-than-stellar presence. Remorsefully, Clio concedes (as perhaps the voice, fractionally wounded, implies) that in doing so she has been ignoring beauty.

Q: *Briefly explicate Rilke's lines, "All of you undisturbed cities / haven't you ever yearned for the Enemy?"*

A: When that voice says, "Selfish us, we've kept you up too late. You're tired," Clio, not yet ready to confront the source, steadies the bowl of her wineglass between two fingers and a thumb, observing the rhythm of her pulse in the concentric wine rings. The voice qualifies, thoughtfully, "No, *sad*," italicizing with the pleasure of nailing emotion to its right name, and for this ventured precision, Clio feels the agitated relief of the solitary, whose emotions, seldom articulated for another, mostly live and die nameless. Immediately following relief comes panic, not an unusual progression, for there's no panic quite like the panic of having found something you'd hate to lose. Now we come to that oddly asocial moment when the inkblot of private gesture, proof of exigent emotion, stains the unfolding social contract: Clio can't look at this woman. Not yet. Realizing it must appear rude, she closes her eyes. A person whose composure is not only a professional asset but an actual cast of mind may become a connoisseur of her own panic, just as, for a Japanese gardener, the chance scatteration of cherry petals on freshly raked gravel beautifully illumines the futility of control: so behind her closed eyes Clio experiences, as counterpart to panic, exaltation. The Enemy!

Q: *The absurd and the erotic are mutually exclusive modes of perception. That is, no love object can be both ridiculous and beautiful. True or false?*

A: The voice's owner, perceiving an invitation in Clio's half-empty glass, leans in with the bottle, startling Clio, whose closed eyes have prevented awareness of her proximity. Clio jumps, diverting the airborne artery of wine, which leaps about, bathing her wrist, spattering her dessert plate, splashing from the table's edge into her black silk lap. The voice's owner fails to right the bottle until wine rains from the table's edge, pattering into flexing amoeba shapes on the polished floor, the voice's owner apologizing manically—yet as if she anticipated some need for apology?—and setting the bottle down with a thump. *I'm so so sorrrrry.* It is Clio's lap that the voice's owner bends toward, still uttering wild *sorries,* so that Clio's first image of her is of her hair, red and in torment, copious, strenuous, anarchic hair, writhing, heavy, ardent, gorgeous hair tricked into confinement, knotted at the nape of a neck so smooth and white its single mole seems to cast a tiny shadow. The tip of Clio's tongue so covets the mole, which stands out like one of the beads of Beaujolais stippling her wrist, that she scarcely experiences the swabbing of the napkin at her lap—thus, for the sake of the imagined, missing out on the thrill of the actual, and immediately repenting this, the first loss within the kingdom of true love.

"This is *so* not working," says the woman, turning to blot at Clio's wrist while Clio memorizes every detail of the profile of her future. Too much forehead, baldish and vulnerable-looking, as is often true of redheads, a long nose with a bump at its tip, the smart arch of the lifted eyebrow, thick eyelashes dark at their roots, fair to invisibility at their tips. A fine chin. A neat and somehow boyish ear exposed by the tension of the trammeled hair. Why boyish? Unearringed, Clio notes, not even pierced, a sexy virgin petal of lobe. Under the fine chin, the hint of a double, a faint softening in a line that should ideally run tensely along the jaw to the downcurve of the throat. This is true of redheads as well, Clio thinks, this appearance of laxness in certain secret places, as if the body, where it can, resists the severity of the contrast between pale skin and vivid hair, and asserts a passivity, a private entropy, counter to the flamey energy of red. Clio is forty-two to the other's twenty-something: fact. Fearful fact.

"Don't worry, we can get you cleaned up," says the younger woman, "so come on," standing to take Clio's wrist, leading Clio down a long and shadowed hallway, the din of apologies—everyone's, chorused yet random, like Apache war cries—fading behind the two of them, then gone entirely, Clio surrendering to the sexiness of being *led*, for the other hasn't released her wrist and hasn't turned around, and for the length of that fatal hallway Clio obediently pursues this most unexpected of persons, the Beloved. Under Clio's hot gaze the knot of passionate hair at the Beloved's nape, screwed so tight in its coil, releases red-gold strands flaring with electricity.

Q: *The following quotation is taken from Wittgenstein's* Philosophical Investigations:

> . . . *a face which inspires fear or delight (the object of fear or delight) is not on that account its cause, but—one might say—its target.*

> *Discuss.*

A: Prof. Mitsak's new condominium comes with its own scrap
of California, backyard enough for two spindly fruit trees,
a futon of gopher-harrowed turf, and an inherited compost heap. It's still winter, the trees' tracery of bare branches
unreadable as to kind, but Prof. Mitsak thinks of them as
plum trees because sex, for her, was born with a theft: of her
grandmother's plum jam, the old woman watching, from the
corner of an eye, the child's fingers crooking over the jar's
rim, sliding into lumpish, yielding sweetness, the old woman
giving the plaintive laugh peculiar to that kind of vicari-
ous delight, witnessing a pleasure one essentially disapproves
of, which costs one something—in her grandmother's case,
a steely domestic rigor and a wicked Methodist conviction
about the virtue of self-deprivation.

It will be spring by the time the trees, if their blossoming
proves they're not plum, can disappoint Clio, and by spring
she hopes to be eating and sleeping again, done with writing and rewriting letters, actual, insane, ink-and-paper letters that she never sends, done with twisting herself into yoga
asanas meant to impress the younger, suppler Beloved, who
will never observe her contortions. In Clio's previous experience of heartbreak, she's been its cause. On heartbreak's
receiving end, she proves hapless, self-pitying, wincing,
vindictive. A forgetter of goddaughters' birthdays, a serial
umbrella-loser. Winter rains down on her head, pelting her
with the icy spite of finality: she will never tip a baby bottle
toward the mouth of a Mei or Ming, or click wedding ring
against steering wheel in time to Mozart. Her most paro-
died gesture becomes the convulsive shake of the head with
which she assumes the lectern, flicking raindrops across her
notes, rousing the microphone to a squalling tantrum as

water pings against electronics. In each lecture Clio seems to be trailing after some earlier, more brilliant Clio, even as she had followed the Beloved, she of the *sturm und drang* hair, down the fatal hallway. How can love do this, alienate one from oneself? One's necessary, tenured self? All winter, this is the lone relief built into every pitiless week: white-knuckling it at the podium, Clio suffers the loss of something other than the Beloved.

Fridays can be very bad. As junior faculty, the Beloved isn't always required to attend faculty meetings, but sometimes she must. So there is this torment, certain Fridays, of having to sit on the far side of a slab of exotic wood from some plundered rainforest, studying the span of the Beloved's cheekbone, a revelation of human perfection. Like human perfection, shadowed. The corner of the Beloved's mouth has an unwarranted tendency to break Clio's heart. That is, the corner of this mouth now and then deepens into a near smile. Suppose everyone were capable of disarming everyone else thus, by the merest turn of a head, by the flicker of an eyelid or the premonition of a smile: then all relations would be grounded in wonder, then everyone would be taken hostage by the immensity of what it is possible to feel.

Q: *True or false: In narrative, desire is scarcely born before it encounters an obstacle; neither can exist without the other.*

A: Following the Beloved down that fatal hallway, *you*, in your Questioner's detachment, would have kept your wits about you, and would have observed, on the fourth finger of the Beloved's left hand, the diamond whose flash was hidden by the wonder veiling Clio's mind. Well: she is only a character, much of her own story is lost on her.

In that multiply mirrored ladies' designed for blissful immersion in one's reflection the Beloved rinses Clio's trousers under a golden faucet. She twists and wrings out the trousers, then carries them to a dryer on the wall, tapping its round silver button, dangling the black legs in the sirocco so they weave happily, gusting into the Beloved's own body, then fainting away.

"Really, you don't have to do this. You should be out with the others."

"*I* spilled the wine all over you."

This washerwomanly penance is cute, they both think.

"Why did you say, before, 'sad'?" Clio asks.

"Maybe everyone is, when a dinner party drags on and on. If we had a reason to leave, we'd leave. If we don't have a reason, that's sad. You don't seem to have a reason. Or"—she catches herself—"is it rude to say that?"

When she turns Clio makes a fig leaf of her hands. "No, honest."

"And I was surprised, you know? One always thinks of famous people as having everything figured out. Here. I think you can try these now."

Q: *Susan Stewart writes:*

The face becomes a text, a space which must be "read" and interpreted in order to exist. The body of a woman, particularly constituted by a mirror and thus particularly subject to an existence constrained by the nexus of external images, is spoken by her face, by the articulation of another's

*reading. Apprehending the face's image becomes a mode of possession.
. . . The face is what belongs to the other. It is unavailable to the woman
herself.*

A: What was the question?

Q: *What do you make of that?*

A: Clio, hiking her trousers up, finds the Beloved stretching
   lazily, her real and mirrored arms uplifted, fingers interlaced,
   palms ceilingward, fox-red tufts of underarm hair bristling,
   black dress hiked midthigh-high: flirtatiousness or ravishing unself-consciousness, and for her watcher, no knowing
   which. So exigent is Clio's confusion that she cracks her
   knuckles and then remembers how she had hated it when
   her *mother* did that. The memory stamps out several little
   wildfires of desire, Mother's is so derisive a shade, and Clio
   was never out to her. The perfect antidote to desire, skinny
   Mother materializing, upright backbone and the witty inci-
   sion of her neat, ungiving Methodist smile. Just *try* thinking
   back through this woman.

   It's then that two blazing wings of sensation touch down
   on Clio's nape, and the Beloved's palms begin to move in
   circles, massaging, worrying at the tension they discover,
   digging in, the Beloved's thumbs bookending the axial ver-
   tebra, so that Clio feels the three-dimensional puzzle-piece
   of bone turn as distinct as if newly wedged in place, her
   entire skull balanced upon the knife's point of sexual alert-
   ness, Clio afraid to move or make a sound for fear of dislodg-
   ing the hands, startling them into flight. She is aware that

savage loss is the counterpart and shadow of this raw arousal and yearning, which she can scarcely trust even as she leans into it, wondering what this means, this sensual charity.

"Shiatsu."

"Shiatsu," echoes Clio.

"Mmm. Good for what ails you."

The Beloved's reflection squints at the real-world Clio over her shoulder, to which she administers a comradely slap. Dismissed.

What ails me? Clio wonders. *Loss. Aging. Regret.*

So this is Eros' dark side. Always before it was Clio who inflicted the first reality check. The pangs foreshadowing abandonment, the subtly poisonous forewarning: Clio dealt those out.

Now we come, though it's timed wrong, to our epiphany, for Clio, academe's androgynous roué, contriver of seductions, far-flung affairs, and prolonged breakdowns—here and now, Clio encounters a possibility never before entertained: she's been unkind. Careless with others' hearts. A waster of time, a despoiler of affection. As of this moment, that Prof. Mitsak is dead. Just ask Clio, absorbed in this mirror's vision, herself and her at-last true love, the radiant-haired object of all future dreams, now rubbing a finger across a front tooth. Clio puts her hands on those shoulders and turns the slender black-sheathed body around. She feels the weird cessation of her breath in her throat—heart-stopping, she thinks— and then all self-narration, even the stabs at description that accompany the worst emergencies, stops. Though the red mouth tilts toward her, lips parting, the eyes remain open. Dazzling, desirous, repelled, unreadable.

Q: *Compare/contrast the roles of "body" and "soul" in the act of kissing.*

A: This eyes-open kiss is clumsy: neither body nor soul can readily forgive that. Seduction, it turns out, requires an almost Questioner-like detachment to ensure grace. To become a character in the story is to fall from grace. It's as if Clio, in her previous affairs, was always narrator, never simply down in the story, at the muddy, helpless level where she understood only as much as anyone else. Or less. It could be that the Beloved needs a narrator, not simply a floundering fellow character. Clio's teeth grate against the Beloved's, a terrible, nails-on-blackboard sound from which they both recoil.

Q: *Comment briefly on the following quotation:*

Perhaps it was to that hour of anguish that there must be attributed the importance which Odette had since assumed in his life. Other people are, as a rule, so immaterial to us that, when we have entrusted to any one of them the power to cause so much suffering or happiness to ourselves, that person seems at once to belong to a different universe, is surrounded with poetry, makes of our lives a vast expanse, quick with sensation, on which that person and ourselves are ever more or less in contact.

A: All that drear winter of La Niña, Clio feels as if she's trying to keep a wine cork submerged in a bathtub using only one thumb, so dodgy and unpredictable is this love. Tamped-down love means not only sublimated energy but also ranting, pointless impatience: before long, she's sick of obsession's two-lane Nebraska highway. She welcomes any distraction, even this folder, thwacked down on her desk by a junior colleague, younger even than the Beloved. Fading back toward the doorway, this colleague announces in an injured tone: "We really need to talk at some point after you've read this." "About?" "About Nadia." The Beloved, up for tenure. While junior faculty can't vote on tenure decisions, they do a fair amount of lobbying—if that's what this is—on behalf of favored candidates. Renee strains for ease, a gauche, brain-driven woman whose particular mix of ethnicity baffles Clio. African American? Vietnamese? And Czech? Irish? Dutch? Some unprecedented cat's cradle of deoxyribonucleic acid granted her that shapely mouth, pugilist's menacing nose with flaring nostrils, oily fawn skin marred across the cheekbones by an orange-peel stippling of adolescent acne. That acne, severe and untreated, suggests a raisin-in-the-sun, down-home poverty, valiantly tackled and, at this point in her young career, stringently repudiated. If Renee ever had an accent, it's gone. Or not quite: some suggestion of backwater lulls and daydreamy delta vowels remains, despite that impressive will. To suggest a chic she's far from possessing, Renee's left ear is multiply pierced; adorned with wires and rings, it seems more alert than the other, more attuned to signals and nuances. It is to this ear that Clio says, "I'll read it. We'll talk."

"You don't *get* it. We expected so much from you." *We*, the nine who held the dinner in her honor, that memorable evening.

In this chilly pause, Clio, love's insomniac, fails to suppress a yawn. Renee, fervent with insult, closes in, hurling herself into Clio's office's only unoccupied seat, a meanly proportioned straight-backed chair designed to discommode students who would otherwise linger in Clio's aura of disdainful indifference. Throwing one leg over the other, leaning in, slapping the folder, Renee begins, "You were supposed to—"

Clio says, " 'To'?"

What the hell is the expression stamped on those fine, ethnically inscrutable features. "To change things! To, not *mother* exactly, but at least *care* about our careers. If you hear the word going around that 'Nadia's publications are a little *scanty* to qualify for tenure,' you're supposed to have her back, but no one's heard a peep from you, and Nadia—Nadia's some kind of demoralized shadow of her former self."

"Shadow?"

"Me, I fantasize obsessively about burning down this building."

"But Nadia? She's a demoralized shadow?"

"Even to confess this fantasy probably gets me on about five different lists right now."

"I haven't noticed anything wrong with Nadia."

"Well: you seem to be avoiding her."

"No. No, no. Not avoiding her. Why would I avoid Nadia? No."

"Avoiding all of us, then."

"You appear to have found me."

"Right at home in this building I burn down ten or eleven times a day."

"If you burn it down, what will you do?"

"Ha! Even in daydreams I blow out the match. Even in my head, where you'd think I'd have no fear, I can't touch the flame to the shitty carpet. This place! Can't you get a little more involved? Unless you're willing to get your hands dirty, her tenure meeting's gonna go in a truly ugly direction. 'Scanty'! She has two books! Would you like the figures on just how many junior female faculty this place has *ever* tenured? Because I find that figure impressive. It's a very round number. Zero! And, excuse me for noticing, but the last male this department gave tenure to had only one— uninteresting, I think—book and a couple of *derivative* articles, yet his shit was never called 'scanty.'"

"Okay," Clio says.

"Okay what?"

Down the hallway, a door opens, closes, and is locked, the homeward-bound deconstructionist whistling, the melody trailing down the floor before vanishing into the elevator, not before lodging itself in Clio's mind. *Miss my clean white linen, and my fancy French cologne.*

"I'll peep," Clio says distractedly. "I'll get Nadia's back."

"Her books are *really good*. You've read them, right? Look, did I—?"

"Did you?"

"Offend you."

"There's truth in what you said. I haven't been very engaged." Gently, but sick of gentleness, disliking the baiting way this woman hangs her sentences in the air.

"Your advocacy will be a game changer, you know that, right?" A pause while this antagonist wonders how far she can push her luck. "Nadia *really needs you*, is the thing."

"I'll do what I can." *But it's really not my ho-ome.*

"I would open a florist shop," Renee says. "After I burned this building down. Since you ask."

"You know what I think about?" Clio says—not, in the moment, even faintly surprised, though in retrospect she will marvel at this question, at having done, next, something so unlike herself, telling a truth, and why, when no good comes of such slips? "A bookstore on a downtown corner in some rinky-dinky town. Rare books, first editions."

"But you're famous. You can make waves. You're not at their mercy." *You have everything I want.*

"There are days, lately, when I don't love books."

"You're losing your soul."

Clio reflects on the justness of this observation. "People open bookstores because they want their souls back."

"It works. I know bookstores whose owners have *gotten* them back."

They laugh, and then don't know what to do with the silence that follows.

"Does Nadia know you came to me?"

"Nadia. Girl is *losing* it. Sleepless, skinnier than ever, keeps printing out articles about former professors who end up homeless or hoarding cats or whatever. But, no, we've never talked about you. I think she thinks you've got reservations about her work."

"What gave her that idea?" In fact, it's true: in the cool scholarly part of her soul Clio doesn't much like Nadia's books. Trusting this secret assessment, with the rest of her judgment compromised by love, would be unwise, and Clio has intended all along to vote yes, has meant, in short, to do the right thing, or at least the least *wrong* thing. Whichever way it goes, next week's meeting will cause pain: either the pain of Nadia's being granted tenure and remaining near but unpossessable, or the pain of her being refused tenure, thus vanishing forever from Clio's life. If not even a starry glimpse of the object of fear and desire is possible, what will become of that life?

And yet, freed on this, the first afternoon in our story

that can safely be called *spring*, lugging her laden briefcase, Clio surrenders to the lightness of soul hidden within each Friday, taking the stairs in long-legged, traipsing descent, her voice pitching *up!* and *up!* precariously, caroming off cinderblock as if the stairwell were a gigantic cement shower stall, quick with resonance, echoing and amplifying:

"Oh, I

"Could drink

"A case

"Of you!"

You! flung into the rainy outer world as Joni Mitchell, trailing rags of her ethereal voice, charges across the asphalt only to find, wading in a slow circle around a rusted-out wreck of a car in the flooding parking lot, Nadia, head bent under the assault of the rain, carrying something, now and then pausing to hammer with her fist at the car's Bondo-dappled hood. Clio suffers a twist of emotion she can't at first recognize. Before, encountering Nadia unexpectedly, she has experienced a number of emotions—shame of a particularly rich, basking intensity, or a pitiless, wired kind of happiness—but never before has any response to Nadia been as temperate as this: disappointment.

"This is all I can *fuck. Ing.* Take." *Fuck* and *ing* are blows.

It's been two months since they have exchanged more than cautious *hi*'s, passing in the hall.

"Keep doing that, you'll hurt your hand."

"I locked myself out, can you believe it?"

"Come get in my car. You can use my cell."

"This had to happen in front of you." Nadia begins to cry. "When all I want—"

"All you want—?" More baiting sentences? Did the junior women catch this from each other?

"Is to be like you. So to*gether*. So far above the shit and disarray."

Nadia wants not to *have* but to *be* Clio, it seems. "I lose keys," she says, and tries to catch Nadia's wrist before she can bang on the old car again, but too late: a racket of reverberating metal, and the rain drumming on the Chevy's roof and hood, Clio sheltering Nadia's head, now, under an impromptu roof of briefcase.

"Get in my car and we'll figure out what you should do."

"I can't get in, I'm soaked, I'm a mess."

"You're shivering. Come on."

In Clio's BMW, with its kid-glove leather and customized quiet, German engineering exerts its power to heal the psyche, and Nadia grows calmer. As she ducked into the passenger side after Clio unlocks its door, she had absently relinquished an old shoebox with bulging sides, wound around with duct tape and curiously heavy. Covertly, Clio tries shaking the box.

"Hey!" Nadia cries, and snatches the box away, giving Clio a look full of accusation and darkening sorrow. "This box has my heart in it," she confesses.

"Your *what* in it?"

Nadia bends forward in her seat and rests her forehead against the lid of the box, communing with whatever's inside. After a moment she says clearly, "My cat." Droplets chase down the spiraling madrone twigs of wet red hair to patter onto the box's cardboard, where they appear as fuzzy, dilating dots. "Who loved me for *me*."

There is nothing to dry either of them with, Clio the

bad, the negligent mother in this impromptu family in the quasi-domesticity of the car's interior. Wanting to help but unable to think how, Clio sets the wipers going. Fans of visibility flash open and swipe shut, melodically. Around them, the drenched and shining asphalt reveals streaks of brilliance, as if light were drilling down into a medium infinitely soft and black, and the other cars stranded here and there across the lot possess a wet, sharp-edged distinctness. Clio turns on the heat, not just because Nadia is still shivering; suddenly it seems important that they not be fogged in by breath, and she's worried about the weirdness of Nadia's behavior. "The cat is," Clio says delicately, "*in* the box?"

"Dead," Nadia says to the box.

"Nadia, I'm sorry."

"Fuck, what a word," Nadia says. "*Dead*. Onomatopoetic."

"I'm so sorry."

At last, to Clio's relief, Nadia sits up. "I sensed something was wrong all night, and I took her in first thing this morning. To the vet. It was an okay experience, really. They give her this shot and she goes limp in my hands. This little velvet sack from which all fear just, *sssst*, leaks away. I'm holding her, I'm stroking her. They give her the other shot then. The death shot."

Q: *In the light of your answers to the previous questions, formulate a definition of "beauty."*

A: "I'm sorry," Clio says again, meaning to convey empathy, though she can't help it: such grief seems ridiculous to her. Is there a fugitive whiff—carnal, musky?—of decay in the car?

She hadn't known Nadia had a cat, but in her experience cats, belonging to lovers or exes or lovers' exes' exes, come with relationships—never before sealed in a box, though. Clio longs to apply the balm of her cool hand to Nadia's forehead, to the temple, where new hair grows in a minute clockwise whorl, like the illustration of the birth of a star, the tiny hairs strung with fine condensation. For no reason a phrase of Woolf's comes to Clio: " 'Reality' . . . beside which nothing matters." Reality for Clio seems born of that fine, nearly invisible star on the Beloved's temple, and if she wants more than anything to touch it, for the sake of what the other must be feeling, she resists.

Q: *"At the center of each person,"* D. W. Winnicott writes, *"is an in-communicado element and this is sacred and most worthy of preserva-tion." Can this belief be reconciled with erotic love, and if so, how?*

A: She resists. "Where can I take you?" she asks, hating to inter-rupt this communing silence, which, however dreary, is still the easiest closeness they are ever likely to achieve.

Provoked by sympathy, her instinct to redeem herself in Clio's eyes warring with the wretchedness of grief, Nadia begins to cry again. "Hey, hey, come on, it's all right, it really is," Clio says. "I can take you wherever you need to go."

Monotonously, Nadia weeps, not with her hands clasped to her face but rubbing and swiping at it compulsively, as if her hands wanted to *work* on grief, to knead and knuckle it out. This at least—the loss or death of cats being a staple of lesbian discourse—*is* familiar.

"I don't know where to go. Or what to do with her."

Nadia's voice has a rasp in it, deprivation meeting and marrying remorse, the tone of the truly, bitterly disconsolate. The dead-cat smell is stronger now. Nadia says, "I live in this apartment, seventh floor, there's no garden, not even really a lawn. No place she can go into the ground." She clears her throat. "I thought of trying to sneak in to bury her on campus, maybe in one of those old eucalyptus groves. That's why I brought her. I was actually walking around with her under my arm, looking. But I thought, what if the campus police find me burying this little box of cat? Won't it be ludicrous, won't it get me in trouble, won't they just anyway stop me? Plus what can I dig with? It's not like I own a shovel. What a fucked-up *life*. I hate my *life*. I can't even call someone and say, 'My cat died,' because everyone I know would feel some kind of irony about the situation, like they would never be caught driving around with their cat in a box. Even Billy. He wouldn't mean to, but he'd convey his— I'm sorry, I'm ruining your beautiful leather."

Billy, Clio remembers, is the boyfriend, who teaches at Columbia and seems to be mostly a phone presence in Nadia's existence but, as such, sufficient to thwart other entanglements. For example, with Clio.

"He would convey his what?" She can't help this little viper of voyeurism, uncoiling.

"He never liked the cat. So—his re*lief*."

"Oh, no."

"He's going to try not to show it, but he's going to be *glad*."

"Surely not, Nadia."

"He's going to think, ah, now we can live together, no impediments."

"The cat can't have been much of an impediment."

"He can be *fussy*. The cat liked peeing in his shoes."

Doesn't the cat have a name? Clio wonders. "Listen, I think we should go to my place. I have a backyard. Maybe you'd like to bury your cat there. It's a nice backyard. With plum trees."

"You'd want my cat in your backyard? Why?"

"You need to get her into the ground, right? I don't mind if your cat gets a tiny piece of my backyard. I think it's a good use for it."

"How can we bury her in rain like this?"

"Under umbrellas?"

Umbrellas are what they use, taking turns digging and sheltering, Clio glad to break in her Smith & Hawken spade, the soil yielding pebbles of asphalt and shards of glass but mostly giving way easily enough, not difficult to excavate a fair-sized hole in, though the bottom has begun to seep before Nadia lowers the sodden box, and because she begins to cry again, it's Clio who shucks the first spadeful onto the darkening coffin, petals, borne in by a gust, sticking to the cardboard, Nadia crying harder, Clio's lower back beginning to ache and her own eyes to brim.

When Clio is done tamping the earth over the little grave, she asks Nadia if she'd like to come in, and Nadia assents. Barefoot, she prowls past the floor-to-ceiling bookshelves with scarcely a sideways glance. Clio can't help registering her failure to read titles or pull out a single one of the Woolf firsts, with their fragile, charming Vanessa Bell jackets. In the kitchen Nadia pauses at the refrigerator door. "Wow. Chinese babies."

"My godchildren." Each morning, with her first cup of coffee, she stands before the collage of fat-cheeked faces, snowsuits and tutus, trying to make sure she's not forgetting another birthday.

"All girls?"

"In China girls get abandoned so the parents can try for a boy."

"Do you like kids?"

"Only those."

"I can't imagine what it would feel like, abandoning your baby." She imagines: "Like tearing your heart out with your bare hands." She taps several pictures. "These are cute, these tiny violins."

"Suzuki method."

"I want kids."

"Why don't you get out the wine? But let me pour."

"Ha."

Bringing two wineglasses filled to the brim, she sets one down by Clio and sits in the nearer of two cubes of chrome and black leather.

Clio says, "I'll make a fire. Get you warmed up." Thinks *Dolt!* for the double entendre. She busies herself with crumpling newspaper and arranging kindling into a tipsy pyramid—reminded, as the lit match wavers, of Renee—and she's in luck, the fire catches nicely, and Nadia comes to sit cross-legged beside her, the bath towel now slung over her shoulders boxer-style. She rubs the back of a freckled hand across her cheekbone, leaving a streak of wet grittiness. Clio looks away so she won't be tempted to take the towel's corner and erase that streak. She doesn't want to ask if she can, but simply for things to unfold, or not, as Nadia wishes. Nadia hugs her shins, fire-gazing, and says, "I was crazy, out there in the rain. You came along and saved me." In her voice, the definite note of flirtation.

"I want something for you."

"Something *for* me? What?"

"You might not understand this, or think it has anything to do with me—and probably it doesn't—but what I want is your happiness. However you want to go about obtaining it. Whatever shape it takes in your imagination. The funny thing is, I can want this without knowing the specifics. How you'd define happiness. Whether you even think it exists."

"What about your happiness?" Nadia says. "You know, supposing something happened with us. Would you be all right if it happened only once?" So, when it comes down to it, she's a person who likes to know what she's getting into. Clio had believed, wrongly, that she would prefer not-knowing, risk, improvisation.

"I don't know." She rues her honesty. "Yes."

"You would? Even if we can't see each other after this?"

"Yes."

"Because this can't turn into a *thing*." Nadia sticks to interrogation: reluctantly, Clio realizes she might be good at it. "I don't want you to get hurt, do you see that?"

"I'm fine."

"Because I'm straight."

"The essence is that I love you," Clio says, "that I loved you the moment I saw you," and then she says, "and that's never happened to me before," and hugs her own shins, the two of them fire-gazing in parallel universes, waiting for what will come next.

Q: *Tell me.*

A: The Beloved's nipples are terra cotta, her vagina is coral, her hair, floating as it dries, a torrent freed from gravity, roams the air around her face with an unruly will of its own, her high forehead serene in spite of this changeling hair, her small breasts swinging and bumping her whippet rib cage, the mole on her neck vivid, her kneecaps flushed bright pink by the fire's heat as she crouches above Clio, and if Clio wants to believe this night the most beautiful she will ever live through, who can disagree? All conspires to ensure the Beloved's tenure, Clio's argument ("The last male this department gave tenure to had only one—uninteresting, I think—book and a couple of *derivative* articles"), the *yes* Clio scrawls on a slip of paper, one of several dozen slips collected by the chair, doubly, triply inevitable. Let's agree that no love should be judged by its duration, and that what Clio learned that isolated night, never before having experienced its like, is of incalculable worth in what Keats calls the school for souls. But there is another vantage point, the future, which finds Clio dreaming she's lost something and can't regain it, no matter how she searches. She wakes to find she has bitten her lip until it bleeds. Spots of blood dapple the pillow slip, and when, later that day, Clio discovers the wedding invitation lurking in her departmental mailbox, she tears it to pieces, only to end up taping them together and magnetting the frankenstein card among her goddaughters. Nadia's bridegroom is composedly handsome in his tux—maybe there is, in fact, a slight fussiness in the shine of his shoes and the primly satisfied set of his mouth; of the two of them, bride and groom, his is the more conventional prettiness. After a boomingly musical interval, all heads turn to follow the bride's progress down the aisle, getting farther and farther away, and the only thing Clio wants to do, there in her pew, is claw at her arms, bare for the beautiful May weather, to smear ashes across her face, to maul and mark her body forever, but a hand clasps hers. This clasp conveys restraint, forbearance, calm. It's Renee's hand, for not long after Clio sat down, Renee slid into the pew beside her, craning her neck to take in the fanciness of the flowers at the altar, concluding, "Swanky." Then, in a whisper: "Mimosa. Unusual choice."

The two trees in Clio's yard prove to be not plum but cherry, merely ravishing. Even the inexhaustible Woolf, in the following days and weeks, holds no fascination for Clio. Much, much later it will occur to Clio that though the box seemed to her to possess sufficient weight, and seemed to hold something both lolling and stiff, she had never actually seen the cat. The lid had been taped down, the box wound around and around again with duct tape. Did Nadia, unaware her conniving was redundant, scheme for Clio's *yes*? If it wasn't the cat in the box, what else can it have been? Something with the density of the once-alive, with a certain compactness, the weight of dark muscle—say, Clio's heart. It might as well have been her heart, she parted with it so completely that night, and it's so long—so bitterly long—before she sees *that* again.

Q: *Does she ever see it again?*

A: Sweet Questioner, you care. If we skip ahead to the morning two years later when, rolling over in bed, lifting herself on an elbow to gaze down her pugilist's nose at Clio, Renee reels off the ingredients for her fawn skin, handsome mouth, and eerie green eyes—African American, Lakota Sioux, Welsh, some Norwegian—we can call that the moment Clio sees it again. And, look, beyond the ken of this exam they never run out of things to say to each other, though one spends her days leafing through old books, the other up to her elbows in sweet peas and tuberose, cattleya and quince.

Q: *Read the following quotation from Simone Weil's "On Human Personality."*

If a child is doing a sum and does it wrong, this mistake bears the stamp of his personality. If he does the sum exactly right, his personality does not enter into it at all.

Argue that this does, or does not, have implications for love.

Nobody You Know

Only a divorce but she can barely get out of bed, she needs a cocoon or echoless cave, the phone rings on and on despairing, every clock in the twilit house ticks further into the future.

You're a survivor.

It disturbs her to be called *survivor* when she knows she is not—not in the sense that's intended, of belonging to a superior, blessedly resourceful class of human being. When she lived through the experience, she had been a child, and that is what children do, they live through things if they can. In that sense, *survivor* is like *breather*. Breathing is what every child does and keeps doing until some force or other rules out breathing. Which is all that *survivor* amounts to, too.

I didn't want to be the one who tells you this. He's her lawyer. He has to tell her. *Bruce is involved with someone.*

Disbelief resembles distress, maybe, because he says *Hey?*

She says *Look, it can't be true. I would have known.*

Evidently not.

He said the survivor thing by way of preface to this news. Before this afternoon she has been, not enigmatic exactly, but not particularly readable, and he'd liked the challenge. No tears in her eyes till now. Silently he parts with his idealized version of her: interesting slash almost beautiful, a painter whose work nobody really likes, who is somehow famous anyway, or at least well known.

Who is it?

"Nobody you know." Each of the three words given its pat of emphasis, either because this is a lie or because it's a truth, she can't tell. It's not so much English-as-a-second-language that is the problem, it's the inflections and subtleties that would confide truth or its absence if she were a native speaker. In the heat of argument, once, Bruce told her she needed to *get a grip*, and her bewilderment had magically turned anger to laughter, and the two of them back into lovers.

"Nobody I know?"

"So I'm assured."

"Nobody I know? He told you that?"

"It was conveyed. Look, X." Her husband's nickname for her; the lawyer is trading in overheard intimacies now well out of date. "This is a small town. You should think about that job offer. Get the hell out of Dodge."

"Dodge?"

"What the sheriff tells the—. Joke. Bad joke. Meaning, basically, elsewhere could have its attractions about now. In terms of not running into them."

A nameless emotion is born the moment she learns he has slammed the door of an excluding love in her face. It can't be true that she can't see in. That she *can't know the story*. This is her life she's been shut out of! Throughout their relationship they have been each other's great explainers and interpreters, and silence is completely and annihilatingly unlike him. There was nothing they didn't tell each other, no subject that had been out of bounds. The other side of her need to know the story will be his longing *to tell her the story*, and what do you do, how can you live, if the one you tell everything to, who tells you everything in return, disappears? What happens to their stories now? And how does this severance feel to him? What does it cost *him*? Does the new lover announce outright *No talking to Ximena, not ever*? Or is she the sort who doesn't explicitly forbid but simply makes her fragility clear? After Ximena, the *survivor*, might fragility have its charms? What had the new woman told him, who was she, what were her eyes like, her mouth? It would be a huge leap toward understanding what had just happened if Ximena could only see the new lover's eyes. Those eyes would tell Ximena what Bruce thinks he sees, because they have always come to the same conclusions about other people. They were close that way, and after all Ximena knows what he likes in faces and what he has seemed attracted to in the past, though he wasn't the inconsiderate kind of husband who often calls other women beautiful, and in fact Ximena believes he did not find very many women beautiful, and when he did it was because of intelligence, or soul, something seen in the eyes. Chief among the deprivations of divorce is this awful, inscrutable facelessness of his new lover. Ximena searches her memory for a face interesting enough to have caught his attention. The lawyer is right, theirs is a small town; Ximena must have waited behind the new lover, who was not yet the new lover, in a checkout line, or scoffed at her stupid marginalia in a book in the secondhand bookstore, or brushed past her on a sidewalk, or sat down at the table where she had left her empty coffee cup, or resented the future lover not taking off her perky beret in a movie theater. Ximena can't ask Bruce, who is the expert on her life, just as a husband should be; she can't ask him whether she ever encountered the lover, and no one else can clear up the mystery of whether the lover really is unknown to Ximena or say with authority *Actually there was this one time.* Not knowing is like a ravenous O right in the middle of her mind, crying for the truth. An O like that could turn a person into a stalker. Ximena is not that far gone. She will not haunt Bruce and the new lover, not in real life, not on the Internet. Only, look who they have caused her to understand: menacers, skulkers, crazy people.

Divorce is not linear. One morning there is peace of mind, the next there is wrath. So what if she packed and left, so what if she *behaved well* and let him keep the house instead of forcing him to sell it and settle up, that doesn't make her *forgiving*, it doesn't mean she feels anything but contempt for the lover and basilisk rage toward him. Good thing they are far away. Just let her see them once more and she will ruin their lives if she can.

Welcome to Iowa, you survivor you. Ximena walks through the emotionless atmosphere found only in new houses. She owns a kitchen sink, electrical outlets, bare walls, a cat brought home from the animal shelter so there will be another heart adapting to this strangeness. Thanks to an oversight by the finish carpenters or whoever, the stairs have not been swept, and the sawdust records her ascent in good peasant footprints, one per tread. See the cunning peas-in-a-pod lineup of her toes, clear as if printed in beach sand. Up comes the cat. Ximena crouches to let the striped cat rub against her knee, her shin, the knuckles of her hands, first the left and then the right. The cat will work methodically, taking small breaks from the project of rubbing its cheek against every new corner and facet of home, and what is Ximena's project? Should she try rubbing her cheek on facets and corners? Maybe this is a space she can work in, this attic. Skylights permit cloud shadows to roll purposefully across the planks. Bird shadows, too, handfuls of them splashed across her floor, wheel and tilt and vanish. Summer. It's enough, for now, to be kept track of by a cat, it's plenty. This is a bare-bones existence, not bare in the sense of poor because she's not, but bare in the sense of involving minimal contact with other human beings, intelligently bare, Agnes Martin minimal, and the one thing she misses is her studio behind the house in Smoke River. Bruce's carpentry had proved inadequate to the more fantastic, Russian-dacha elements of the sketch she'd done on a napkin in answer to his question, *If you could have the perfect place to paint what would it look like?* Because that had been their first cup of coffee, their first conversation, she had not understood he was serious. She had not foreseen his saving the napkin and setting out to translate romance into two-by-fours, and he had not foreseen that romance would not prevail over a lack of competence. Windowpanes cracked for no reason, the roof was always shedding shingles, the door never completely closed, but for her it was the safest place she had ever known, every single nail driven for love of her, and now she will never see it again. Abandoned, its floor pattered over by mice, she supposes, its spire (that was crazy, that he'd built her a spire) waiting for lightning to strike, whimsical little shipwreck rotting in the field behind the house where Bruce lives with, with (   ). The lover's name is still unknown to her.

The dean who, on first hearing a rumor of her divorce, had sought Ximena out, wooed and reassured and faxed, describes the Indian mounds of a nearby state park, mentions the Art Deco theater featuring indie films, says how pretty spring is in Iowa, how astounding after seemingly endless winter, and Ximena says she looks forward to it, and in fact certain discoveries please her: figs drizzled in honey in the town's organic restaurant, gingko leaves turning a uniform raincoat yellow, a yoga instructor saying *open* or *softly* directly to her knees or knotted shoulders, cajoling Ximena's body as if that relationship, his with her body, was subject to laws different from those of minds' polite, slowly accreting acquaintance. Divorce, it turns out, means severance not only from certain cherished versions of oneself but with *disliked* variants. In particular there is a suffering, slightly famous self that Ximena is glad to forsake. Here are acquaintances who have never heard Bruce narrate the death of Ximena's father to an entire quieted table of his doctor friends. Now she wonders why he had ever believed he had a right to tell that story. Why keep talking when by staring down at her plate she'd made her resistance plain? Why did he like stories in which harm was done innocence, and why had it taken her so long to wonder why? In his absence, the world's murderousness continues: the eleven-year-old schoolboy caught abusing five-year-olds; not just one baby found dead in a dumpster, but twins. Bruce believed it was essential to keep abreast of coups, smuggling, assassination. He was one of those catastrophe-literate Americans who knew immediately, from her name, whose daughter she was, and if that had been part of her appeal for him, she had never minded until now, six months into divorce: and now she hears, or rehears, the accusations that had been part and parcel of their intimacy, the failure to engage with her past, the resistance that he stopped short of calling cowardice, her need *to paint the same thing over and over again*. To break through to the next subject would require courage. She didn't want to raise her voice with him, not about courage, and not about painting, and not in her studio, because that would have been like screaming in church. There had been one final, bad confrontation. Softly she said that she was already doing what she wanted to and it was the only thing she wanted to do, and under her softness she meant that he should cut it out, this thing of telling her what to paint, but he persisted: "Baby, why not work closer to the bone?" Which, it takes her a moment to understand, means *Why not use your own life? Use.* He should have said *use*. "My hown life," she said—hearing, through anger, the emergence of the accent that will make her seem more perversely authentic to him. "I could hopen a vein and paint with the blood and you'd be *pleased*, I could paint my father's shirt with nineteen bullet holes, the shirt left at night on the doorstep for my aunt to find so she could fall to her knees screaming, paint that and you and everyone can say *That really happened*, and it would make you feel so good, right?, because you would have a little piece of this terrible thing, a piece you can handle, which makes you feel more alive, because what you want me to use my father's death for is *to make you and everyone feel more alive*, and that makes you a stealer, a *leech* of emotion, a thief—"

She had screamed in church, and from then on, whenever he came out to the shed to see a new painting, he was no longer honest. Even now she misses his confrontational stance before a painting, his boxer's glower, brow creased, chin down. He had held nothing back, and if the painting failed to change his life he blamed it, and he was right, she understood now, in the relentlessness of his extraordinary expectations he had been right, more than right, *rare*, because once one has ceased to be a child there is not nearly enough visceral loathing of complacency. It's an aspect of their marriage that has come to seem, in retrospect, a treasure: the dictatorial rightness of his obsessiveness, his crazy conviction that she is a genius, or would be if she would only listen to him.

One night when the full moon and too much wine keep them awake after sex, the yoga instructor asks if he can see her work, and she can think of no real reason to say no. The good part of this is that while following him up the stairs she can admire the high rounded puckish symmetrical ascending cheeks of his ass, the cleft of their clean division curving in to the shadow where the scrotum, like some sad, worn, withered shaman's bag he must carry everywhere, lolls between long-muscled thighs. Not that women think this way, she thinks, but this man is far more beautiful than Bruce, who was getting soft around the middle when she saw him last, whose wispy hairline exposed his temples, sharpening his air of braininess and worry, and why had she loved those qualities, why was he real to her, more real than anybody else? Down the length of the attic, in and out of shafts of moonlight, the bare-assed yoga instructor named Daniel drifts, and—sure that she is about to be lied to—she stands watching his easygoing unawareness, his innocent shambling failure to *feel what he is feeling.* He says some nice things and for the first time she grasps that he believes her to be obscure and a failure, that concealed within his attraction is the desire to rescue: *to help her out.* This boy! Help her! While the cat rubs his left ankle, Daniel asks, "One thing I don't get."

She gives him no encouragement. If he wants to say it, let him say it.

He says it. "Why paint the same thing over and over?"

More than a year later Bruce turns up, one hazy midsummer morning, in the form of a letter. Envelope, stamp, handwriting. A letter.

> Hey X,
>
> I'm hoping you won't just rip this into little pieces.
>
> I want to believe you can look back on what we had without pain, but you would say that like always I am imposing my version of how things should be, without asking you. For the pain I caused you, I would like your forgiveness. Please forgive me.
>
> Occasionally somebody says you're doing well out there and I'm glad. There are developments in my life, too. This is Robin holding Clem, who just said his first word. He had me wrapped around his finger from day one.
>
> Listen X, make them treat you right out there in the Heart of Darkness and if you get back this way give me a call.
>
> > p.s. Happy 37th—be well.

She's no expert at telling babies' ages, but this one has to have been conceived long before they broke up. For *months* he had kept this secret. In those months she had kissed him, she had told him what she dreamed last night, she had done his laundry, she had confided her fears. He must not have known what to do; he must have been torn, hearing, under their domestic small talk, the ticking clock of his predicament. The baby wears the kind of ominous knit cap favored by perpetrators of muggings and assaults. She makes a halfhearted attempt to tear the picture in two, but it's tough and flexible and destroying it would require scissors, and besides it's as if this picture has infinite depths and she can't see deeply enough, but that has to be shock. Disbelief, which causes this simple picture to seem strange. The baby's expression—opaque, lordly, insolent, dire—suggests the laser-beam confidence of the utterly beloved. He has been caught in the middle of a lunge, resisting the arms that hold him.

It is degrading to have lost him to so white a face, pale to its barely-there lashes and with the pointy rat nose sometimes seen on the monochromatically fair. But the mouth! The mouth is done in lipstick of a carnal, crude, trashy red, a third-world mouth, a Cuban mouth, and Ximena can't help wondering if the lover feels the need to mitigate her whiteness, if the ethni-fication of her mouth is owed to competitiveness with Ximena, about whom he must tell stories, feeling as he always has about Ximena's life, that its tragedy rubbed off on him and persists even now as an aura, the tingling persistent glamour of violent death. Ximena packs, biting her lower lip as she shoves note-books and BlackBerry and reading glasses into her messenger bag, needing at last to confront him, to tell him that his theft of her life, his lover's theft of her *mouth*, has to stop, fifty miles of highway vanishing before she pulls over to dig out her cell, cancel her birthday dinner with Daniel, and ask can he feed Bad Cat while she's gone? Sunk deep between walls of corn, the yellow line sucks toward an irresistible vanishing point.

———

Ximena paints moonscapes across which the lunar wind blows
esoteric litter, a tumbling bowler hat, a black dress, glowing
rubber balls, flying scraps of paper bearing scribbled handwriting. They don't work for everyone, far from it, but her paintings
are sought after, collected, given the minor awards that foretell
greater awards in the future, deemed sufficiently *interesting* to
justify lucrative visiting-artist stints and, out of the blue, the associate professorship at Iowa. No doubt her story plays a part,
and the famous photograph. *LIFE* had caught her father, three
days before his death, resting his bearded cheek against Ximena's hair while she toyed with his watch. She remembers this
photograph from inside. That is: the feelings whose outward
expression makes this photo memorable—the feelings that cause
anyone seeing it for the first time to pause—were her feelings.
Or: half of them were hers, the other half her father's. Usually undemonstrative, he had laid his cheek against her hair, his
contentment in his child's presence, contentment of the kind
almost anyone can feel, combined with weariness almost beyond
comprehension. The tiny deliberate steps that undid his wrist-
watch were the most intimate actions Ximena had then ever
performed on or with another body, and she loved him for letting her do them. Without the watch his forearm was a rak-
ishly black-haired length of wild creature, tendony, bony, full of
authority and life force, capable of great quickness, of (she had
sensed it even then) violence. A man's arm, which she had set
free. Ximena made the watch glide snakelike up her own thin
arm, concentrating with a child's rapture in sensation—which
can appear in a photograph as mere reverie—on bringing time
to a halt.

Her aunt, the older of two, a black-browed, haggard, natural-

born martyr, led Ximena through a strange world of tin roofs
and dusty alleys to the site of her father's death. Across a wall
of adobe bricks tottered gigantic letters in fresh paint, reds and
blues and blacks unmediated, as yet, by dust. Wasps clambered in
and out of the holes in the wall. Each emergent wasp, posing on
the rim of a bullet hole, took an instant to compose itself. Wit-
less witnesses to her father's death, had they cowered inside their
holes, or flown out enraged? Her father's name reeled across the
wall in letters whose haste suggested peril, but someone had run
the risk. Once written, the name had been embellished, paid
homage, annotated with signs and slogans. It was only a question of time before it would be found by obscurers and erasers
of history; it was bound to be a brief-lived salute, but while it
lasted it was as brave as paint could be, as loving and outraged as
hands could contrive. Here was a language Ximena spoke. She
needed to press against that paint, to wet her fingertips and leave
an imprint of her own, but her hard aunt, seizing the thick tail
of the girl's hair, yanked her back.

The girl was handed over to the younger aunt, the smarter
aunt, who managed to get them both to the country across
which Ximena drives, high on the sense of destiny that attends
certain self-destructive decisions. Caffeine sweeps every mote
of delusion from the white room of consciousness. *Now* she understands. Bruce was still sleeping with *her* when that baby was
conceived with the lover, when he came inside that albino with
her little smile who probably told him she was going to keep it,
she was going to have this baby *with or without you*, and Bruce
would have looked from one to the other of the two women
in his life and seen one whose sorrow was unrelenting and one
whose need had a beginning and an end. A kind of end. As Ximena's grief never will.

The town has gone ahead without her: a new traffic light on Highway 1, a McDonald's painted a shade of blue sanctioned by the Coastal Commission, a hotel at cliff's edge where once a grove of towering shaggy eucalyptus had sifted the wind. In a dim room smelling of latex paint she opens the window for the evening breeze and leans out: yes, tatters and coils of beige-green bark litter the margin of bare ground between cliff and raw hotel. Ximena slides between newish sheets, and after a time realizes that she has been awake far too long. After such a long drive sleep is rightfully hers, but this paint-stinking room withholds it, the rustle of clean sheets repels it, impersonal pillows offend it. She tosses and moans and scratches fleeting itches, waking in wan eleven A.M. light with a headache and a weird chemical taste in her mouth.

Which could be guilt, or the premonition of guilt.

As in: doing something that leaves a bad taste in your mouth. Or planning to.

Having driven halfway across the country in order to.

If she packs now and heads back to Iowa no one will get hurt. Breakfast—no, lunch—and she'll gas the car up for the long drive back across the flat states. Finally she grasps the essential rightness of signing over Smoke River to Bruce and his lover: to have stayed would have inscribed her obsession with the two of them in the marrow of her bones. As it is, she has been free—more or less free. Out over the ocean, a horizon-wide brushstroke of fog bides its time, but until it advances on the town every edge and outline has the chill clarity of coastal light, every little shingle on every little roof diamond-exact. Even the McDonald's is pretty. Where Highway 1 is, briefly, Main Street, logging trucks roar through, leaving a wake of diesel fumes and dancing evergreen twigs. Ximena turns pages in a bookstore, the rustle of suffering, herself older than the last time she turned pages in this corner, wiser, tucks of disappointment around her smile. Even if she did want to call Bruce, she no longer has his cell number. That smallest, most ordinary token of acquaintance, and she doesn't have it. Fuck someone for ten years. She's not even thinking about love. Not love. Just all that fucking. Think how much fucking was involved. How many times and how nakedly, fucking till he tells you you're an angel. She buys a couple of paperbacks and after paying for them can't remember their titles or what they're about. On the sidewalk she contemplates the new streetlights the town has paid for, black cast-iron columns ascending to frosted globes meant to evoke the gaslights of an earlier, more genteel thoroughfare. Who are they kidding: Smoke River had always been the surly, xenophobic logging town. Its streets had never been lit. Yet among the improvements is a storefront advertising handmade *local* ice cream.

She's sitting at a table when, on the other side of fogged plate glass, a woman pauses to stare, the baby on her hip. Bruce's new wife, from the photograph. Staring at Ximena? No. Of course not. At the menu. Wondering if the ice cream's organic, if it's safe for baby, or for her given the allergies that must come with that pallor. See her private half-smile, because the baby's tugging on a lock of her hair and that's cute—it feels cute, Ximena can almost feel how it feels. Tug, tug. If this is hate it is small-scale, tight in its focus, and not fun, not energizing: it simply means you see clearly. You concentrate. Because here she is. Her eyebrows have been replaced with the single moronic band of her backward baseball cap, her hipster jeans try too hard, her Converse sneakers say she's already afraid of getting older, but in this war, which this girl has no idea is a war, it's Ximena who's the loser. This girl has a greater claim on the world than she has. First there's the baby. That is a claim. Then there's Bruce. This girl can be awkward and foolish and inept, and still when he wakes and yawns and rolls over this is the face Bruce sees, those are the eyes looking back at him and not Ximena's, and as long as he wants her eyes looking back at him she has a hold on this world, and Ximena, who has lost his gaze forever, has no hold at all.

It's true what her lawyer said. Ximena has never met this person before. This person squats. The baby dismounts. Across black-and-white checkerboard tiles the toddler advances with the lordly shamble of a drunk who finds himself charming. Advances toward *Ximena*, his surreal little monkey hand with its actual greedy fingers seizing the cup on her table just as she jerks it away, their grabs clashing, the chocolate orb slobbering down her shirt to her lap, cradled there till she jerks her legs apart and lets it plop to the floor, his slow mother dragging the toddler back, vehemently apologizing, but it's clear she hopes for interruption, forgiveness, kindness, because he's a baby after all and maybe what happened was even kind of funny. But Ximena wipes theatrically at the chocolate Rorschach blot. She can't help thinking this person is a bad mother, letting this kid walk right up to strangers, steal *food* from them, and then expecting to hear *Don't worry about it* even as the kid picks up the orb from the floor and dabbles it at his mouth, which causes his mother to say *Don't sweetie that's nasty.* At her sharpness the baby throws the lumpen chocolate, which skids along the winding smear of its own melting. They all watch. Suddenly the mother thumps down on her ass with her legs stuck out on either side of the baby, letting her exhaustion show, and Ximena, who has had no intention of pitying her, feels the swift unfolding of empathy, this woman or girl close to tears from embarrassment and not knowing what to do. No lipstick today, her lips barely a shade darker than her skin, fair except for the grainy redness flaming up her throat, an odd way to blush but interesting to watch. "Look, I am sorry, it's his age, there's a lot going on at one year old, all day he's been crazy to get away from me, I'd like to buy you another ice cream, please let me buy you another ice cream, what were you having?"

"Oh no, no, really, no need for that, it's all right." She didn't intend to say anything so nice and is surprised.

"I'd like to. Chocolate, right? Please. It would make me feel better."

Ximena doesn't say *Look, the ice cream cost a dollar seventy-nine, the shirt was three hundred bucks and is maybe my favorite piece of clothing in the world.*

An aproned girl has emerged from behind the counter to crouch with a wet rag and dustpan, muttering *No problem, no problem, you guys, no problem.* In the relief from tension afforded by her mopping, the two strangers look right at each other. When their eyes meet there's the kind of click you get when your gaze meets a gaze of equal, kindred but not rivalrous, intelligence. Likeness like this—likeness of minds? in the slant taken on the world?—is rare, the affinity arising from it unmistakable, yet in this case it is worse than useless. Nothing can come of it. The baby sucks his fist, and his mother says to Ximena, "Let me make this up to you." Ximena shakes her head. "But your shirt is ruined." Fine, it's fine, really, she's got to get on with her day, seriously don't worry about it, Ximena self-conscious as she stands, dismayed that her blotched shirt has engendered this fresh round of apologies, saying it's nothing, deciding to get out of there but wanting a last glance at this person she meant to dislike—to hate—and looking over her shoulder she walks right into an entering customer who says, "Oops," and then, "Hey," and then, "Wow," and she is staring up into the eyes that are Bruce.

He has gone bald.

He didn't write this in the letter.

They are in the doorway.

The matched intensity of their stares—hers upward and his down, the hanging nearness of his face causing the slackened musculature around his unsmiling mouth to bulge ever so slightly downward, the flicker or play of recognition versus bewilderment in his non-smile, the expressive dark holes of his nostrils, the tiny beady lights of extra liquidity that cause his eye-whites to seem especially luminously clear, the distinctness of eyelashes and their strangeness when looked at closely and how warm he is and how the same old detergent used on his clothes has a different smell from his skin and how well the smells go together, their not knowing what comes next, their happiness, the feeling of being part of a true story again, their unwillingness to look away—adds up to a feeling of *at last: us again*.

There's a chance that inside the store Bruce's wife has not seen what has just taken place, and collecting her wits Ximena says, "Sorry." Her tone claims they are strangers. Right away she knows it's odd she lied, but he accepts her having done so.

He is even, she sees, relieved.

He says, "Hey, no problem."

The new lover may or may not have witnessed their encounter, she might have been talking to the baby, she may have been spooning ice cream toward his gaping hole of a mouth with a plastic spoon. There's a chance she didn't notice what happened in the doorway, but even if she had, she might have understood their mutual stare as jolted apologetic curiosity, natural when someone has just bumped into you. Ximena walks away with a quickening sense of guilt: recognized for what it was, that stare could cause problems with the new wife. She walks fast, willing him to get away with it. To be okay with the crazy intensity that overcame them in that doorway and not to let it show. Detachedly she thinks he looked good. Lucky his skull is a nice shape. The pushy cranial roundedness suits his height, his doctorliness, his air of being slightly out of it. This, then, is the other side of the betrayal coin, the way the two of them must have felt about *her*: she wants not to cause pain.

She turns around to see if she's the one being called out to.

"It felt so wrong seeing you walk off," the younger woman says. "And then I thought, dinner. I can buy dinner, to make up for the shirt, because I can tell from your face that—well. Or cook. I can cook. Say yes."

To be a guest inside one's own old house: it's like being a guest inside one's own body, the way you feel on a doctor's examination table, outwardly polite, inwardly full of offended resistance and asocial impulses—to insult, to make an escape. Only Robin appears at ease, her hair disciplined into a high ponytail, arms bare, lipstick on. The wine is good—"organic," Bruce says—and the food, too, salad with grilled figs and goat cheese followed by a risotto that keeps Robin in the kitchen while Bruce and Ximena stare and stare and look away and stare again while disliking this deception, the pretense that it is not extraordinary for them to find themselves across a table from each other again.

For the sake of deceiving Robin, Ximena's style has changed. This new style is more breathless and glancing than her own, funnier, free of sorrow. More likable in general. Strangely, given that she is repressing a number of strong emotions, her English is better. Her faked detachment permits close study of the couple Bruce-and-Robin: their marriage is of the endearing kind, not so good that you feel intimidated, but not so bad that you worry for them.

When Robin had followed Ximena into the street and asked her to dinner, Ximena had said, "Look, you don't want that," and Robin had said, "Why?" and Ximena had said, "I'm Ximena, you know, who he was with before," avoiding the word *wife* the way she would have avoided driving a knife through the other woman's heart, as a fatal action whose aftermath would be mess and confusion, but Robin had said only, "You are? Really, you are?" and then "Why did he act like that?" and then, "Okay, this is weird. Me asking you to explain some idiotic thing he did," and Ximena said, "I'm not great at explaining him," and they had laughed. And Robin said, "Wrong time to say this, prob-ably, but I love your work. I've always sort of wanted to tell you, but I never thought there would be a way. Really love it."

Which is not something Bruce had included in his letter. But she doesn't know about the letter.

There in the street, Ximena had said, "You're kind to ask, but I don't want you to go to any trouble, and it's maybe not such a good idea, my coming to dinner," and the other woman said, "No, it will be lovely. It's the right thing, you know, for people who've mattered to each other like you and he have, it's important for you to find some way to talk and not just to disap-pear forever. He was scared that you were gone. I don't know what it is like for you, and I don't mean to intrude or seem to pressure you, but if he lost you again now it would hurt him so much. Please come. It will turn out all right—it will, trust me."

From this whole speech, Ximena fastened onto one assertion. "He was scared?"

"Of never seeing you or talking to you again, yes, really scared. He didn't think I knew that, but I did."

"Well, wow, this is very understanding of you," Ximena had said, and meant something mildly slighting, like *Are you some kind of pushover, don't you get jealous?* But this implication was lost on her, and the younger woman's smile made Ximena repent of her meanness and say, "So okay, I'll come. Tell me when to be there."

If, after her second or maybe third glass of wine, Ximena starts to flirt with Robin, it's partly because they were able to laugh with each other like that in the street. Women flirt: it means nothing, it means you are alive. She feels the elation of playacting, she is being lovely to them, but something is wrong: the conversation is haunted by a triangular stiltedness that drives Ximena a little crazy, which she wants to remedy, because they are trying this new and daring thing of talking with each other, three people who have been in various ways badly hurt by each other, except that Robin has not been hurt, Robin got what she wanted, and Robin has never once granted Ximena a long unguarded gaze, and suddenly, somehow, that is the gaze Ximena needs, and not Bruce's. By what alchemy has desire changed its object—is this even really happening? Robin has the grace of a person who doesn't second-guess herself, whose aims are mostly kind, and you would think she is not available for flirtation, and yet here it is, quickening the air, Ximena alert to the other woman's least gesture or the minute tightening of her lips that suggests she is, sexually, no fool, and has registered what is happening, and is at a loss how to repress it, unused as she is to repressing impulses, honest and aboveboard as her life is. In truth, Ximena thinks, those qualities are rarer than rare in a person she now recognizes is very, very beautiful. This is what Bruce had seen early on and why he wanted her. There is a kind of shelter obtainable from Robin's attention, a tiny house she can make for you where you can take refuge, and suddenly this is what Ximena wants.

Bruce is not aware anything is happening.

None of this occurs in language. The advance and swift deepening of attraction take place at the older, deeper level of recognition, down where the unsaid lives, and art.

After clearing the dinner plates Robin retreats to the kitchen and returns with a torte that she sets down on the table, and Bruce and Ximena glance away from each other because Ximena loathes birthdays and always has.

"It's amazing," Ximena says. "It must have taken you hours."

Lighting the candles—one two three, Ximena sees, a token cluster, or one for each decade—Robin explains, "It's meant to sort of redeem chocolate for you."

"What?"

"After having it smeared down your shirt. I'm nervous about how this turned out. I'm going to close my eyes while you take your first taste."

Did that need to sound so sexy?

It's Bruce who asks, "Why three candles?"

Robin says, "All I could find. Left over from the last cake, I guess."

From upstairs the baby howls. Robin hesitates. Such hesitation is uncharacteristic of her, surely—the adoring mother. "I'll go," Bruce says, having caught on at last, and Robin frowns, upset with herself for letting it show that she is tired of the baby's demands, shaking her head but letting her husband ascend a flight of stairs whose every creak Ximena knows, as she knows his particular rhythm of stair-climbing, the habitual fraction of an instant's pause (caused by what?) on the fifth stair, the sturdy tramping tread that finishes the flight, the silencing of his foot-falls by the hallway's carpeting. The baby must be in the small bedroom under the eaves. They used to talk about turning it into a bathroom.

How oppressed she has been by his watchfulness, what a relief that he's gone, even if only for a few minutes.

Ximena lays down her fork. Robin lays down her fork. They face each other undefended. It's sex. It's the laying down of forks. Ruin, chaos, sex, and recklessness, we live and breathe for what you will do with us. The candles burn between them. Robin says, "I don't believe this," and Ximena says, "You don't believe what," and Robin says, "This. What's happening. Whatever it is," and Ximena says, "You can't believe it?" and when there is no answer she says, "Do you want to believe it?" and she could say *I can help you feel how true it is*, but who is she to say such a thing to this woman, when did she acquire the power to convince this other of a truth that could ruin or at least fuck up her life, which seems well worth protecting, something someone like Ximena, whose motives if viewed even in the best possible light would have to be described as mixed, should stay completely out of? But that is the last thing she wants to do: to stay out of this woman's life. She's not *capable* of staying out of her life. Worse, stranger, Robin is not capable of *keeping* her out. They are in it now. How did they do that with eyes and faces and voices, come as far as this, get in such trouble?

They can't kiss while Robin's baby is crying upstairs, that

can't be the sound track for their first kiss because it would be too crazy-making for both of them and for Robin too inevitable a source of guilt, and even supposing they could shut their ears to that they can't kiss across the table. One of them will have to stand and lean across, palms flat on the table, careful not to put a hand in a piece of cake, straining, and the combination of effort and delicacy would amuse both the person leaning forward and the one being leaned toward, and the furtive comedy would undercut what they would otherwise be sure to feel, the full unexpected force of their attraction. Its power to take their breath away, that is what is most deeply longed for, and they can't get at it by ridiculous leaning across this table even if the baby has stopped crying, and he has, but that means too that they have only a minute or so left to figure this out, whatever it is. Five minutes tops. How will this play out after Bruce comes back down the stairs? He may not have caught on yet but he isn't blind. He'll look from one to the other and the truth will gradually become more and more *felt* among the three of them, and the pretense that everything is all right will collapse.

In Robin's eyes the decision has been made. She stands. She leans across Ximena's own old dinner table with all its memories. Bruce didn't even bother to replace it, he didn't fear the ghosts of their life together, and if he didn't fear those, how much can it mean to him, that old life? Nothing. Not if he can sit down at this table, lift his wineglass, smile across at her without fear and trembling. The fear and trembling is done by his new lover as her lips meet Ximena's. Candle flames warm their forearms, their throats, as Ximena tilts her head to allow room for the other woman's nose, as she tastes her tongue, as she tries with her tongue to suggest the palace of inventiveness and aggression and complicity that would be sex between them, as the two of them ease apart from each other to allow for looking—for the assessment they need to do of what this means and how things have changed. And that look is enough, more than enough, because it tells Ximena that lives can be ruined beginning right here, right now, and that the worst of the damage won't be done to her, but to these two—no, three—others, whom she might as well love, because without them she's alone in the world.

For strangeness, for fucked-upness—no kiss has ever come close. For the power of the unforeseen taking over.

Before Bruce comes down the stairs she has altered the course of the future, standing up, collecting her things, keys, the coat she pulls on though Robin says behind her, "Was that wrong? Ximena? Was it wrong?" With luck she can get out of the house before he can glimpse her expression. He couldn't hear from upstairs if she tried to explain to Robin why she has to go, and probably it would be a good thing, less memorably hurtful, if Ximena tried to give some explanation for this decisive fleeing-the-scene, but she can't both explain and mobilize her resistance to the other woman. It would be unwise even to turn and take a last look at that face. She's given Robin reason to believe that they will get away with this, that the two of them have felt something and even acted on it and now Robin can choose how much, if anything, she wants to confide to Bruce about what just happened, only why would she say a thing? Now she is almost out the door, Ximena who believes there is a way to stop time but she has not found it, Ximena who is about to do, just this once, the right thing. And painting—not the moon, not anymore. Not the moon: a face. To inscribe it more deeply in memory, she looks over her shoulder. From now on, that face.

The Wilderness

Her students are the devotees and tenders of machines. Some of the machines are tiny and some of the machines are big. Nobody wrote down the law that students must have a machine with them at all times, yet this law is rarely broken, and when it is, the breaker suffers from deprivation and anxiety. Machines are sometimes lost, sometimes damaged, and this loss, this damage, deranges existence until, mouseclick by mouseclick, chaos can be fended off with a new machine, existence regains harmony, interest, order, connectedness. Sleeping, certain machines display a dreamily pulsing white light meaning *this machine is not dead.* Images, icons, passages of text: even in a silent room the machines are continually storing these up. The students never advance into a day or even an hour without the certainty of messages awaiting them, without the expectation of signals and signs. Rendered visible, the embrace of hyperconnectivity would float around their heads like gold-leaf halos. During class the machines grow restless and seek students' attention. Certain machines purr, certain machines tremble; certain machines imitate birdsong. Whoever invented the software that causes the machine to sing like a bird must have foreseen not only bewilderment like the professor's but also the pleasure her mistake, if visible (it is! Flushed from her lecture notes, her gaze swerves around the room), gives to those in the know—that is, her students. For the fraction of an instant that either makes or breaks her authority (she would say she is not interested in *authority*)—the fraction when exhilarated hardwired startlement tips into that laughter-inviting cognitive slough, bewilderment—the professor can't make the correct attribution. For her and her alone, among the two hundred and forty-three listeners in the lecture hall, that realistic sequence of ascending trills equals "bird." To observe her puzzlement is to know that a bird flits through the wilderness of her brain, to understand that in the professor's experience song emanates from a creature. Her students find this endearing: she can't help letting it show that she belongs to the world that preceded theirs.

Her face gives her trouble as a teacher. Irony has inscribed certain lines; insincerity, others. The insincerity is estranging—estranging her from herself, that is, for she feels, inwardly, like the most honest person on the planet. Inwardly she is plain and kind, emotionally Amish. But outwardly, no. Outwardly she is a professor. With a mocking lift of her brows, she has more than once accidentally silenced a student, and been stunned that it happened so fast. Now she strives, facially, for serenity. As a child in the depths of a great museum she was struck mute by the impersonally eloquent eyes painted onto the linen wrapped over the face of the mummy—no detachment, no trace of aversion, rushed to defend her huge, vulnerable heart from the perfect painted face tenderly laid against the true, hidden visage whose corruption seduced the imagination into graphic detail. That was going on right below the painted face whose uncanniness told her *I was alive*, whose individuality, almost completely submerged in stylization, was more poignant for having barely made it through. For the first time she comprehended death. Once, a real person had spoken through those lips, *a person* had looked out from those eyes pointed at both ends. That was why they took children to museums. She had been meant to understand this great thing they all understood, whose inevitability they could somehow (she did not see how) bear, which they expected her to spend the rest of her life knowing: death, first recognized in the depths of the museum, would be alive for her now her whole life long, and could never be un-seen. They had afforded her neither preparation nor protection, and this treachery, this cold willingness to let her see what she saw, could not be explained. Inconceivable, the demented precision of this blow aimed at her by forces pretending to be benign. Hours later, in the backseat of the station wagon trundling south on the highway leading away from the city, she had fallen asleep. When she woke, she was looking out of eyes pointed at both ends.

Once another professor, a handsome old charmer and taunter, had asked her by way of flirtation what she wanted on her gravestone. For years, long after losing touch with this professor, who had left for a university on the opposite coast, she thought about the question. She wrote and rewrote her gravestone, always with him in mind, recalling that particular moment at the party when he had come up to her and with two fingers touched the inside of her wrist, exposed because of the way she was holding her glass, and then, as if his somewhat intrusive but tolerated touch required its counterweight in charm, he had smiled a beautiful male smile within a dark beard and asked his question, and she has been answering him ever since, though he died years ago.

Her by-now-experienced soul (but her heart is no bigger than it was when she was a child) gazes out through pointed eyes at students whose great museum is all of literature. Her corner of the museum is in English, which she has always loved—which she will love to her dying breath. Here come students. Why do *they* love it? What do they want? Is the end of such love inevitable, will there be a last English major? Will he be eyebrow-pierced and tattooed, a prowling, scanning searcher-boy invoking the name David Foster Wallace, could she be that raggedy ann–haired anorexic cross-legged in the last of four chairs in the hall-way outside the professor's door, this girl with tattered *Golden Notebook* upheld? They come. They are enthralled. The professor likes how enthralled they are. It is an old thing, a deep thing, to be enthralled. While enthralled they are beautiful. She could swear that an enthralled reader nineteen years old is the most beautiful animal on earth—at least, she's seen one or two who were, in their spellbound moment, the incarnation of ex-tremest human beauty. They were not themselves. Literature looked back at her from their eyes and told her certain things she was sure they ought not to have understood at their age. They had gotten it from books—books with their intricacies and the things they wanted you to know about love and death that you could have gone a long time not knowing if you had not been a reader, and which, even when you were a reader, you saw as universal truths that did not apply to *you*.

When the professor sees that a student loves a certain sentence, her heart lifts as if she's been told *Great news! You will never die!* Why does it feel like this? That book in that student's hand has nothing to do with her. It's just luck she's in the same room.

In the center of a roundabout, a paved orbit around a central island whose white gravel is set with concentric circles of a kind of agave she happens to know are called foxtail after the slender oblong upheld sleekness of their array of pointed leaves, the professor watches while bicycles skim past within arm's reach, hundreds of bicycles. If she stood here long enough she could easily witness the whirling transit of a thousand bicycles, with her as their still center. Either extinction or a drastic diminution of population worldwide is inevitable within their lifetimes, according to research well known by the students. Here we can make some really big, really simple connections: we can cease to care, for a moment, how it *looks* to make big simple connections instead of subtle small ones. So. The same world that warns them of extinction bestows toys for them to carry, to key, to rub with their thumbs in swift ovals, to insert into those apertures called, in *Hamlet*, *the porches of mine ears*, natural distance between brain and music annihilated, the cacophony nudged deep, close, too close to the species' most exquisite bones. That is the point of the ten thousand toys. They are not about strangeness and newness after all. They seek innateness, sensual invisibility,

the body's quality of being not-there to itself. In their insinuated proximity they elude the soul's attempt to differentiate between soul and soulless. Which is basically all that literature has
ever cared about, and why it will *never cease to be loved*. Sure,
tell that to yourself, the professor tells herself. The strap of her
heavy leather messenger bag rests on her left shoulder, crosses
her chest, and fits below her right armpit, an arrangement com-
pleted with an inevitable creasing of her jacket, which is black
or any of the dozen shades of gray in her closet; not much varia-
tion there, not much risk. The bag itself is revolved until it rests
snugly against her back, a trick learned from students in the
nick of time, just before her neck acquired a permanent ache
from one-shouldered weight carrying. Calculate it sometime,
the weight of the books you have lugged in your life. Would it
equal that of a house, a ship, a small mountain? Bicycles rush at
her from nineteen directions. No one hits anyone. Just how this
is accomplished—by what unerring divination of one another's
intentions and how many hundreds of swift corrections—she
wants to know, to see, or if she can't see it, if she's not quick
enough to perceive the glance that averts disaster, and she's not,
then she wants at least to be close to it, she needs to know that it
happens, that it goes on and on happening.

Her heart has always been the same size as it was that long-ago
Sunday when she first saw those eyes pointed at both ends, and
she has always felt the same to herself. Secretly, because people
are supposed to go through enormous changes, to mature, she
wonders if there is something wrong with her, to feel such con-
sistency between who she is now and who she was then when she
looked down into those alive-dead eyes. Is something wrong with

still being who she was as a child, or is she fine? What book can answer that? Many of them seem to intuit the existence of this question *from her*, however far away she is in time from the writer of the book, however remote, and in this context the right adverb to modify *remote* is *impossibly*. A great many of the books she loves most *hold* this question. It's in there somewhere, the question, if not the answers, and why is it enough, in reading? Why is it beautiful simply to find your own questions?

Long ago, when she was a new professor with a new professor's keen motivation, she took the trouble to think of really good answers to certain questions students asked, and the trouble she took then has paid off ever since, because the answers can be revised according to the times, some needing more revision than others, but her original responses continue to strike her as sufficient, and form a sort of core around which revision can take place, and the questions haven't changed. Really there are only twelve or so main ones, at least in her life. Around those, a haze or shimmer of worries and intimations that can't quite materialize into questions. Anxieties like droplets lacking the particles of dust or grit they need to coalesce into clouds. Things they fear. Questions she could not answer anyway.

In her mind she answers the professor, who is no longer alive to hear what she wants on her gravestone—not that she plans to have a gravestone, because she wants to be cremated, and despite her fear of death is consoled by the notion of ending up as ashes, why she's not sure: their vulnerability to dispersion suits her, as does their incorruptibility, the fact that nothing further can

be done to ashes, that in their lack of ambition regarding im-
mortality ashes are the opposite of those eyes she gazed into in
the museum. In her mind he asks his question, which for all she
knows he's in the habit of asking as a disconcerting, cut-to-the-
chase, *what are you really like?* refinement of flirtation whose bad-
boy contempt for the usual niceties at least some women would
respond to. She had responded, not in the way he hoped, not
with equal and opposite impudence, but with the awkwardness
of needing to think before talking, an awkwardness despised at
her university, a trait she mostly hid, but not that evening and
not with him, and he hadn't liked that, and hadn't liked her
answer, so they parted and not long afterward lost touch and
she was left answering him in her mind, saying yes, there was
something she'd like, just one word, on her gravestone. *Reader.*
And in her mind he loves this answer.

For instance, a student will ask whether reading critically and
interpreting—beginning to study *literature*—will cause the student to stop loving reading, because the student thinks there's
a risk of this, and that is what the student never ever wants to
happen. And what is the answer? Is it right to reassure the student, when after all the professor doesn't know how it will go
for that student, she knows only how it went for her? Well, she
says, in my experience, she says, the more someone learns about
an intricate thing, like, say, the human heart—the more a sur-
geon knows about that heart, right?—the deeper *in*, the more
beautiful the thing seems, and by *thing* I mean a heart or a book,
either one. Then the student says thank you and goes away. But
the professor does not know any heart surgeons and has never
asked any of them if what they feel is wonder. She made that up.

Only when she is well away from that roundabout, settled into her favorite corner of the couch in her office; only in this quiet, narrowing her pointed eyes in pleasure in an interval of aloneness she has no right to, because they should be here, the students, they've said they're going to come by and one of them will knock on the door any second, meaning the value of this interval, the preface to losing oneself in a book, is heightened by her awareness of its likely end; only in the particular space created by unexpected liberty (in which thinking her own thoughts has a stolen or illegitimate savor) does she grasp the real reason for her love of standing motionless in the bicycle onslaught, in the student whirlwind. As usual, the real reason has been expertly swaddled in and obscured by false, lesser reasons, attractive in and of themselves. Oh yes there is pleasure in being unmoved in the midst of an every-which-way assault. But also, this is like her life. They come at her from every direction! They never touch her! No. That's not it, not the bottommost layer, not the meaning revealed only when other meanings are peeled away, whose existence you only ever discover if peeling is a habit, if you love this deft quiet work of lifting away length of gauze after length of gauze to find the true face. Down down down down down and down. They mean something, these almost-winged cyclists, in their seriousness and lightness, their concentration, in their searchingness that must discern every signal *or else*, in their absorption. This is reading. No wonder she loves standing there: in the middle of a steady cascade of virtuoso reading on which their lives depend.

It could be, she tells herself, that apart from your work and your teaching you do not have enough going for you, that you need to get out more, that due to your aloneness—which we're not going to call loneliness because it's not that; it's a deliberate, cultured, desirable, nonnegotiable state, necessary if you want to get work done, intelligent aloneness, *good* aloneness; it has a point!—your students matter too much. At least you have to ask yourself once in a while, you have to check in regarding whether or not it is wrong, what you feel for them, the students. Without fail you need to recognize that the easiest transition love ever makes is into coercion, and that your most useful quality as far as students are concerned is *dis*interestedness. You've said often enough that you love teaching, but you have never said the truer thing, which is that you love your students, because it would only worry everyone to hear it, it would worry even you, and it might not even be true, because there is, remember, the risk that aloneness has exaggerated what you feel for them. Which may not be love, but some minor, teacherly emotion that nobody has ever bothered to give a name. Who were they, the people who figured out what the emotions were, and how many of them would be recognized and named, and which shadings or gradations could safely be ignored—who were they, these feeling namers, and what did they have against shades of gray?

The students rarely embark on a difficult or painful subject without some sort of rhetorical exit strategy. There is almost no sorrow they can't disown with an immediate laugh, designed to prevent the professor from realizing that she has glimpsed genuine emotion. After many years as a professor it still strikes her as unnatural that students, that *people*, fear what she might think: Who the fuck is she? But they watch her eyes for what she's thinking. Will she say something actually useful to them, or something they in their desperation (because sometimes it is desperation) can *twist* into usefulness, which will be more useful for coming from her, the professor? What can she tell them about what comes next?

In the corner of the couch, with a titanium-sheathed machine balanced partly on the arm of the couch and partly on one raised knee, the professor clicks through the forests and clearings of a few contested acres. Mild and unexceptional except for being somewhat forlorn, these acres, sad in the way of woods that don't thrive, lacking the cannons, the plaques, the bronze generals on horseback that tell you blood was shed here. The Wilderness, this battlefield is called. Walmart wants this particular scrap of the Wilderness for a supercenter whose aisles will be lined with toys for the children of tourists drawn to other, already protected acres of battlefield. There is no telling from these unphotogenic, scantily wooded hills that her great-great-grandfather was badly wounded here. If he had died, he would have been one among thirty thousand, and she, of course, would never have existed. He lived—the War Department records his new status as prisoner of war, sent by train to Fort Delaware, also known as Pea Patch Island. The professor both likes and hates the irony, the sunny potager promised by the name Pea Patch Island and the reality of filth and exposure and fever and starvation, tainted water and maggoty flour, that befell him at nineteen. Was he *as alive* to himself as she is to herself, did he feel *as real*? If he flexed his fingers or studied the lines intersecting and diverging in the palm, did he marvel? The deepest despair, the blackest pitch of

disillusion about humankind: those are what she imagines, envisioning his emotions in the prison camp, but these conjectures
could be wrong. He is remote in time and culture. Consola-
tions that seem to her the most childish lies and self-deceptions
might have been his salvation. Not books, but Book, the King
James Version. He might, if time were transcended and he could
know her and what she thinks and what she teaches her students
and her preference for ambiguity over conviction and her god-
lessness, turn his savage Civil War eyes on her, his billy goat
beard, his cavalryman's uprightness, his gaunt authority, and re-
nounce her, his distant child. A cousin emailed the professor the
only known photograph of him, a slouch-hatted elderly figure
astride a sorrel horse, and even in this image, no bigger than a
matchbook, and even in extreme old age, he is plainly someone
to reckon with. From the year 2015 she gazes into the pixels
that comprise his gaze. Back to the home page of the historical
trust fighting Walmart, and with several clicks of the mouse, she
"buys" an acre of these woods where he lay wounded, and while
she is aware such ownership is merely honorary, a contribution
toward the trust's large-scale purchase, she chooses to believe
her mouseclick has saved the exact patch of earth once stained
with her great-great's blood from becoming a parking lot. Her
in-box *dings* with instant thanks from a computer in the trust's
distant offices. It's *his* thanks she wants to come dinging in. She
is amused at herself, though there are tears in her eyes, for longing to connect to that long-ago, unknowable, very likely hostile old man. For whom she's somehow as lonely as if she had
once been a child cradled in his arms, as if, leaning down so his
mouth was close to her ear, he had said her name, and then said
Listen, and then told her the story that was the story within all
the other stories of her life, the oldest and most beautiful and

farthest back, the one that would elude death forever and ever and ever amen.

Me. Say you lived at least partly for *me.*

This is the story that must exist somewhere; this is what she never finds to read.

Never Come Back

This was his life now, his real life, the thing he thought about most: his boy was in and out of trouble and he didn't know what to do.

Friday night when he got home late from the mill Daisy made him shower before supper, and he twisted the dial to its hottest setting and turned his back to the gimmicky showerhead whose spray never pulsed hard enough to perform the virtual massage its advertising promised—or maybe at forty-three he'd used his body too hard, its aches and pains as much a part of him now as his heart or any other organ, and he had wasted good money on an illusion. Ah well. He rubbed at mirror fog and told the dark-browed frowner (his own father!) to get ready: she'd had her Victor look. Whatever this development was, it fell somewhere between failing grade in calculus and car wreck, either of which, he knows from experience, would have been announced as soon as he walked through the door. Whatever the case, the news was bad enough that she felt she needed to lay the groundwork and had already set their places at the table and poured his beer, a habit he disliked but had never objected to and never would. When she was a girl, Daisy's father had let her tilt the bottle over his glass while the bubbles churned and the foam puffed like a mushroom cap sidling up from dank earth, and if she enjoyed some echo of the bliss of being in her daddy's good graces while pouring *his* beer, Sean wasn't about to deprive her.

Daisy told him:

Neither girl seemed very brave, yet neither seemed willing to back down. Not their own wounds, but a sturdy sense of each other's being wronged, had driven them to this. They had a kind of punk bravado, there on the threshold, armored in motorcycle jackets whose sleeves fell past their chipped black fingernails. A flight of barrettes had attacked their heads, pinching random tufts of dirty hair. They were dressed for audacity, but their pointy-chinned faces—really the same face twice—wore the stiff little mime smiles of the easily intimidated, confronting her, the tigress mother, bracing their forlorn selves as best they could, which wasn't very well at all. There was nothing to do but ask them in. As she told it to Sean, Daisy wasn't about to let them guess that A, she pitied them, and B, she understood right away there was going to be some truth in what they said. Victor's favorite sweater, needing some mending, lay across the arm of the sofa, and when one of the twins took it into her lap—talisman, claim—Daisy hardly needed to be told that girl was pregnant. As the twins took turns explaining that not just one of them was in trouble, both were, an evil radiance pulsed in the corner of Daisy's right eye, the onset of a migraine.

A joke, Sean said. *Because, twins? Somebody told these girls to go to V's house and freak out his parents.*

Drinking around a bonfire, Daisy said, *and they wander into the woods and stumble across this mattress. They have a word for what happened. Three-way. They have a word for it, so ask yourself what else these girls know. Why they have no sense of self-worth. Their mother's in Arizona, their daddy's a trucker, never around.*

Across the table Sean shook his head, his disgust with his son failing, for once, to galvanize Daisy's defense of the boy. In the harmony of their anger, they traded predictions. Victor would be made to marry a twin, maybe the one whose dark eyes had acquired a sheen of tears when she petted his old sweater, because she seemed the more lost. Victor would be dragged under.

"When's he get home?" Sean said.

"Away game. Not till two A.M." It was Daisy who would be waiting in her SUV when the bus pulled up at the high school to disgorge the sleepy jostling long-legged boys.

"We hold off on doing anything till we hear his side of the story."

We hold off? If she hadn't loved him she would have laughed when he said that. It wouldn't be up to them to hold off or not hold off, but if Sean was slower to accept that reality than she was, it was because he hated decisions being out of his hands.

However disgusted he'd been the night before, in the morning Sean was somber, mindful, restrained, everything Daisy could have wished when he sat Victor down at the kitchen table for what he called *getting the facts straight*. The reeling daylong party was true, and the bonfire, and the rain-sodden mattress in the woods where a drunken Victor had sex with both girls, though not at the same time, which was what *three-way* meant. They must have claimed that for dramatic impact, as if this sce-

nario needed more drama, or because they had been so smashed
that events blurred together in their minds. The next several
evenings were taken up with marathon phone calls. Sean asked
most of the questions and wouldn't hand the receiver to Daisy
even when she could tell he'd learned something especially
troubling and mouthed *Give it to me!* By the following weekend
they had established that only one twin was pregnant, though it
seemed both had believed they were telling the truth when they
sat on Daisy's velvet couch and said the babies, plural, were due
July fifth. The sweater-petting girl told Sean she had liked Victor
for a long time—*years*—and had wanted to *be* with him, though
not in the way it had finally happened. Questioned, Victor remembered only that they were twins. He knew it sounded bad
but he wasn't sure what they looked like. Nobody was quote
in love with him: that was crazy. And no, they hadn't tried to
talk to him first, before coming to the house, and was that fair,
that they'd assumed there was zero chance of his doing the right
thing? And why was marriage the right thing if he didn't want
it and whoever the girl was *she* didn't want it and it was only
going to end in divorce? The twin who was pregnant had the
ridiculous name of Esme, and what she asked for on the phone
with Sean—patient, tactful Sean—was not marriage but child
support. If she had that she could get by, she insisted. She'd had
a sonogram and she loved the alien-headed letter *C* curled up
inside her. At their graduation dance she shed her high heels
and flirted by bumping into the tuxes of various dance partners.
Victor followed her into the parking lot. Below she was flat-
footed and pumpkin-bellied; above she wore strapless satin, her
collarbones stark as deer antlers. He backed her up against an
anonymous SUV hard enough that their first sober kiss began
with shrieks and whistles.

———

In the hushed joyous days after the baby was born Sean made a mistake he blamed partly on sleep deprivation. The narrow old two-story house had hardly any soundproofing, and because Victor and Esme's bedroom was below his and Daisy's, the baby's crying woke them all. He had stopped in the one jewelry store downtown and completely on impulse laid down his credit card for a delicate bracelet consisting of several strands of silver wound around and around each other. Though simple, the bracelet was a compelling object with a strong suggestion of narrative, as if the maker had been trying to fashion the twining, gleaming progress of several competing loves. He was the sort of husband who gets teased for not noticing new earrings even when his wife repeatedly tucks her hair behind her ears, and any sort of whimsical expenditure was unlike him, but he found he couldn't leave the store without it. He stopped for a beer at the Golden West, and when he got home the only light was from the kitchen where Esme sat at the table licking the filling from Oreos and washing it down with chocolate milk. Her smile hoped he would empathize with the joke of her appetite rather than scold the late-night sugar extravaganza as, he supposed, Daisy would have done, but it was the white-trash forlornness of her feast that got to Sean—the cheapness and furtiveness and excessive, teeth-aching sweetness of this stab at self-consolation. With her china-doll hair and whiter-than-white skin she was hardly the menace to their peace they had feared, only an ignorant girl who trusted neither her new husband nor her sense that it was she and not her mother-in-law who ought to be making the big decisions about the baby's care. Esme wet a forefinger and dabbed the crumbs from Daisy's tablecloth as he set the shiny box down next to her dirty plate. She said, "What is this?" and, that fast, there were tears in her eyes. She didn't believe it was for her, but she'd just understood what it would feel like if the little box *had* been hers, and this incredulity was his undoing: before those tears, he had meant only to ask Esme if she thought Daisy would like the bracelet. Now he heard himself say, "Just something for the new mama." As soon as she picked the ribbon apart, even before she tipped the bracelet from its mattress of cotton, he regretted his impulsiveness, but it was too late. She slid it onto her wrist and made it flash in the dim light, glancing to invite his admiration or maybe try to figure out, from his expression, what was going on. In the following days he was sorry to see that she never took it off. Fortunately the household was agitated enough that nobody else noticed the bracelet, and he began to hope his mistake would have no ill consequences except for the change in Esme, whose corner-tilted eyes held his whenever he came into the room. Then, quick, she'd turn her head as if realizing this was the sort of thing that could give them away. Of course there was no *them* and not a fucking thing to give away. Sean began to blame her for his uneasiness: she had misconstrued an act of minor, impulsive charity, blown it up into something more, which had to be kept secret. The ridiculousness of her believing he was *interested* was not only troubling in its own right, it pointed to her readiness to immerse herself in fantasy, and this could be proof of some deeper instability. He didn't like being looked at like that in his own house, or keeping secrets. He was not a natural secret keeper, but a big-boned straightforward husband. Since he'd been nineteen, a husband. Daisy came from a background as rough as anybody's, her father a part-time carpenter and full-time drunk who had once burned his kids' clothes in the backyard, the boys running back into the

house for more armfuls of sweatshirts and shorts, disenchanted
only when their dad made them strip off their cowboy pajamas
and throw those in too. The first volunteer fireman on the scene
dressed the boys in slickers that reached to their ankles and bundled their naked teeth-chattering sister into an old sweater that
stank of crankcase oil, and to this day when Sean changes the oil
in his truck he has to scrub his hands outside or Daisy will run
to the bathroom to throw up.

As Esme alternated between flirtation and sullenness, he
tried for kindness. This wasn't all her fault: he was helplessly
responsive to vulnerability, and—he could admit it—he did
have a tendency to rush in and try to fix whatever was wrong.
Therefore he imitated Daisy's forbearance when Esme couldn't
get even simple things right, like using hypoallergenic detergent
instead of the regular kind that caused the baby to break out in a
rash. The tender verbal scat of any mother cradling her baby was
a language Esme didn't speak. Her hold was so tentative the baby
went round-eyed and chafed his head this way and that, wondering who would come to his aid. More than once Esme neglected
to pick up dangerous buttons or coins from the floor. She had
to be reminded to burp him after nursing and then, chastened,
would sling him across her shoulder like a sack of rice. Could
you even say she loved the baby? Breastfeeding might account
for Esme's sleepy-eyed bedragglement and air of waiting for real
life to begin, but, Daisy said, there was absolutely no justifying
the girl's self-pity. Consider where she, Daisy, had come from:
worse than anything this girl had gone through, but had Sean
ever seen her spend whole days feeling sorry for herself, lying in
dirty sheets reading wedding magazines, scarcely managing to
crawl from bed when the baby cried? It wasn't as if she had no
support. Victor was right there. Who would have believed it?

He was attentive to Esme, touchingly proud of his son, and even after a long day at the mill would stay up walking the length of the downstairs hallway with the colicky child so Esme could sleep. For the first time Victor was as good as his word, and could be counted on to deal uncomplainingly with errands and show up when he'd said he would. Victor's changed ways should have mattered more to Esme, given the desolation of her childhood. Victor was *good to her.*

Esme could not explain what was wrong or what she wanted, Daisy said after one conversation. She was always trying to talk to the girl, who was growing more and more restless. They could all see that, but not what was coming, because it was the kind of thing you didn't want to believe could happen in your family: Esme disappeared. Dylan was almost four, and for whatever reason she had concluded that four was old enough to get by without a mother. That much they learned from her note but the rest they had to find out. She had hitchhiked to the used-car dealership on the south end of town and picked out a white Subaru station wagon; Wynn Handley, the salesman, said she negotiated pleasantly and as if she knew what she was doing and (somewhat to Wynn's surprise, you could tell) ended up with a good deal. Esme paid in cash, not that unusual in a county famed for its marijuana. She left alone—that is, there was no other man. None that Wynn had seen, at least. The cash was impossible to explain, since after checking online Victor reported that their joint account hadn't been touched, and they hadn't saved nearly that much anyway. Esme had no credit card, of course, making it difficult to trace her. Discussion of whether they were in any way to blame, and where Esme could have gone, and whether she was likely to call and want to talk to her son, and whether, if she called, there was any chance of convincing her to come back, was carried on in hushed voices, because no matter what she'd done the boy should not have to hear bad things about his mother.

With Esme gone, Victor began to talk about quitting the mill. The ceaseless roar was giving him tinnitus; his back hurt; some nights he fell asleep without showering and woke already exhausted, doomed to another day just like the last, and how was he supposed to have any energy left for the kid? Had Esme thought of that before she left, he wondered—that he might not be able to keep it together? No doubt his steadiness had misled her into thinking it was safe to leave, and when he remembered how reliable and fond and funny and tolerant he had been, anger slanted murderously through his body; and it was like anger practiced on him, got better and better at leaving him with shaking hands and a dilated sense of hatred with no nearby object; and he began to be very, very careful not to be alone with his little boy.

Dylan understood this. After nightmares he did not try his dad's room, right next to his, but patted his way through the dark house up the narrow flight of stairs to the bedroom where he slid in between Sean and Daisy. More than once his chilly bare feet made accidental contact with Sean's genitals, and Sean had to capture the feet and guide them away. This left him irritably awake, needing to make the long trip to the bathroom downstairs, and when he returned the boy was still restless and Sean watched him wind a hand into Daisy's long hair and rub it against his cheek until he could sleep. Worse than jealousy was the affront to Sean's self-regard in entertaining so contemptible an emotion. This was a scared little boy, this was his tight hold on safety, this was his grandfather standing by the side of the bed looking meanly down. Protectiveness toward his own flesh and blood had always been Sean's ruling principle, and if that went wrong he didn't know who he was anymore. He rose to dress for work one cold six A.M. and noticed the tattoos running cruelly down the boy's arm. Had an older kid got hold of him somehow, was this some kind of weird abuse, why hadn't he come running to his grandfather? Sean bent close to decipher the trail of descending letters. *I LOVE YOU.* Not another kid, then. Not abuse. But wasn't Daisy aware a boy could be embarrassed by that, wouldn't the ink's toxins be absorbed through his skin, didn't she understand that was going too far, inscribing her love on the boy while he did what—held his arm out bravely? Time, past time, for Sean to try to talk to Daisy, to suggest that daycare would be a good idea, or a playgroup where the boy could meet other kids. When Daisy was tired or wanted time to herself she left the boy alone with the remote, and once Sean walked in on the boy sitting cross-legged while on the screen a serial killer wrapped body parts in plastic, and how could you talk to a child after that, what could you tell him to explain that away? All right, they could do better. He supposed most people could do better by their kids. Maybe her judgment in taking a pen to the boy's arm wasn't great, but if that was the worst thing to befall him, he'd be fine. If Daisy adored this boy, Sean could live with that. More than live with it: he admired it. He admired her for being willing to begin again when she knew how it could end.

Maybe Victor's mood would have benefited from confrontation—a kitchen-table sit-down where, with cups of reheated coffee to warm their hands, father and son could try to get at the root of the problem—but envisioning his own well-meaning heavyheartedness, and guessing that Victor would take offense, Sean was inclined to ignore his son's depression. In most cases, within a family, there was wisdom in holding one's tongue. Except for one thing: Victor could, if he concluded his chances were better elsewhere, take the boy with him when he left. This gave a precarious tilt to their household, an instability whose source, at bottom, was Victor's fondness for appearing wronged. He came home with elaborate tales of affronts he had suffered, but Sean knew the foreman and doubted that Victor had been shown any unfairness. When Victor needed to vent Sean steered clear and Daisy, rather than voicing her true opinion—that it was time he got over Esme—calmly heard him out. Victor could ruin his mother's peace of mind by ranting at the unbelievable fucking hopelessness of this dead-end town, voice so peeved and fanatical in its recounting of injustice that Sean, frowning across the dinner table, thought he must know how crazy he sounded, but Victor kept on: he was only waiting for the day when the mill closed down for good and he could pack up his kid and his shit and get out. What were they, blind? Couldn't they see he had no life? Did they think he could stand this another fucking day? From his chair near his dad Dylan said, "Are we going away?" "No, baby boy, you're not going anywhere," said Sean, at which Victor did the unthinkable, pulling out the gun tucked into the back of his jeans and setting it with a chime on his dinner plate and saying, "Then maybe this is what I should eat." Daisy said, "Sean," wanting him to do something, but before he could Victor pushed the plate across the table to him and said, "No, no, no, all right, I'm sorry, that was in front of the kid, that's taking it too far, I know I know I know, don't ask me if

I meant it because you know I don't, but I swear to god, Dad, some days it crosses my mind. But I won't. I never will." Gently he cupped his boy's head. "I'm sorry to have scared you, Dyl. Daddy got carried away."

"I want that gun out of the house," Daisy said.

Sean had gone out into the chilly night and folded the passenger seat of his truck forward and tucked the pistol, a lightweight Walther .22, into the torn parka he kept there, thinking that if Victor had meant to carry through on his threat he would have gotten a more serious gun. In bed that night Daisy turned to Sean, maybe needing to feel that something was still right in their life, and while he understood the impulse and even shared it he found he was picturing Esme's pointed chin, her head thrown back, her urchin hair fanned out across a mattress in the woods, an image so wrong and *good* he couldn't stop breathing life into it, the visitation no longer blissfully involuntary but nursed along, fed with details; the childish lift of her upper lip as she picked at the gift-box ribbon came to him, the imagined grace of her pale body against the stained mattress, her arms stretched overhead, her profile clean against the ropy twists of dirty hair—no she wouldn't look, she wouldn't look—and he came without warning, Daisy far enough gone that momentum rocked her farther, Sean relieved when she managed the trick that mostly eluded her while also, in some far-back, disownable part of his mind, judging her climax too naked, too needful, and at the same time impersonal, since she had no idea where he was in his head, and this, her greedy solitary capacity, bothered him.

In the slowed-down aftermath, when their habit was to roll apart and stretch frankly and begin to talk about whatever came to mind, a brief spell, an island whose sanctity they understood, where they were truly, idly, themselves, their true selves, the secret selves only they recognized in each other, she didn't move or speak and he continued to lie on her, worrying that he was growing heavier and heavier, her panting exaggerated as if to communicate the extremity of her pleasure, and for a sorry couple of minutes he hated her. There was something offensive in her unawareness of his faithlessness. If he was faithless, even in his mind, he wanted it to matter, and it couldn't matter unless she could sense it and hold him accountable and, by exerting herself against him as she had a right to, remind him he belonged to her and her alone. That was her responsibility. If she couldn't do it then he might continue to be bewilderingly alone and even slightly, weirdly in love with the lost girl Esme, indefensible as that was, and astounding. Daisy squirmed companionably out from under, turned on her side, a hand below her cheek, the crook of her other arm bracing her breasts, her smile confiding, genuine, her goodness obvious, the goodness at the heart of his world, the expression on his face god knows what, but by her considering stillness she was working up to a revelation. With Daisy sex sometimes turned the keys of the oldest locks, and he could never guess what was coming, since years and decades of wrongs and sorrows awaited confession, and even now, having loved her for twenty years, he could be blindsided by some small flatly told story of a terrible thing that had happened when she was a kid. Damage did that, went in so deep it took long years to surface. Tonight he had no inclination to be trusted, but could hardly stop her. "This thing's been happening. Maybe four or five times. This thing of the phone ringing and no one being there. 'Hello.'" The *hello* imitated a voice not hers. "And no answer. And 'Hello.' And no answer. Somebody there, though. Somebody there."

Such a relief not to have to travel again through the charred landscape of her childhood that he almost yawned. "Kids. Messing around."

"No," she said. "Her." His frown must have been baffled because she said, "Esme."

"Esme."

"Don't believe me, then, but I'm right, it was her. And the last time she called I said, 'Listen to me. Are you listening?' and there was no answer and I said, 'Never come back.' I didn't know that was about to come out of my mouth, I was probably more surprised than she was. But I meant it—I've never meant anything more. Just—pure. From deep down. 'Never come back.'"

"And then what?"

"Well, she got it. People get it when you say a thing from real deep down. And she hung up." Daisy scratched one foot with the toes of the other. "And I was left thinking, what was that? Was that really me?" Rueful smile. "If I'd said, 'Honey, where are you? Are you in trouble?' that would have been like me, right? And maybe she would have told me, maybe something is wrong and that girl has nowhere else to turn. She's the kind of girl there's not just one filthy mattress in the woods in her life, but last time she was lucky and found us, and we let her come live in our house, and we loved her, I think—did we love her?— and I'm guessing if things got bad enough for her she'd think of us and remember we were *good* to her—weren't we good to her?"

"Yes."

"Yes, and now it's like I'm waiting for her to call again. Or turn up. I think that's next. She'll turn up. And I don't want her to. I never want to see that girl's face again."

He couldn't summon the energy for *I'm sure it wasn't her,* even if that was probably the case. He could also have accepted Daisy's irrational conviction and addressed it with his usual calm. *Of course you're angry. Irresponsible, not just to her little boy, but to us who took her in, who cared about her—she left without a word. It's natural to be angry.*

He lay there, withholding the reassurance that was his part in this back-and-forth, until she turned onto her back and stared at the ceiling.

I made a serious mistake with Esme once. Gave her a bracelet. If he could have said that. If he could have found a way to begin.

Dent Figueredo wasn't someone Sean thought of as a friend, but this sweet May evening they were alone in the Tip-Top, door open to the street alive with sparrow song and redolent of asphalt cooling in newly patched potholes, Dent behind the bar, Sean on his bar stool worrying about taxes, paying no attention until he heard, "I want your take on this."

"My take."

"You're smart about women."

Women? But Sean nodded, and when that didn't seem to be enough, he said, "Hit me."

"See, first of all, despite her quote flawless English, she utters barely a word in the airport, just looks at me like I saved her life, which you'd think I would be a sucker for, but no, I'm praying *Get me out of this*, ready to turn the truck around and put her on the next flight home, and like she knows what I'm on the verge of she unbuckles and slides over and you know Highway 20 twists and turns like a snake on glass, I never felt so trapped before in my life, just because this itty-bitty gal has hold of my dick through my trousers and you *know* she's never done that before and I should've remembered that at this late date I'm not good husband material, but naw, I had to get melty when I seen her doe-eyed picture on the Internet. Shit."

"Husband material."

"What you got to promise if you want a nice Filipina girl," Dent said. "She's some kind of born-again. Dressed like a little nun, baggy skirt and these flat black worn-out shoes. No makeup. Won't hold your eye." When he caught Sean's eye he looked down and away, smiling, this imitation of girly freshness at odds with Dent's bald sun-spotted pate and the patch of silvery whiskers he missed on his Adam's apple, and Sean couldn't help laughing.

"What happens to her now?"

"Stories she tells, shit, curl your hair." Dent used his glass to print circles of wet on the bar. "America still looks good to a lot of the world, I tell you." He crouched to the refrigerator with his crippled leg stuck out behind. "She's staying in my house till I can figure out what comes next, and you should see the place, neat as a picture in a magazine. Hard little worker, I give her that. If any of my boys was unmarried, I'd drag him to the altar by the scruff of his neck." He levered open his beer, raising it politely. Sean shook his head. "Course before long," Dent continued, "one of them boys will shake loose."

"Meanwhile where does she sleep, this paragon?"

"Nah, Filipina."

"And you two, have you been—"

"Ming. Cute, huh?" Dent drank from the bottle before pouring into his glass. "Took the upstairs room for her own, cleared out years of boy shit. Jesus won't let nobody near her till there's a ring on her finger. Twenty-two, looks fifteen. That's the undernourishment."

When, sitting down to dinner that night, Sean told Daisy about the girl, she said, "You're kidding," and made him tell the entire story again, then said, amused, "Poor thing. You *know* he lied to her. And do you think he ever sent his picture? He's, what, a poorly preserved sixty, a drinker, a smoker, hobbling around on that leg, and he talks this child into leaving her home and her family, and now he won't do the right thing?"

"His lack of any feeling for her came as a shock, I think. And in his defense he is leaving her alone."

"Of course he's terrified of any constraint on his drinking. Dylan Raymond, we are waiting for your father."

Dylan put down the green bean he was trailing through his gravy and said, "Why?"

"Yeah, I think that's maybe more to the point. Because she's a born-again, and might start in on him."

"Is she pretty?"

"He says she has drawbacks." He bared his teeth. "Primitive dental care."

"Oh, and he's George Clooney."

"But she's sweet, he says," Sean said, prolonging his bared-teeth smile. "Good-natured."

Victor came to the table then in his signature ragged black T-shirt and jeans, his pale workingman's feet bare, dark hair still dripping wet, and he stood behind Dylan, kneading the boy's shoulders. "Who're we talking about?"

"My mom is pretty," Dylan announced, then waited with an air of uncertainty and daring—the kid who's said something provocative in the hope the adults will get into the forbidden subject. Victor conceivably could have said *What mom?* He conceivably could have said *You wouldn't know your mom if you passed her in the street.* He conceivably could have said *That bitch.* Sean knew Victor to be capable of any or all of these remarks, and was relieved when Victor calmly continued to rub the boy's shoulders. Not answering was fine, given the alternatives. When Dylan started drawing in his gravy with the green bean again, his head down, he inscribed circles like those his dad was rubbing into his shoulders, in the same rhythm. How does he understand his mother's absence? Sean wondered. Surely it's hard for him that his father never mentions his mother, worrisome that nobody can say where she'd gone. Daisy has not made up any tale justifying Esme's desertion. Sean understood the attraction of lying consolation; he felt it himself. The boy's relief would have been worth almost any falsehood, but Daisy had insisted that they stick with what they knew, which was virtually nothing. Daisy said, "Yes your mother is pretty," with a glance at Victor to make sure this didn't prompt meanness from him.

Victor changed the subject: "Who were you saying was sweet?"

Ming had no demure, closed-mouth smile, as he'd expected from an Asian girl, but a wide, flashing laugh whose shamelessness disturbed Victor, for her small teeth were separated by touching gaps, the teeth themselves incongruously short, like pegs driven hastily into the ground. The charm of her manner almost countered the daredevilish, imbecile impression made by those teeth. Seated on a slab of rock at the beach, he peeled off his socks. Flatteringly, Ming had dressed for their date—not only a dress, but stockings and *high heels*—while he had worn jeans and his favorite frayed black T-shirt, but he figured this was all right, she would know from movies that American men complained about ties and jackets. Ming's poise as she stood one-legged, peeling the stocking from her sandy foot, was very pretty, and the wind wrapped her dress—navy blue printed with flying white petals—tightly around her thighs and little round butt. Her pantyhose were rolled up and tucked into a shoe, her shoes wedged into a crevice of the rock. In the restaurant earlier Victor had observed her table manners and found them wanting. It wasn't so much that she made overt mistakes as that she observed none of the grace-note pauses and frequent diversions—a smile, a comment—with which food is properly addressed in public, but instead chewed steadily with her little fox teeth. Her manner began to seem quick and unfastidious and he was curious about what that would translate to in bed. He had been trying not to think about going to bed with her, because he knew from what Dent had said—first to his dad and then, when Victor called, to Victor himself—that she was a virgin, and it seemed wrong to try to guess what she would be like, sexually, when the only right way of perceiving her was as a semisacred blank slate. Respect, protectiveness: he liked having these emotions as he slouched against the rock, the wind bothering his hair, the bare-legged woman turning to find him smiling, smiling in return. There: the unlucky teeth. Guess what, she's human. He jumped from the rock and took her hand and they walked down the beach.

For nearly a year Victor was happier than his parents had ever known him to be, even after he was laid off from the mill for the winter. Not the time you'd want to get pregnant, but Ming did, and when she miscarried at five months, they both took it hard. "She won't get out of bed, Dad," Victor confided in a late-night call. "Won't eat, either." When he got off work early the next day Sean decided to swing by their place, a one-story clapboard cottage that suited the newlyweds fine except that it didn't have much of a yard and lacked a second bedroom for Dylan; all agreed the boy should continue living with his grandparents. *Two birds with one stone*, in Sean's view. Not only was the continuity good for Dylan, but once she saw she wouldn't have to negotiate for control of the boy, Daisy was free to be a relaxed, non-meddlesome mother-in-law. Privately, Sean has all along believed he is better than the other two at relating to Ming. To Daisy, Ming was the odd small immigrant solution to the riddle of Victor, the girl who had supper waiting when he got home, who considered his paycheck a king's ransom, who tugged off his boots for him when he was tired. The miscarriage was a blow, but such things happened. Ming was sturdy and would get over it. Basically Daisy was only so interested in anyone other than Dylan, and Victor—well, could you count on Victor to bring a person flowers to cheer her up? Or ice cream? Even if Ming won't eat anything else, she might try a little of the mint chocolate chip she loves. Safeway is near their cottage, so Sean turns into the parking lot and strides in, wandering around in the slightly theatrical male confusion that says *My wife usually does all this* before finding what he wants, remembering Daisy had said they were out of greens, deciding on a six-pack of beer, too, craving a box of cigarettes when it was time to pay—that habit kicked decades ago, its recurrence a symptom of his sadness about the lost baby, and he was standing in the checkout line with tears in his eyes, recognizing only then that the girl thrusting Ming's roses into the bag was Esme.

She seemed to have been trying not to catch his attention, and he wondered if she'd been hoping against hope that he would finish his business and walk out without ever noticing her. She could reasonably hope for that, he supposed: a job like hers could teach you that the vast majority of people walked through their lives unseeing. The checker was hastening the next lot of groceries down the conveyor belt, loaves of bread and boxes of cereal borne toward Esme as Sean hoisted his bags and said, "So you're back."

"Not for long."

"Not staying long, or you haven't been back long?"

Over his shoulder, to the next person: "Paper or plastic."

"You're staying with your sister?"

None of your business, her expression said.

The woman behind squeezed past Sean to claim her bag, frowning at him for the inconvenience. No, he realized, she was frowning because she thought he was bothering Esme, who scratched at her wrist, then twisted a silver bracelet around—*the* bracelet, now part of her repertoire of nervous gestures. Because this was Esme, fidgeting, forlorn, scared, and guilty, probably guilty more than anything, ready to construe his mildest question as a reproach. She and Victor really were two of a kind. Nonetheless he tried: "Come to see Dylan."

"Paper or plastic."

"He wonders about you, you know."

"Plastic."

To Sean, who had edged out of the aisle and stood holding his bags, she said wretchedly, "Does he?"

Sean said, though it was far from the case, "No one holds anything against you. He needs you. He's five years old."

"I know how old he is," she said.

"Or I could bring him by if that's easier."

Abruptly she stopped bagging groceries and pressed the heels of her hands to her eyelids. It was as if she'd temporarily broken with the world and was retreating to the only sanctuary possible in such a place. It was as if she despaired. He was sorry to have been a contributing factor, sorry to be among those she couldn't make disappear; at the same time he felt formidably in the right, and as if he was about to prevail—to cut through her fears and evasiveness to the brilliant revelation, from Esme to herself, of mother love, a recognition she would never be able to retreat from, which would steady her and bring her to her senses and leave her grateful for the change that had begun right here and now in the checkout line at Safeway. Because lives had to change unglamorously and for the better. Because he had found her.

"Would you really do that?" Esme said.

"Yeah, I could do that."

She tore a scrap from the edge of the bag she was filling, reached past the glaring cashier for a pen from the cup by the register, scribbled, and handed Sean the leaf of brown paper, which he had to hunt for, the next day, when it came time to call her, worrying that he'd misplaced it, finding it, finally, tucked far down into the pocket of the work pants he'd been wearing. But Esme wasn't there when he called; instead he got her sister, who told him Esme would be home from work at four. Sarah was this one's name, he remembered. "You know, she said you were really nice. Kind. So I want to thank you. She might not tell you this herself, but I know she can't wait to see the little guy. Me, either." Fine, they would come by around five.

Sean hadn't yet broken the news of Esme's return to Daisy, much less Victor, partly for his own sake, because he wanted to conserve the energy needed to cope with Daisy's inevitable fretting and Victor's righteous anger, partly for Dylan, because he wanted the boy to meet his mother again in a relatively quiet, relatively sane atmosphere, without a lot of fireworks going off, without anyone's suggesting that maybe it wasn't the best thing for the boy to spend time with a mother so irresponsible. Was there, in this secrecy, the flicker of another motive? Something like wanting to keep Esme to himself? Sean, driving, shook his head at the notion, and beside him Dylan asked, "Am I going to live with her now?"

"Honey, no, this is just for a little while, for you guys to see each other. You know what a visit is, right? And how it's different from *live with*? You live with us. You are going to *visit* your mom for a couple of hours. Meaning you go home after. With me. I come get you."

"What color is her hair?"

"Don't you remember? Her hair is black. Like—" He felt foolish when all he could come up with was "Well, not like any of ours."

"Not like mine."

"No, yours is brown." Sean tried to think what else Dylan wouldn't remember. "Your mom has a sister, a twin, meaning they look just alike. That'll be a little strange for you, maybe, but you'll get used to it, and this sister, see, is your aunt Sarah, and this's your aunt's house I'm taking you to. Because your mom is staying there. With her sister."

Too much news, for sure, and for the rest of the brief drive Dylan sucked his thumb as he hadn't done in years, but Sean didn't reprimand him, just parked the truck so the two of them could study the one-story white clapboard house with the scruffy yard where a bicycle had lain on its side long enough that spears of iris had grown up through its spokes. If this had been an ordinary outing, Sean would have explained *They built all these cottages on the west side for workers in the mill, and they don't look like much, maybe, but they're nice inside, and the men were allowed to take home seconds from the mill and they made some beautiful cabinets in their kitchens*, because he likes telling the boy bits of the history of his hometown, but he kept that lore to himself, and when the boy seemed ready they climbed the front porch steps together and stood before the door. "You want to knock or should I?"

"You."

Sean used his knuckles, three light raps, and then Esme was saying through the screen to Dylan, "Hey, you," smiling her pained childish smile, and Dylan couldn't help himself, he was hers, Sean saw, instantly, gloriously hers because she'd smiled and said two words. She held the door ajar and Dylan went past her into the house and he never did things like that—he was shy.

"Coming in?"

"I'll leave you two alone. To get—" *Reacquainted* would strike her as a reproach, maybe. "So you can have some time to yourselves. Just tell me when to come for him and I'll be back." He paused. "His bedtime's eight o'clock and it would be good if I got him home before that." *In case he needs some settling down.* Sean doesn't say that, or think about how he's going to keep the boy from telling his grandmother where he's been, but he will find a way, some small bribe that will soothe the boy's need to tell all.

"Barely three hours," she said.

"It's not a great idea to feed him a lot of sugar or anything, cause then he gets kind of wired."

"I wasn't going to," she said. "I know how he is."

"It would only be natural if you wanted to give him a treat or something."

"To worm my way back into his affections."

"Not what I meant," he said, and he suffered an emotion bruising but minor, too fleeting or odd, maybe, ever to have been named, nostalgia for a miserably wrongheaded sexual attraction. Not regret. He repeated, "Not what I meant."

"So maybe you won't believe this, I can see why you wouldn't, but I wanted to see him so bad. Only I thought you-all would for sure say no. Blame me. Not, you know, trust me. And instead you've made it easy for me, and I never expected that, and I don't know how to thank you, I don't, but this means everything to me, it's kind of saving my life. It's really basically saving my life." Running the sentences together, so unaccustomed was she to honesty, afraid, maybe, of the feeling of honesty, scary if you weren't used to it, and Sean reached out to lay a finger on her lips, ancient honorable gesture for *hush now*, no further explanation was necessary, he got it that to see your child again was like having your life saved, he would have felt the same way in her shoes but also chastened and rebellious, confronting someone like him who was doing the real work, continually, reliably present for the boy, and he wanted to convey the fact that none of this mattered if she was here and could give the boy a little of what he needed, a sense of his mother: but now it was Sean who was inarticulate, moved by the girl softness of her mouth, Sean whose finger rested against her lips until she jerked her head back and he was blistered by shame, the burden of impossible apology and regret shifting from her shoulders to his. He waited for her to say something direct and blaming, scathing, memorable, and when she did not he was relieved. But he wasn't fooled, either. She knew exactly what had happened and where it left them. This girl believed she now had the upper hand, but must use her leverage tactfully, however unlike her that was, if he was not to instantly deny what had taken place. What he understood was that he was in trouble here, but that she was going to collude with him because, basically, he could give her more of what she wanted. The child. His agreement was necessary for her to continue secretly seeing the child. And Sean did not know how to set any of this right, only that he needed to keep his voice down and not do any further harm—not scowl in dismay or do anything else she could construe as a sign of problems to come. He told her, "Seven thirty, then, okay? See you at seven thirty," and she said in a voice in no way remarkable, "We'll be here."

But they were not. "She has rights," Sarah told Sean, who was in her kitchen, in a rickety chair she had pulled away from the table, saying, "She has rights," saying now, "It's wrong for him to be kept from his *mother* the way you-all have done."

For some reason, when she'd pulled the chair out for him, he'd taken it and turned it around and straddled it. Maybe he had needed to act, to take control of something, if only the chair. This is her sister—or closer than sister, twin—and he keeps his voice down. "Ask yourself why I brought him by? I'm her best friend in this mess, but what she's done is damage her own cause. This isn't gonna look good."

"To who?"

"Do you know where she's going?"

"To who won't it look good?"

Trailer trash, Daisy called the sisters once. "The thing is to make this right without having anybody else get involved."

"You're threatening me."

"I'm the opposite of threatening you. I'm saying, let's work this out ourselves. You tell me where she's gone and I find her and we work it out like reasonable people and there's no need for anybody else to know she abducted a five-year-old child."

"*Abducted*. Like my sister wasn't in labor eighteen hours. Like

she never chipped a tooth from clenching or left claw marks
on my hand. Tell me you ever even really knew she was in the
house. Ever once really talked to her. Victor hit her upside the
head so hard the ringing in her ear lasted a week. Do you know
he told her he'd kill her if she tried to leave? It was my four
thousand dollars. So she ran, you know, she took the money and
she ran and there was never any phone call and it kept me up a
lot of nights. It wasn't the money, it was not knowing she was all
right—they say twins know that, but I didn't, not till I saw her
again. And I never saw her look at anyone like she looks at that
little boy when he says *I want to stay with you*, and it's not like
she planned this, but after that how was she going to let him go?
I'm not saying she makes great choices, but you were unrealistic
thinking she could give him back."

The chair wobbled as he crossed his arms on its backrest.
"Maybe so. She and I need to talk about that. Work out what's
best for all involved."

"It sounds so reasonable when you say it."

"I am reasonable." He smiled. "Families need to work these
things out."

"Now you're family."

"Like it or not." Still smiling.

Esme was driving north toward Arcata to go to college there.
"None of you thought she was good enough for college."

An outright lie, but he let it pass. "How long ago did they
take off?"

"Not long. She had to get her stuff. She was just throwing
things into the car. Dylan helped. Laughing like they were both
little kids." He continued to look at her and Sarah shook her
head before saying, "Twenty minutes ago maybe."

"What kind of car?"

"I don't know kinds of cars." He won't look away. "Smallish. A Toyota maybe. Green, maybe." Not smiling now: he needs her to get this right. "Yeah. Green. A bumper sticker. *Stop fucking something up.* That really narrows it down, hunh. Trees. *Stop Killing Ancient Trees.* Trees are her thing."

"You're sure about Arcata."

"See, she's wanted that for years, an apartment and classes and her little boy with her. Botany. Redwoods, really. Did you know that about her? She loves redwoods and there's this guy there who's famous, like *the* guy if you want to study redwoods, and she met him, and she might be going to be his research assistant this summer. She said—" But she'd told him what he needed to know and he was out the door. Lucky that it was north, the two-lane highway looping through the woods without a single exit for sixty miles and few places to pull over, lucky that after dark nobody drives this road but locals and not many of those. As long as he checks every pull-off carefully and doesn't overshoot her then it comes down to how fast he can drive, each curve with its silver-gray monoliths stepping forward while their sudden shadows revolve through the woods behind, the ellipse of shadow-swerve the mirror image of his curve, evergreen air through the window, no oncoming lights—which is just as well given his recklessness, the rage he can admit now that he's alone, the desire just to get his hands on her, the searing passage of his brights through the woods like the light of his mind gathered and concentrated into swift hunting intelligence that touches and assesses and passes on because its exclusive object is her. At this speed it's inevitable he will overtake her—nobody drives this road like this—but now he has bolted past a likely spot, a rutted crescent rimmed with trees tall enough to shade it from moonlight: there. He brakes and runs the truck backward onto the shoulder, passing an abandoned car whose color, in the darkness, can't be discerned, and pulling in behind it he reads *Stop Killing Ancient Trees.* Such fury, such concentration, and he almost missed it. An empty car. Here is his fear: that she has arranged to meet someone. That Sarah was lied to, and Arcata was a fable, and there's a guy in this somewhere, and Esme told him she would go away with him if she could get her kid. Nobody to be seen but when he gets out in the moonlight it is as if the air around Sean is sparkling, as if electricity flashes from his skin and glitters at the forest, as if he could convey menace even to a stone.

When he checked in the backseat there was the boy curled up, sleeping in his little shirt and underpants with nothing over him, no blanket, not even an old sweater or jacket, and cracking the door open—its rusty hinges alarming the woods—Sean ducked into a cave of deepest, oldest life-tenderness and took the child in his arms and backed out, loving the weight of him and the shampoo smell of his mussed hair. He set him down barefoot and blinking, his underpants a triangular patch of whiteness in the moonlight, the boy as shy as if it was he who'd run away, keeping a fearful arm's length from Sean and blinking when Sean said, "Where's your mom?," seeming not to trust Sean, confused and on the brink of tears, and there was no time for that. "Get in the truck," he told the boy, "and I don't want you coming out no matter what. Your job is to stay in the truck and I don't want you getting out of that truck for any damn reason whatsoever, do you understand me?"

"I have to pee."

"Come on then."

Watching from behind, Sean felt the usual solicitude at the boy's wide-legged stance. Dry weeds crackled.

"She had to go pee in the woods," he said. Solemnly: "My mom did, in the woods." That was a new one to the boy.

Sean said, "What happened to your clothes?"

"I threw up and she made me take 'em off and throw 'em out the window cause the smell was making her sick too."

"All right, now you get in my truck and you *stay* in the truck. What did I just say?"

"*Stay* in the truck."

"What're you going to do?"

"*Stay* in the truck."

He had to boost the shivering boy up to the high seat. Sean took the flashlight from the glove box and checked to make sure the keys were in his pocket. He motioned for Dylan to push the lock down, first on the passenger side, then, leaning across, on the driver's. Sean nodded through the window, but the boy only wrapped his arms around himself and twisted his bare legs together, and Sean remembered the old parka stuffed down behind his seat and gestured for the boy to unlock again and leaned in and said, "Look behind the seat and there's a jacket you can put on," and his flash framed twigs and brambles in sliding ovals of ghost light, stroking the dark edge of the woods, finding the deer trail she must have followed. By now she had to be aware that he was coming in after her, and he took the shimmer of his own agitation to mean *she* was scared, and somehow this was intolerable, that she would be scared of him, that she would not simply walk out of the woods and face him. That he is in her mind not a good man, a kind man, but instead the punisher she has always believed would come after her, and whether he wanted to cause fear or didn't want to hardly

mattered, since that role was carved out ahead of him, narrow
as this trail: coming into the woods after her, he can't be a good
man. He can't remember the last time he felt this kindled and
all-over passionate, supple and brilliant, murderously *right*, and
when his flash discovered her she was already running, but it
took only two long strides to catch her. She broke her fall with
her hands, but before she could twist over onto her back he had
her pinned. If she could have turned and they could have seen
each other, it might have calmed them both down, but this way,
with her back under his chest, his mouth by her ear, he was talking right to her fear-lit brain, and what he said would be indelible, and he felt the exhilaration of being about to drive the truth
home to her, and he said *What is the matter with you* and then *You
took my kid* and she said *He's not your kid* and he said *My flesh and
blood* and they both waited for what she would say next to find
out whether she had reached the end of defiance but she hadn't.
If you take him away I'll just come back. Even now she could have
eased them from this brink if she had shown remorse, and he
was sorry she hadn't, and he said *What do I need to do to get through
to you.* She thrashed as he rolled her over and her fist caught the
flashlight, sending light hopping away across the ground. In the
refreshed darkness he reached for her neck, and she was screaming his name as his hands tightened to shut off her voice. Where
his flashlight had rolled to a halt a cluster of hooded mushrooms
stood up in awed distinctness like tiny watchers. When she
clawed at his face, he seized her wrists and heard twigs breaking
under her as she twisted. The twining silver bracelet imprinted
itself on his palm: he could feel that, and it was enough to bring
him to himself, but she did not let up, raking at his throat when
he reared back, and now her *Fuck you fuck you fuck you* assailed
him, its echo bandied about through the woods until, feeling

her wrath slacken from exhaustion, he rolled from her so she would understand it was over, and they fell quiet except for their ragged breathing, which made them what neither wanted to be, a pair, and as he sat up something nicked the back of his skull in its flight, frisking through his hair, an electrifying noncontact that sang through his skull to the roots of his teeth and the retort cracked through the woods and there was the boy, five feet away, holding the gun with his legs braced wide apart. Behind him rose a fountain of sword ferns taller than he was. "Don't shoot," she said. "Listen to me, Dyl, don't shoot the gun again, okay? You need to put it down now."

He turned to Sean then to see how bad it was, what he had done, and in staring back at him Sean could feel by the contracted tensions of his face that it was a wrecked mask of disbelief and no reassurance whatsoever to the boy.

"It was a accident," the boy said. "I'm sorry if I scared you."

"Just you kneel down and put it on the ground," she said. "In the leaves—yes, just like that. That was good."

"It was a accident."

"Sweetie, I know it was." She sat up. With her face averted she said to Sean, "It could have been either of us. Did it nick you? Are you bleeding?"

He felt through his hair and held his hand out and they both looked: a perfect unbloodied hand stared back at them.

"A fraction of an inch," he said in a voice soft as hers had been: conspirators. "I left the damn gun in the car. Fuck, I never even checked the safety, I was so sure it wasn't loaded. It would've been my fault and he'd've had to live with it forever."

"He doesn't have to live with it now," she said. "Or with you."

She was on her feet, collecting the flashlight, and playing

through the sapling audience the light paused and she said, "Jesus," and he turned to look behind him at a young tan oak whose bark was gashed in sharp white.

She told the boy, "It's okay. Look at my eyes, Dylan. Nobody's hurt. You see that, don't you? Nobody got hurt."

"You did," he said.

"Baby, I'm not hurt. Pawpaw didn't hurt me, and you know what? We're getting out of here. You're coming with me."

Dylan looked down at the gun and she said, "No, leave it." Then changed her mind. "I'm taking it," she told Sean, "because that's wisest, isn't it?"

"You can't think that," Sean said.

"Tell me you're okay to be left," she said.

"A little stunned is all."

"That's three of us, then."

Dylan was staring at him and Sean collected his wits to say clearly, "You know what a near miss is, don't you, Dyl? Close but not quite? That bullet came pretty close, but I'm okay. Are you hearing me say it didn't hurt me? Nod your head so I'm sure you understand." The boy nodded. "We're good, then, right? You can see I'm all right." The boy nodded.

Esme said, "We need to go, Dylan. Look at you. You're shivering."

"Where are we going?"

"Far away from here, and don't worry, it's all right if we go. Tell him now that we can go."

This was meant for Sean, and they watched as he took the full measure of what he had done and how little chance there was of her heeding what he said now: "Don't disappear with him, Esme. Don't take him away forever because of tonight. From now on my life will be one long trying to make this right to you. To him, too. Don't keep him away. My life spent making up for this. I need you to believe me. I can make this right."

"I want to believe you," she said. "I almost want to believe you."

Before he could think how to begin to answer that, the mother and child were gone.

He knew enough not to go after them. He knew enough not to go after them yet.

Mendocino Fire

One time in the library in town a boy has a rat inside his shirt. Its head pokes out under the boy's chin, its clawey hands clinging and whiskers quicked forward. It is as if Finn has never wanted anything before: this, *this* is her destiny, to be a girl with a rat inside her shirt. Wherever she goes the rat will hang on, the alert small subject of her gigantic solicitude. *How long do you think a rat will last in the woods against foxes and ravens and owls and hawks.* But if I was really careful and kept it in a cage and was really careful. *Do you think a rat wants to be your little Gitmo prisoner, or do you think a rat wants to be free like you are.*

Nights when the fog holds off they laze around the illicit summer fire, smoking and telling stories and feeding twigs to the flames for the love of seeing small things burn, story after story, and there is Finn, almost seven, riding the high end of a canted redwood log in the dark. Mary, too, tells stories. Whenever Mary tells how Finn was born, Finn feels both beloved and ashamed, her helpless, ridiculous baby-self held up for them to dote on. That story ends with Mary crying in ever-renewed astonishment: *Finn you were so beautiful!* Finn works her arms from too-long sleeves and pulls her knees to her chest under the sloppy tent of Goodwill sweater smelling of the grown man who gave it away. Who smoked. Who was not her father, because she's asked and Mary shook her head. The baggy sweater hem covers the boots so only their toes show, and she evens the boot toes so neither is ahead, neither is winning, not the left, not the right, old black boot toes in a setting of moss and fingerlength ferns and upthrust mushrooms whose caps are pale, pushy, tender, mute. A boot toe edges into the gang of mushrooms. One is uprooted and maimed by the slow back-and-forthing of the toe of the boot. Then she is sorry. Finn shuts her eyes and fills up with sorriness.

That is *killing*, Finn.

For a while she is absorbed in accusing herself, then blame loses its electrical charge and if she wants that absorption again another mushroom will have to die. Boredom nudges her boot toe close to another cocky little button of rooted aliveness.

What is that like: not to be able to move out of the way.

Another night, that summer or the summer after. If firelight flashes high enough there's laughter, first because it's a freaking *face* up there in the dark, then because it's a *little kid*. Now and then Finn has come down when coaxed, and that was a mistake. They may not intend it thus, but their solicitude is an oblique condemnation of Mary. Finn resents this even if her mother doesn't.

Aren't you cold in just that sweater and your poor legs bare? And Jesus look how scratched up.

How long since you seen chocolate?—I think I got some somewhere.

My little girl is your age just about and she can say her ABCs, can you say your ABCs?

In this full-moon circle there's a stranger, though the grown-ups don't at first know that, each person assuming the lean bearded dude with the hostile vibe arrived with somebody else. Afterward no one will own up to having told him about the circle, but that could have been from remorse at showing the kind of piss-poor judgment that fucks up everyone's night. Finn who can go a long while unseen has been found out: he has noticed her. He has called, "What's your name?" and gotten no response. The wiry dark shrub of his beard parts again, the teeth asking, "What's your name?" Finn's hesitation lasts long enough to offend him down there in his bared-nerve world and he shouts, "Don't answer then you autistic little shit, not like I give a fuck." Finn is being, for the first time, *hated*: her nerves memorize the shock. And him: she memorizes *him*, this shirtless shaven-headed hater, brows heavy and meaningful in contrast to the round gleaming exposure of his forehead, and, inked on the left upper slab of his chest, a tattoo, a spiral, big as her handprint would be if she left a handprint on his bare, slightly sweating, hard-breathing chest.

"Hey," someone, not Mary, commands gently. "Hey, come on now. Hey."

Another voice says, "Way disproportionate, man, going off on a kid like that."

Someone else says, "Look, she never answers." Adding, "But it's not autism."

Someone says, "Maybe, man, you should apologize to Finn."

He says, "Finn."

Mary, at last: "You know her name."

"Finn," he calls up to her. "Finn, man, I'm sorry, I lost it."

The others wait for an utterance equal to the scale of his offense. He too, for reasons of his own, seems to want to say more. He calls, "You not telling me your name, it just hurt my feelings, I lost it."

At this skewed sincerity they laugh, and he sits down and reaches to accept the joint, and everyone in the mended, redeemed circle relaxes. Finn is almost asleep when she hears his voice again: "You know what I saw on TV last night. This bear. Polar bear. It teeters on this little dwindling *raft* of ice and it can't stay where it is and it can't go because there's no other ice in sight, it's swimming and swimming, this small, like a dog's, polar bear head in a world of water, forever and ever water, this bear swimming hard against the drag of its fur with nowhere to swim to, nothing to climb out onto, ice gone, ice melted, and it's despair, what he feels, what we feel, *that* is despair and *we all know it*, you think Mendocino is different, your safe hole to hide in, well wake the fuck up, they're coming for the last scraps, who stops them? Us? Have we stopped them from screwing over the planet? Let me tell you their ideology. Want me to tell you their ideology? *Take take take take take take take. Kill kill kill kill kill kill kill.*" When he says *kill* they hear not only *fucked up and pissed off*, there's a personal element, some provocation an ordinary person could tolerate, which he, being crazy, can't endure. "What's coming should terrify us. Tell me this. Why aren't we fucking *terrified*. Why don't we do *a fucking thing* to stop them." He gets to his feet. "Now it all falls on *children*." He tilts his face up but the fire has died down and Finn doubts he can make her out against the darkness. He says, "She's gonna see—," and means *her*. He's forgotten her name.

He tries again. "She's gonna live to see—"

He's forgotten the end of the sentence.

With soft concern, the kind that doesn't presume to insist, someone drawls, "Come on, man, sit down, why don't you sit down"—and other voices, fastidiously soft, tug at him. "Come on, it's all right, sit back down, good, that's good, don't cry, it's a beautiful night, you're among friends, there's the moon."

Finn has things to fix—terrors, gaps in knowledge—that wolves can help with, and for a time, alongside her love of Mary, her passion for her mother's weather-roughened fair skin and the wealth of her never-cut hair and her habit of rubbing a leaf between thumb and forefinger and asking the plant *What's wrong here? Am I missing something?* and her woodsmoke, damp wool, and patchouli scent and her voice and the millet-flour pancakes she makes in their cast-iron skillet when she's in a good mood with wild blackberries that burst and bleed inky streaks through the batter, alongside all of that Finn's love of wolves runs parallel. Protective yellow-eyed posse: Agnes, Bone, Donedeal, Moody, Sid. Slipsliding through the woods with her. Finn can't remember mentioning their existence ever, so how does Mary know? Mary says *Sometimes it's like that, beloveds from the life before stick with the child into the child's new existence, and ignorants call them*

imaginary. Because they regard human doings with supreme contempt, there are limits to what the wolves can teach Finn. And
one day Mary says *Outgrow the fucking fairy tale, Finn. There are no*
wolves. There never were.

Not a road, you can't call it a road, just the dirt ruts someone
would drive down when the orchard needed attention. That
time, the time when these trees badly needed pruning, came
and went years ago, and now thickets of water shoots, pretty
much impenetrable, swarm once-elegant branches. Mary's lover,
Teague, says the orchard is *asleep.* The last four or five winters
were too warm, with so few chill hours that the trees—who
break into blossom only after experiencing what they believe to
be a whole winter's worth of cold—never wake from dormancy.
They have been stranded by global warming in a kind of dream.
Teague likes explaining things about his land, even troubling
things that keep him awake at night. *Listen when I'm talking to*
you, Teague says. Finn *was* listening. He doesn't like it when she
tells him so. *Why do you have to piss him off,* Mary says, pressing a
rustling bag of frozen peas to Finn's jaw. After a couple of tries,
Finn perfects a listening expression. Finn has to climb several
trees before finding an apple. She twists it from its twig. Where
some old trees were taken out there is a shaggy clearing sheltered from rough wind, hidden from low-flying planes, perfect
for Mary's little darlings. From her loft Finn hears Teague say
There's shit kids need, and when Mary says *Like what* he says *Like*
has she ever had a birthday cake? Wherever Mary goes, Teague's
dog follows at a bowlegged pitbull trot. *The handsomer the man*
the uglier the dog, Mary says. *Do your thing, goofball goonface,* Mary
says, scratching what's left of a torn-off black ear. *Pitbull pee is the*

flashing neon keep-out sign of the animal world. As backup, tarnished spoons clink and tinsel shimmers along strands of salvaged wire strung trunk to trunk in a critter-proof perimeter, the plants leafing out in the grow-bags Finn and Mary drag into new, sunnier configurations as summer progresses. *A real secret is one your life depends on,* Mary says. The apple is as small as Finn's fist, gone in five bites. Finn has taken to counting bites. *Did you remember to feed her?* is one of the accusing questions Teague aims at Mary. If he finds out about the grow, he'll do more than accuse. It's his land, he's supposed to know what's going on. Even if he didn't know, he can still lose the land, that's the law. The bigger danger is the patch being found by accident and ripped off. *Say some new guy came to work for Teague,* Mary said, *then I'd worry.* The beauty of this semiwild sixty-acre slice of Mendocino is that it's too much for Teague to handle without help, and he puts off hiring help because he's paranoid. The downside is that in Teague's paranoia he's convinced Mary cheats on him. They can't stay. *My fucking luck,* Mary says. *Those seeds came from Afghanistan.*

Dev plays guitar in a band with gigs throughout the county and even, two or three times that winter, down in the city, where Mary wears high heels and a vintage dress with pansies on it and they eat Chinese. In potholed parking lots outside bars in Arcata and Hopland and Forestville, Finn finds quarters, earrings, condoms she knows better than to touch, a lipstick whose red Mary likes, a dog collar complete with tags, a real bullet, a run-over T-shirt that, uncrumpled, says *Mendocino Fire* and was a fireman's, Dev says, and then says *We should look for a puppy to go with that collar.* Someone, a drunk, breaks the van's left taillight with a baseball bat. For no reason, Mary says. Wrapped in an old flannel shirt of Dev's, zipped in his sleeping bag against the cold in the rear of the van, Finn sleeps alongside instrument cases and the sawdust-sweet carpentry tools of Dev's day job. All night the van is a tin drum for the rain. Most mornings she gets to school. A cough ransacks her chest and scrapes her throat raw. When the shoplifted thermometer says 104, Dev sings *If that mocking-bird don't sing, Daddy's gonna buy you a diamond ring* and by dawn her forehead is cool under Mary's palm. Far out in the country a curve of road stampedes her heart and right there is the dirt drive that winds to Teague's house. She studies Mary's profile. Nothing. When Dev likes the song on the radio, he turns it up high and they all sing.

Mary is still asleep inside. At the table of recycled redwood near Kafka's trailer, Finn is fed tea and slice after slice of toast dripping with honey by Kafka, fresh from her shower, the mown contours of her crewcut pinheaded with glisten, all six feet of her clean and slender and unbothered in cargo pants and a white wifebeater that exposes the zoo sleeving her forearms. Ocelot, macaw, monkey, winding vines. From this intricacy Kafka's hands emerge naked and in need of something to do. A near-drowned bee orbits the bowl of Kafka's spoon. Does Finn know about bees? "Because this is some ominous shit. By far the most important pollinators on the planet, disappearing. Flying away, never coming back, hives *empty*. No one knows why. So now, if I see a bee flounder-ing around in my teacup, I'm like, 'Sister Bee, just you take hold of the tip of this spoon, just you rest a while, calm down, dry your wings.'" Since Kafka keeps talking, Finn's confusion plays out exclusively within her own head, where it can't complicate the good impression she hopes to make. In case they're staying.

Rick is a tattooed sea urchin diver who has custody of his eleven-year-old daughter, and Maddie and Finn share a pink room looking out over unmown fields and patchy woods to the barn that still has its old copper running-horse weathervane. On Maddie's laptop they research sex and try what they find out. In a cinderblock room they're forbidden to go into, she and Maddie run their hands over sleekly wrapped bricks of cash and fit their index fingers into triggers. From a FedEx box slithers a dream of a dress and Rick tells Mary try it on. Bare-legged she spins around and he says what's it like wearing five thousand dollars on your back. Finn squints from down below: daylight rays through bullet holes in the horse's chest. Inside the barn, down the lengths of parallel benches, the long-fingered leaves bask under metered lights, in rainforest warmth, to the music of Mozart. Music Finn can't believe Mary has known about all along.

Finn's hair turns pink. A friend's older brother gives her the Earth First! shirt she wears under a baggy old-man cardigan, whose pockets hold crusts for sparrows wintering in the woods behind the school. Fall of sophomore year she writes a history paper on the FBI's involvement in the attempted assassination of Judi Bari. That spring Finn hides the rats from another student's science fair project in a pillowcase under her oversize hoodie and saunters from the school. When she stops to peer in, they're scrambling and clutching, whiskers vibrating with fear. Finn kneels in the woods. She holds the first at eye level, his hind legs scrabbling, and checks the petal of chest under the albino fur. "Hello after all these years," she tells it. "You thought I wouldn't come back to save you?" A heart batters against her thumb. *Live! live! live! live! live!* thuds the heart. You've been asleep, Finn! Half as alive as this rat! Dreaming, while death after death streams out from your existence like ripples when a finger touches a river. Fed from a slaughterhouse, Finn, educated with cunning lies, your clothes stitched by enslaved children. Mr. Hahn seeks her out. Nobody's accusing her. It's not as if anyone saw who took the rats. But, hypothetically. Hypothetically, even if one student holds extremely strong views, other students are entitled to do projects for the science fair. Right? Can she accept the fairness of that? She likes Mr. H, his unfunny jokes and love of zombie movies, the surfboard on top of his Jeep when the sets are good. He wants her to assure him that for the duration—meaning till she graduates—she will respect others' property.

"Living beings can't be property."

"Have you thought about college?" Mr. Hahn says.

"My family couldn't afford it." In general the word *family* suffices to fend off intrusiveness.

But it doesn't deter him. "Trust me, Finn, it can happen," he says. "Bright mind like yours. All you have to do is want it."

Jared's black hair goes unwashed week after week, Jared buys his *Scarlet Letter* essay off the Internet and argues he deserves more than a B+, in the boys' locker room Jared holds a lit match under the tick in his armpit, then wears it in a glass phial around his neck till it withers into tick dust. His dad is the foreman at the lumber mill, and when he was eleven Jared was supposed to have talked someone's little sister into taking off her underpants at Abo's company picnic and to have been caught by her older brother and beat up pretty bad. Finn's outward appearance—

kohl eyeliner, slip dress, combat boots—isn't what moves him. This goes way deeper. When they share a match—his cigarette, then hers—his world is rocked by her presence, her being, the Finn-ness of her eyes and nose and mouth and hard-beating heart, she can tell. Her skin can tell. No part of her doesn't love him, nothing holds its tongue. God, that he is alive! While she was in the woods he was playing *World of Warcraft* on the flat-screen TV in his room. If only she could go back and tell her little kid self *Hold on because your soul mate exists, you just have to live long enough to get to him.* Bliss, this is what they mean by bliss. Or it would be if she could forget the death awaiting the two of them and all living beings. *Everything for me's not all melting arctic ice, Finn, not all dead birds falling from midair and viruses spread by monkey rape,* he says. *I'm not you. Sometimes I need it to be a sunny day with no problems.* What won't go away is one sentence. *I'm not you.* That stops her in her tracks. What is wrong with him that he can say *I'm not you.* They spend a night in zipped-together sleeping bags with stars transiting the gap between redwood spires and he says *Tell me again how you made up the wolves and their names and what they said.* For as long as it takes to tell him about the wolves, she's not lonely.

Rubber bullets have been fired, five protesters seriously in-jured, two others dead. Rumors tremor through the group of nuns in the van with Finn, who bends forward uncomfortably, her bound hands wedged against the small of her back. River and Trespass and the others were muscled into a different van, leaving Finn the only Earth First!er among nuns. The crush of ambulances and police cars and rescue vehicles allows no exit from the bridge, and for an hour after the doors are slammed on them they swelter and wait. Marshaled on the tech plate of the van's floor, eleven pairs of practical black lace-up oxfords and one set of dirty red high-tops, the chorus line of black skirts and fawn stockings interrupted by Finn's filthy jeans, a tear exposing her banged-up left knee. Her wrists aching, Finn makes small talk with an elderly sister whose gaze is magnanimously fond behind cat's-eye glasses, and whose upper lip sports a wispy Frida Kahlo mustache Finn finds endearing, the righteousness of the calm white superior face undercut by this roguish touch of androgyny. She's never been this close to a nun before, and is worried about giving offense, not by saying something inappropriate, because she means to keep a close watch on that, but merely by being dirty and young and an anarchist. The cat's-eye nun's inquiries break the ice, and soon Finn is the object of their concerted attention. It is a van full of mothers, Finn thinks. It's nothing to do with today's protest, but she ends up explaining the threat to the last remaining old growth in Mendocino County and confesses that she believes a treesit is her destiny and there's some redwood, as yet unmet, she was born to save. Neat coiffed heads, dark or graying, nod benignly. The van rolls a few feet, and the women sigh in approving relief, but then it jolts to a halt, and a nun says, "Oh, nuts." Finn closes her eyes, thinking that when she tells River about this, she will report, *The worst expletive they allow themselves is "nuts."* One of the nuns sneezes repeatedly, but nobody can offer her a tissue since their hands are locked behind their backs. The van jolts forward again, and Finn is thrown against the cat's-eye nun, and rests close against her a fraction of an instant longer than she needs to, for the skin-and-bone kindness of the woman—to take that in.

She's been warned against it—subjected to detailed lectures on safety—but on her third day Finn abandons the ropes that are her only insurance against a fall. She free-climbs into the vaults of this aerial brazil, gardens of licorice fern, couches of moss, single boughs as grand as reverend oaks, thickets, hidey-holes, moths indistinguishable from bark till they flutter away, dewy arboreal salamanders insinuated in crevices, forest after forest ascending this five-hundred-year-old tree whose lightning-charred pinnacle, visible only when fog melts away, looms far above. Finn wants to climb that spar, but decides to practice more before attempting it. The sun slants *thus* across a continent of cloud, igniting its upper verge in flaring platinum, streaking through space, silvering the drops beading a cobweb wide as a bedsheet, so that the spider legging it down the shining strands is forced to step high. A satellite blinks across the gray chasm between two cloud summits.

About dealing with the human threats, there have been other lectures, equally detailed. *How you conduct yourself reflects on the movement. Defuse aggression, don't feed it*, Trespass told her. *Try to connect.*

They are Smoke River boys, the fallers, they catcall, invite her to get naked, accuse her of being a dyke, ask how long since she's had a bath and how bad she smells, unzip their pants and urinate on the tree, promise her pizza if she comes down, say hey why don't we all just go out for a beer, say they'll marry her if she cleans up good. And why not come down and get it over with, this tree's gonna die one way or the other, either rotting out from sheer age or because they cut it down, and why shouldn't they get the wood while it's still worth something.

Finn answers according to the doctrine of nonviolence, hanging out over the platform's edge or walking barefoot down the tree as she leans back into her ropes, trying for rapport, smiling twelve stories down with her hair falling every which way around her face, her smile slipping at *Fuck you, cunt, I'm just trying to feed my kids.*

The original treesit, improvised from salvaged and secondhand finds, has mostly disappeared, supplanted piecemeal by newer, safer, higher-tech materials. River says it's like the ax in the fable whose handle gets replaced three times and head gets replaced twice but is still the same ax. Still the same treesit, the fallers thwarted for going on two years by a series of sitters. Within, the shelter is clean-swept and orderly, the medley of jars comprising Finn's garden of alfalfa, lentil, and sunflower sprouts positioned to catch the sun, her climbing gear stashed, sleeping bag aired out and lashed tight, lanterns, laptop, cell phone, radio snug in the waterproof locker, clothes mended and folded *like the housekeeping of an Amish control freak*, River teases over brown rice with goat cheese and shiitakes on his next visit, adding, when Finn doesn't laugh, "This is what comes of raising a kid around a bunch of potheads, right? This kind of rage for order." He licks his chopsticks clean, studying her tattered shirt. "Why 'Fire'?"

Finn, who has never been sure why, doesn't answer.

"Be mysterious then."

He lights the joint, draws the smoke in and holds it, slouching into a more restful pose against Tara's trunk, and so embracing is his well-being that Finn breaks the fundamental law of her private universe, taking the joint from between his fingers, sipping the smoke, angling her head back to rest against Tara's bark alongside his, slipping into the dream he's in the middle of, the dream Mary was continually dreaming, the dream Finn swore she'd never get sucked into, but she's been lonely in this tree whose life depends on her, and he is the lover who's come to spend the night, his closeness so *right*, his company so easeful it makes her want to laugh—she would laugh, except he's talking again. "Interesting being alive. So far it's interesting, though there's been what you'd call long stretches of despair. I forget about them when I'm with you. You're like the anti-despair angel, the way you've held on. The commitment. One hundred forty-three days," he says. "The doubters said you wouldn't last two weeks."

He's older. Emotion has had its way with River's face, strenuously so, inscribing brackets at the corners of the witty mouth. An earring in the ear toward her, a silver lightning bolt visible only when he drags hard and the ember sparkles. Flannel shirt, mussed dreadlocks with the prized loofah-like gnarliness. When she waves it off he smokes the joint down, pinching it out and tucking the tiny burnt tip into the pocket of his jeans. With most visitors she remains covertly vigilant for the clumsiness or oversight that will jeopardize either the guest or her precariously cobbled-together shelter; his meticulousness soothes her. They sit side by side, backs to the tree, no movement in the forest stretching away below them, no wind bothering Tara's branches, the world asleep as far as they can see.

Finn says, "I dreamed I came down and there was this horse waiting for me with a look like *Come on, get on*, and I did and rode it out of the woods into a city with miniature people in it, who came up only to the horse's knees and kept saying *Hurry! hurry!* like I was late." Finn refrains from saying *Late for something wonderful*, though that was how it had seemed in the dream, and why this shyness about *wonderful*, does she think he'll think *wonderful* means him? Such is her trepidation—she's beginning to concede she's in love—that what she says next is equally likely to mislead. "We can't have children, can we? People like us, I mean. Who think, who are aware of what's coming. Who wouldn't want a child to live through that."

River says, "That would keep me up at night, I guess, if I'd ever wanted a kid. But I haven't."

Sounds like you might, though.

Some risks are worth running.

Things she wants him to say, that he doesn't say.

He says, "What do you think, can you get through the winter? They'll mostly leave you alone in the winter. Spring's when they try stuff like siccing the sheriff's department on us, like sending in Climber Dan up in the dark to catch treesitters asleep. Spring is when we worry." River straightens and stretches before saying, "All treesitters dream about the ground. Once you're on the ground you're gonna dream about the tree." After a while he says, " 'Fire.' Whoever wore that shirt before wanted to save live things from fire."

Last night the rain came down so hard a bird couldn't fly through it, literally. You think a bird won't make any sound when it hits, but it cracks like a baseball against the plywood and lies there flattened out with its wings spread wide, so when I picked it up I had to fold its wings in, like wet paper fans that might tear. When it warmed up in my hands, to my complete amazement it wasn't dead. The thing has a heart the size of a dime, you'd think it would make the softest little bumps. But no. The body was so light, but inside it was earthquakes. It's called a fog wren around here, though its right name is marbled murrelet, and it's almost extinct, since what it needs is the sheltered horizontal branch of an old-growth tree. About this it's very particular, it's not capable of adapting to forests devoid of old growth. It doesn't make a nest, just presses its tiny self down into the moss, bringing all its strength to bear, but how much strength is that? The impression it makes in the moss, no deeper than if you pressed your hand against it and counted to ten, that's where it lays its eggs. So you can guess what wind does, any wind at all, and the thing about Tara is, this wren might have wanted one of her branches because there are some nice big horizontal ones, but all her sister trees that once filtered the wind are long gone. She's all alone and gets all the wind. Wind that will for sure roll the eggs right out of any hollow pressed into moss. What else can I tell you? How we are all to blame for that bird's not knowing where to go? How I would have let her nest in my hand if I could have? How you would have too, if only you could have seen her?

Possum, one of the ground crew, came up with Mary's slow-mail address, a post office box in Oregon. Somebody must have told him that Finn had lost touch with her mother. A stroke of luck, this chance to explain, to prove what she's doing is necessary, because that's a contention her mother, no great fan of causes, would be inclined to doubt.

Don't get your hopes up too much, Possum warns. *She may of moved on. I couldn't find the other traces you'd expect—address, phone, credit card.*

But a letter follows a person to her next address, right? Gets forwarded until it ends up in the right hands?

Ink on paper, Possum says, amused by the quaintness. *Could be it has a chance.*

Even twelve stories above the ground, spring throws a great party, competing frenzies of birdsong, fusillades of squirrel chatter—

distracting. The intelligence conveyed to nerve and inner ear by the tree as she exists moment by moment, only that can be trusted, not the transit stored in the map-manufacturing brain even so recently as the last jaunt to the sleeping platform or out along the stargazing branch. Something is *there*. Presence, not absence. Soul, discerned via the disciplined high-wire mindfulness Finn practices. Practices and practices, growing more poised, the muscles of thighs and arms starkly defined, the veins in her feet hypertrophied, the pads of her fingertips schooled in nuances of texture she wouldn't have deemed perceptible. There comes a moment, of course, when she forgets, climbs through the tree of the day before, and where the toehold of the familiar should be, shock blasts a hole. Having stepped off into the void, she adapts. Her feet pedal. She feels a pair of wings flung out from her shoulder blades, beginning to beat. This vision, commensurate with the terror, feels so sure and certain a way out, Finn says "Ah" to it. From deep in her throat, as naturally as in the throes of sex, the "Ah" of being scooped out of the death hole. Yet it's not space that answers Finn, it's the tree, whose soul unfolds time. Time slows and expands, wrapping terrified awareness in a confounded calm, because the tree tells her *There is time*. So she's not afraid—fear is a kind of error stripped from her brain, and what she feels is that she's been taken in by an element so sumptuous she repents, falling, of the waste and foolishness that have so far constituted her relation to time. Finn falls within this sense of cradling infinity, and what will later strike her as the deepest truth about falling, the thing she will never confide to anyone, is that she was *curious*. More mortally *aware* than ever before, thus more profoundly curious. She's still breathing, her heart's still beating—it's a lie, she sees, that the heart stops from shock. Why lie when it's like this: when there's so much that can be comprehended and all the velvet time you need? Lie? When there's this last-breath fearlessness? Within the singularity of the fall, time can be observed, it seems, both backward and forward. In life, it's now clear, consciousness is always so *pinned down*, and time is so much bigger than that pinpoint known as *I*. The vault's been thrown open, and if, eyes narrowed, Finn faces directly into the browbeating updraft, the end of time gleams in through her lashes like a ray of sunset that's shot across space, no stranger than that in its amazingness. It's always had an end, and she was always more or less falling. The ground will claim her. Accepting that, she turns her gaze away and takes up—what? a more ordinary consciousness? her right mind?—where she left off, swimming down through the battering sensorium of glare and dark, passing through a reef of green that shatters around her in a stinging full-body corona, and then Finn is yanked out of the fall, dragged down and whiplashed up. Her hands have seized a branch. The fall roars through her, incomplete.

A pendulum of saved girl, bones scraping their sockets, legs dangling.

A bird veers below her feet, then several birds in their businesslike apartness flash by, their minds on what flushed them out: a shock shudders down through the tree, and the air fills with a staggering, sighing rain of arboreal trash, needles and scrolling ocher dust. An irregular tapping and pattering, aural confetti, Finn's face pelted by dust that smells sharp as fresh-shaved nutmeg, this scent shocked free from the compound of moss, cloud, mold, sap, sunstruck bark warm as horseflesh and evergreen cold as ozone, which together make up the essence of tree. Finn's nose begins to run. She scuffs her nose on the torn sleeve of her taut arm, waiting for the air to clear and incredulity to wear off so she can pull herself up onto the branch. Below, there's a saddle of branch wide enough for her to land on; she measures the distance and isn't positive she can make it. Smarter to climb up, and the branch offers clefts and grooves for finger- and toeholds.

Time has resumed its ordinary momentum.

Cautiously she begins the ascent, relieved to find a smaller branch she can hook her left arm around, leaning forward to ease up onto the major branch, safe, rejoicing. High above in the canopy, at the height she fell from, her cell phone rings. The force of her longing startles her. To answer. To tell what just happened, to say *I almost died.* To say *But I'm all right, I'm all right,* to be believed. Settle down, Finn. *Focus.* It's a long climb back up through the tree, and you need your wits about you.

That night, Finn closes her eyes and broadcasts the keen- est *thank you, thank you* of her nineteen years. *Thank you for my life.* Mummified against the starry cold in her down bag, smell- ing the panic sweat of her underarms—when, falling, had she had time to sweat?—she registers the extent of the damage that proves she's alive, the bruised muscles of her shoulders crying out, the palms of her hands skinned down to nerve. Nicks and scratches everywhere: those would have been noticed on her body if that was all she was now, body. She would have been a body with matted hair and filthy feet. They would have had to find Mary. Mary would have had to say *Yes that's her.* Mary would have had to kneel down, picking needles and twigs from Finn's hair, working frantically, as if nothing mattered but the twigs tangled in Finn's hair, as if Finn could be saved if every bit of debris were combed from her snarled and bloodied hair, and when they tried to tear her away, she would resist, saying *She needs me.* Saying *Live, live, I need you to live.* With her mother's voice close to her ear, Finn sleeps.

"Listen to me, Finn, there's a glacier. An action in Iceland. Crazy beautiful, this glacier, one of the last great ones, and right where they want to put an aluminum smelting plant. Their genius idea is, blow it up. We can go there."

She unscrews the lid of the thermos he handed her when she first climbed into the truck and takes a swallow of bitter coffee. She thinks of saying *What if for a little while you just don't talk* but finds, where the will to deal with Mayhem—with anyone— ought to be, a scraped-bare deficit of interest. She doesn't care how this turns out. It's only an hour's ride, and when she gets back to camp, they'll know enough to let her be. They'll take one look at her and know. Mayhem is the sort of person who doesn't take that look.

In profile, his frown is pained. "Too soon to think about another action," he says. "You're, like, bleeding. Your heart is fucking broke. God, my obsessiveness appalls me, I just start right in. Finn, forgive me, okay? For acting like it's just onto the next thing. You're grieving. I'm insensitive sometimes, I get caught up, I was thinking how great it could be, Iceland. How amazing to do an action there with you, and meanwhile I'm blind to what you're going through here and now, when you're just out of jail and what you need is a bath and something to eat and not me telling you, hey, life goes on, there's this glacier we need to save."

" 'Who stops them?' " she says.

"What?"

" 'Who stops them? Us?' "

After a while he says, "Don't explain. It's okay. It's a strange head space, grief, strange perceptions emerge, I know."

Woods and more woods. No one else on the road, no lights behind or before. There's this reckless blissful aloneness she used to indulge in, on road trips with a lover, the awareness that things are destined to go wrong but that *for now* they're beautiful. Even if he's not her lover he causes that same aloneness and feeling of beauty, as if the world is nearly gone and all that's left is what shows in their headlights. It's sacred. He keeps his hand down low, extending the joint. Finn takes it, inhales, holds it. Mary. Hands it back. His turn.

"Nother hit?"

"No." She says, "You know I have no idea where my mother is?"

"You want her to hear you're down from the tree?"

"Once—this one time when I badly wanted to hear from her—my cell rang and I thought *It's her* but I couldn't get to it in time. When I tried calling back, the number was blocked. Whoever it was never tried again. For all I know, she never even knew I was in Tara."

"Jesus, Finn. She should know you were a fucking hero."

Mayhem drives in silence, now and then checking her profile: not asleep.

After a while he says, "We got it all on film, that climber cussing with his knee in your back—I mean, he should know better than to say *bitch*—and you're trying to reason with him, doesn't he want his grandkids to see a tree like her, and he takes it wrong, he obviously feels guilty, and it's dangerous, him holding you in one arm for the descent while your wrists are cuffed, which is insanely, criminally hazardous. Eleven hundred hits on YouTube, last time I checked."

When she dreams of the tree it's Mary who's there on the platform with her, it's her mother in one of those slapdash outfits pieced together from thrift-shop finds, a sweater collared in mink and missing only a couple of buttons, a satin slip, green wool stockings and over everything, wrapping it up into a single package, the cumbersome military surplus parka, its hood rimmed with another, rattier kind of fur, or maybe not fur but some sort of tufted, partially destroyed dirty synthetic fiber. Out of all the lost things that could come back in a dream, it has to be that dirty parka, Mary's smoke-scented dark hair spilling out from the hood. The hair, though—that, she loves. The hair alone justifies the dream, which isn't an ordeal while it's being dreamed, which isn't painful and strange until Finn wakes enough to remember that her mother is missing. Gone without a goodbye. Mary's hair, swinging into a cave enclosing Finn's face when she was kissed goodnight, was the single aspect of her mother guaranteed to comfort her, no matter how bad a day Mary was having. It was necessary to hide these bad days from customers, though not from her daughter, and to spin stories from her own existence that obscured its precariousness and exalted its triumphs—chief among them, the uniqueness of Finn, whose destiny was obvious to Mary the moment she was born, *because I knew you'd come, Finn. For years I'd known you were on the way,* and Finn has always suspected Mary would have said *to save me* except that it would have come across as frankly egotistical and needy. *Your eyes holding such wisdom, like you had a thousand past lives behind you.* Older, Finn would try to divert her mother from narrating the tale of Finn's birth in the woods, but in storytelling, if nothing else, Mary was immune to distractions. And if no one can say what happened to Mary, why she left or where she ended up, throughout Mendocino county strangers can tell Finn how long her mother's labor lasted, or how, bundled in a raggedy cast-off shirt, the newborn had never cried but only *looked around all calm, like "Planet Earth, you are mine."*

Iceland is beautiful, far-flung cloudscapes sailing over drenched green moors where shaggy ponies prick their ears in wonder before wheeling away, running through the smoke of their own breath.

Narrator

Near the end of what the schedule called the welcome get-together, two women—summer dresses, charm— stood at the foot of the solemn Arts and Crafts staircase where he was seated, mostly in shadow, on the fifth or sixth step. Wasn't it rude, I wondered, to let them keep appealing for some scrap of his attention from below, wouldn't it be nicer to come down? That could have been me his condescension fell on: I had been scraping together the daring to approach. He was leaning back on his elbows, his long legs crossed at the ankles. *This is you in real life?* I said to him in my head. The women at the foot of the stairs were sufficiently unembarrassed in their pursuit that one of them even lifted the camera around her neck and aimed. At the prospect of his rebuking her presumption I was stricken, as if being his adoring reader conferred on me the responsibility to protect us all from any wounding or disillusioning outcome.

And then the worst thing that could have happened, happened: he stood up and turned his back on them. Inspired to document this irascibility of a famous writer's, the camera-holding fan clicked off several shots while he remained immobile, and then both women called out, bizarrely, "Thanks!" before walking off. It occurred to me that they might feel the need to maintain appearances if they were going to be his students in the coming week, as I would not be, having been too broke to enroll before the last minute, and too full of doubt about whether I wanted criticism.

Another student came up to me then, and I made my half of small talk: *New Mexico, yes as beautiful as that, no never been before—what about you, six hundred pages, that's amazing.* My fellow student's confidence was so cheerfully aggrandizing that mine flew below his radar. The full moon would be up before long, and if I wanted we could ride across the bridge on his motorcycle, an Indian he'd been restoring for years—parts cost a fortune. There was a ride like that in his novel and it would be good to recheck the details. I couldn't, I said; I had to read the stories for tomorrow. He said, "Homework, over the wind in your hair?"

Enough students were out, in couples and exuberant gangs, that I didn't worry, crossing through the campus's dark groves of eucalyptus, dry cataracts of slim leaves hanging as still as if they'd just been shushed, low enough in places to whisk across the top of my head. The boy I'd been talking to had implied that, lacking boldness, I wasn't the real deal; listening to him, I had been thinking no real writer could be as imperceptive as he was; who was real, and who wasn't, had been the question preoccupying us—pitiable, unpublished us. He had been right about the moon: sidewalks and storefronts brightened as I walked back to my hotel, followed, for a couple of bad blocks,

by a limping street person who shouted, at intervals, *Hallelujah!*
On the phone my husband told me that a neighbor's toddler
had fallen down an old hand-dug well but apart from a broken
leg wasn't hurt, and he had finished those kitchen cabinets and
would drive them to the job site tomorrow, and our dog had
been searching all over for me, did I want to talk to him? *You big
lunkhead, why did you ever let me get on that plane?* I asked our dog.
When my husband came back on the phone he said *Crazy how he
loves you* and *So the first day sucked, hunh?* and *They're gonna love the
story. Sleep tight baby. Hallelujah.* Bed strewn with manuscripts, I
sat up embroidering the margins with exegeses and genius alternatives—if someone had pointed out that *You should try this*
can seem condescending, I would have been really shocked. At
two A.M., when the city noise was down to faraway sirens, I collected the manuscripts and stacked them on the desk. They were
charged with their writers' reality, the way intimately dirtied
belongings are—hairbrushes, used Band-Aids—and I couldn't
have fallen asleep with them on the bed. Where, in Berkeley,
was his house, and was he asleep, and in what kind of bed, and
who was beside him?

Before leaving the party, I had sat for a while on his step in
the stairwell. All I had to go on were the first-person narrators
whose stubborn cherishing of difficult women imbued his work
with generosity of spirit, but I felt betrayed. Savagely I compared the rudeness I'd witnessed with the radiance I'd hoped
for. How could narrators so prodigal in their empathy originate
in the brain of that withholder? The women had not trespassed
in approaching: the party was meant for such encounters. Two
prettier incarnations of eager me had been rebuffed, was that it?
No. Or only partly. From his work I had pieced together scraps
I believed were *really him.* At some point I had forsaken impartial

immersion and begun reading to construct a writer I could love. Consider those times I'd said not *His books are wonderful*, but *I'm in love with him*. But he had never intended to tell me who he was. *There was no fall from grace, not one page is diminished, not one scene or sentence, the books are as beautiful as ever*, I coached myself. But the sense that something was ruined survived every attempt to reason it away.

The days passed without my glimpsing him again, and besides I was distracted by an acceptance entailing thrilling, perilous phone calls from the editor who was taking the story, whose perfectionism in regard to my prose dwarfed my own. Equally confusingly, my workshop, when my story was up, found the ending unconvincing. The ending had come in a rush so glorious that my role was secretarial, the typewriter *chickchickchickchickchick-tsing*-ing along, rocking the kitchen table on its uneven legs; now I couldn't tell how good it was, and I was anxious to get back to New Mexico and realigned with instinct. A story that was going well set the table jolting, my husband said, like a three-legged dog late for supper. Home was a two-hundred-year-old adobe on a dirt road winding along the contour of a canyon wall: What had I thought would be out here, for me? At the farewell party in the twilight of the grand redwood-paneled reception room, hundreds of voices promised to stay in touch. At the room's far end, past the caterer's table with its slowly advancing queue, French doors stood ajar, and two butterflies dodged in, teetering over heads that didn't notice. They weren't swallowtails or anything glamorous, just drab small airborne slips dabbling in the party air, and my awareness linked with them, every swerve mirrored, or as it felt enacted, by the consciousness I called mine, which for the moment had more to do with them than me. After a while they pattered back out through the doors. Then there he stood, observing their waffling exit. And now it was him I couldn't look away from. His head turned; when he believed I was going to retreat—when I, too, was aware of the social imperative to break off a stare—and I didn't, then the nature of whatever it was that was going on between us changed, and was, unmistakably, a declaration. Triumph showered through me, at finding nerve where there had always been inhibition: I was as delighted with this new self of mine as I was with the man I was staring at. But did he want this? Because who was I? He broke the connection with a dubious glance down and away, consulting the proprieties, since non-crazy strangers did not lock each other in a transparently sexual gaze heedless of everybody around them, and he wasn't, of course he wasn't, sure what he was getting into. If I had been my old shy self, that hesitation would have killed my stare. At last he looked up to see whether he was still being stared at, as he was, greenly, oh shamelessly, by me, and he wondered whether something was wrong with me, but he could see mine was a sane face and that I, too, acknowledged the exposedness and hazard of not break-ing off the stare, and this information flaring back and forth between us guaranteed we were no longer strangers.

We spent the night over coffee in a café on Telegraph Avenue, breaking story-length pieces off from our lives, making a slice of torte disappear in alternating forkfuls. Our waitress's forgetful-ness he explained as distraction; she had a sick child at home. How can you tell? Unicorn stamp on her left hand, he said. How a local pediatrician commemorates non-crying visits. At the next table, two sixtyish gents in identical black berets slaugh-tered each other's pawns. See, I told him, the way when one leans over the board, the other leans back the exact, compensatory distance. When I recognized what I was up to, matching him detail for detail to accomplish what my old anthropology professor would have called establishing kinship—*We are detail's native speakers, and there will be no end of detail, no end to what binds us*—I understood that rapport, which had always seemed to belong among the less consequential social feats, could in fact be revelatory. The most fantastic determination arose, to stay in his presence. At the same time I understood full well that I would be getting on an airplane in—I looked at my watch—five hours. He, too, looked at his watch. Our plan was simple: *not* to sleep together, because that would make parting terrible. We would stay talking until the last minute, and then he would drive me to the airport, stopping by my hotel first for my things. I didn't have money for another ticket and couldn't miss my early-morning flight.

He left it till late in the conversation to ask, "You're, what—?"

"Twenty-four." I stirred my coffee, not sure I should ask the reciprocal question. Forty-two or -three, my guess was, but I was bad at telling ages.

"What's in New Mexico?"

"Beauty." I didn't look up from my coffee to gauge if that was too romantic; the narrators of his books were always in quest of a woman's unedited self. "The first morning I woke up there—in the desert; we'd driven to our campsite in the dark—I thought *This is it, I'm home.*"

Another thing he said across the table: "Your cover is blown, my friend. The story that got taken from the slush pile, that was yours." The workshop instructor, a friend of my editor's, had gone around repeating the news.

"Someone"—the moonlight-motorcycle-ride guy—"told me, 'It's lightning striking, the only magazine that can transform an unknown into a known.' Not that I'm not grateful, I'm completely grateful to have been dug out of the slush pile, but what if I'm not good at the *known* part?"

"Comes with the territory," he said. "Why would it be harder for you than anyone else?"

"Too awkward," I said.

"Pshaw."

"Too foot-in-mouth."

"*Be* the girl wonder."

Which shut me up: I took it to mean that, instead of complaining, I should adapt. I would go on to hear similar corrections encoded in other remarks; this was only the first instance. "You're chipper this morning, kid"—that was a warning whose franker, ruder form would have been *Tone it down*. "You look like something from the court of Louis Quatorze" meant I should have blow-dried my long hair straight, as usual, instead of letting its manic curliness emerge. When he would announce, of his morning's work, "Two pages" or "Only one paragraph, but a crucial one," I heard *And what have you done? Since your famous story. What?* I could be getting it all wrong, I knew, but I couldn't not interpret.

Those first charmed early-summer days he put on his record of Glenn Gould's Goldberg Variations, which I had never heard before, and taught me to listen for the snatches of Gould's jubilant humming. When I was moved to tears by Pachelbel's Canon in D, he didn't say *Where have you been?* He sang Joni Mitchell's

"California" in his bathrobe while making coffee to bring to me in the downstairs bedroom. One morning, sitting up to take the cup, I asked, "Do you remember at the welcoming party, you were in the stairwell and two women came up to you? And you wouldn't say anything?"

He had to think back. "Garance and Lizzie."

"You know them?"

"I was surprised to run into them there, but Lizzie's doing a book, portraits of writers taken from behind. And they just found out Garance is pregnant. Try getting a word in edgewise."

My expression must have amused him. He said, "You have lesbians in New Mexico, right?"

I hadn't caught my flight. Instead we made love in the hotel room I hadn't wanted him to see, since I had left it a mess. "Was this all you?" he asked, of the clothes strewn everywhere, and it was partly from embarrassment that I lifted his shirt and slid a hand inside. When we woke it was early afternoon and the implications of my having not gone home became real to me. My husband had a daylong meeting that prevented his picking me up at the airport; at least he had been spared the ordeal of standing there scrutinizing the disembarking crowd, wondering what could possibly have kept me from making my flight. In five years of marriage we had barely been apart. I imagined him at a conference table among his colleagues in their suits and ties, drawing airplanes in the margins of his legal pad. At our small Ohio college he had majored in art, and when a friend of his father's offered him a position in a Santa Fe firm, he had surprised us both by accepting. I had been selfishly relieved that one of us was able to pay the rent on our Upper Canyon Road adobe. He didn't really have it, he said, and I said he couldn't know that, not now at the very beginning of trying. In an unfinished painting I reclined in our claw-foot tub, paperback book held nearsightedly close, bathwater strewn with lopped-off wildflower heads.

I had feared finding all of California alienatingly new, but where he lived was a comradely neighborhood of mostly neglected Victorians, none very fanciful, shaded by trees as old as they were. His place was the guest cottage—"So it's small," he cautioned, on the drive over—belonging to a Victorian that had decayed past any hope of renovation. The old house had eventually been replaced by a single-story studio-apartment building, and once he bought the place, these rentals became the most reliable part of his income. Whenever he could, he avoided teaching, he said. His minding about precariousness (if it was) was embarrassing. It was proof that he was *older*. Even if they could have, no one I knew in New Mexico would have wanted to use the phrase *reliable income* in a sentence about themselves: jobs were quit nonchalantly, security was to be scorned. With the help of an architect friend—a former lover, he clarified as if pressed; and never do that, never renovate a house with someone you're sleeping with—all that was stodgy and cramped had been replaced with clarity and openness, as much, at least, as the basically modest structure permitted. This preface sounded like something recited fairly often. The attic had been torn out to allow for the loft bedroom, its pitched ceiling inset with a large skylight, its wide-planked floor bare, the bed done in white linen. The white bed was like his saying *reliable income*—it was the opposite of daring. No man I had ever known, if it had even occurred to him to buy pillowcases and sheets instead of sleeping on a bare mattress, would ever have chosen all white. Sleep-lessness and guilt were catching up with me, and there was the nagging feeling any house tour gives, of coercing praise. I was irritated that in these circumstances, to me costly and extraordinary, the usual compliments were expected. "Beautiful light," I said. The narrow stairs to the loft were flanked by cleverly fitted bookshelves, and more bookshelves ran around the large downstairs living room, onto which the galley kitchen and bathroom opened, and on another wall were doors leading to his study and the guest bedroom that would be mine, because, he said apologetically, he couldn't sleep through the night with anyone in bed with him—it wasn't me; he'd never been able to. Would that be all right? Of course, I said. I sat down on the edge of the twin bed. *I can get the money somehow, I can fly home tomorrow.* Even as I decided that, he sat down beside me. "When I think you could have gotten on that plane. I would be wondering what just hit me and how I could ever see you again." In that room there was a telephone, and he left me alone with it.

He had his coffee shop, and when he was done working, that's where he liked to go—at least, before me that's where he'd gone. Time spent with me, in bed or talking, interfered with the coffee shop, and with research in the university library and his circuit of bookstores and Saturday games of pickup basketball, but for several weeks I was unaware that he had altered his routines for my sake. From the congratulatory hostility of his friends, I gathered that women came and went. "Your free throw's gone to shit," said Billy, owner of the shabby, stately Victorian next door whose honeysuckle-overrun backyard was a storehouse of costly toys—motorcycles, a sailboat. "How I know you have a girlfriend." I would have liked to talk to someone who knew him—even Billy, flagrantly indiscreet—about how I was faring in my anxious adaptation to his preferences, whether I was getting anything wrong. Other women had lived with him: What had they done while he was writing in the morning? How had they kept quiet enough? One was a cellist—how had *that* worked? His writing hours, eight to noon, were nonnegotiable. If he missed a day, his black mood saturated our world. But this was rare.

The check came, for the story. Forwarded by my husband, whom I called sometimes when I was alone in the cottage, and blue. "You can always come home, you know," my husband said, and I bit down on the question *Why don't you hate me?* He knew me well. "Look," he said. "People get into trouble. We get in over our heads. It's not only you."

The renovated cottage was close enough to the university that, days when he was teaching, he could ride his bicycle. Covertly, I began to hold it against him that he was honoring his responsibilities, meeting his classes, having conversations about weather and politics. My syllogism ran: what love does is shatter life as you've known it; his life isn't shattered; therefore he is not in love. Of the two of us, I consoled myself with the idea that I was the *real* lover. But, really, why did it matter so much? The question of who was more exposed emotionally would have struck him as crazy, my guess is. But either my willingness to tear my life apart had this redeeming authenticity, or the pain I was causing my husband was callously—even violently—pointless.

By now I had learned something about the women before me, including the Chinese lover whose loss he still wasn't reconciled to, though it had been years. I stole her picture and tucked it into *Middlemarch*, the only book in this house full of his books that belonged to me, and when he admitted to not liking Eliot much I was relieved to have a book which, by not mattering to him, could talk confidentially to what was left of me as a writer, the little that was left after I was, as I believed I wanted to be, stripped down to skin and heartbeat and sex, never enough sex, impatient sex, adoring sex, fear-of-boredom sex.

The immense sanity of *Middlemarch* made it a safe haven for the stolen photograph. Whenever I went back to Eliot's novel, I imagined the magnanimous moral acuity with which the narrator would have illumined a theft like mine, bringing it into the embrace of the humanly forgivable while, at the same time—and how did Eliot manage this?—indicting its betrayal of the more honorable self that, in her narrator's eyes, I would possess. But I didn't go back often; sex and aimless daydreaming ate up the hours I would usually have spent reading, and when I went up to the loft, I left the book behind—I didn't want him noticing it. He had a habit of picking up my things and studying them quizzically, as if wondering how they had come to be in his house, and if he picked up *Middlemarch* there was a chance the photo would slip out. If I fell asleep in his bed after sex he would wake me after an hour or two, saying *Kid, you need to go downstairs.* On the way down I ran my fingers over the spines of the books lining the stairwell. If you opened one it would appear untouched; he recorded observations and memorable passages in a series of reading notebooks.

My scribbled-in *Middlemarch* stayed on the nightstand by the twin bed, and I had hung my clothes in the closet, but that didn't mean I felt at home in the room, with its dresser whose bottom drawer was jammed with photos. What did it mean that this drawer, alone in all the house, had not been systematically sorted? Near the bottom of the slag heap was an envelope of tintypes: from a background of stippled tarnish gazed a poetic

boy, doleful eyes and stiff upright collar, and I wanted to take it
to him and say *Look, you in 1843*, but that would prove I'd been
rifling through the drawer, and even if he hadn't said not to, I
wasn't sure it was all right. His childhood was there, his youth,
the face of his first author photo. Houses and cities before this
one. His women, too, and I dealt them out across the floor, a
solitaire of disparate faces: I wanted to know their stories. No
doubt I did know pieces, from his work, but here they were,
real, and I would have listened to them all if I could, would have
asked each one *How did it end?* When he was writing he would
sometimes knock and come in and rummage through the pictures, whose haphazardness replicated memory's chanciness. As
with memory there was the sense that everything was there, in
the drawer—just not readily findable. Disorder is hospitable to
serendipity; was that the point? When he found the photo he
wanted he didn't take it back to his desk but stayed and studied
it, and when he was done he dropped it casually back into the
hodgepodge. If I opened the drawer after he'd gone, there was
no way to guess which photo he'd been holding.

There were things that happened during sex that felt like they
could never be forgotten. Recognitions, flights of soul-baring
mutual exposure, a pitch of ravishment that seemed bound to
transform our lives. But, sharing the setting of so many hours of
tumult—the bed—and tumult's instruments—our two bodies—
these passages lacked the distinctness of *event* and turned out to
be, as far as memory was concerned, elusive. And there was
sadness in that, in coming back to our same selves. By midsummer, something—maybe the infuriating inescapability of those

selves, maybe an intimation of the monotonousness sex could devolve into, if we kept this up—caused us to start turning sex into stories. Sex with me as a boy, the one and only boy who ever caught his eye, a lovely apparition of a boy he wanted to keep from all harm, but who one day was simply gone; sex as if he was a pornographer and I was a schoolgirl who began, more and more, to conjure long-absent emotions, tenderness, possessiveness, even as the schoolgirl became more and more corrupt, telling sly little lies; the sex we would have if, after ten years' separation, we saw each other across a crowded room; sex as if I had just learned he'd been unfaithful to me with one of his exes; sex as if I'd been unfaithful; the sex we would have if we broke up and after ten years ended up in the same Paris hotel for some kind of writers' event, a book signing maybe, and sometimes it was his book and sometimes it was mine; sex with me in the stockings and heels of a prostitute, with him as a cop, me as a runaway desperate for shelter, with him as a woman, with the two of us as strangers seated near each other on a nightlong flight.

These games always began the same way. Ceremonious, the invitation, proper and respectful in inverse proportion to the derangement solicited. *What if you are. What if I am.* We never talked about this, and though either could have said *Let's not go there*, neither of us ever declined a game described by the other. The inventing of roles was spontaneous, their unforeseeableness part of the game's attraction, but a special mood, an upswell of lurid remorse, alerted me whenever I was about to say *And then after forever we see each other again.* In these scenarios where we had spent years apart, the lovely stroke was our immediate recognition of each other—not, like other emotions we played at, a shock, not a wounding excitement, but an entrancing correction to loss. All wrongs set right. *And we look at each other. And it's like—*

While he wouldn't drink any coffee that wasn't made from freshly ground Italian dark roast and he had a taste for expensive chocolate, he seemed mostly indifferent to food and never cooked. What had he done when he was alone? Was it just like this, cereal, soup from cans, microwaved enchiladas? Should I try to make something—would that feel, to him, to me, stickily wife-y? He liked bicycling to the farmer's market and would come back with the ripest, freshest tomatoes. He taught me to slather mayonnaise across bakery bread, grinding black pepper into the exposed slices before covering them with another slice, taking fast bites before the bread turned sodden, licking juice from wrists and fingertips, the tomatoes still warm from basking in their crates at the market, their taste leaking acid-bright through the oily mayonnaise blandness, the bread coarse in texture, sweet in fragrance. There was at least a chance he'd never told any other lover about tomato sandwiches. After weeks of not caring what I ate, I had found something I couldn't get enough of, and as soon as I finished one sandwich I would make another, waiting until he was out to indulge, and it didn't matter how carefully I cleared away the traces of my feast, he could tell, he was quick with numbers and probably counted the tomatoes.

Really the entire cottage was saturated with his vigilance; his keen eye for detail was now directed at me. When I went elsewhere, tried working in a café (not his) for example, it was as if the house were still with me, its atmosphere extending to the unrocking table where I sat with my books and my legal pad and my cup of coffee with cream and two teaspoons of brown sugar stirred in. At that table I could not do a dirt road in New Mexico. I could not do a wife steeping in cold bathwater while her husband scissored the heads from poppies and black-eyed Susans. Neither could I do my new existence. *He* would not walk into a story of mine. He could not have sat down in an armchair of my imagining, or awakened in a bed beside a narrator in some way me. The world we were in was replete with narration, and it was his. After a couple of hours, I gave up trying.

He was sitting with Billy on Billy's front steps and greeted me by saying, "Everest redux." Billy said, "Can I have a kiss for luck? Leaving for Kathmandu early in the A.M. Oh, and forgot to tell you"—turning to him—"Delia's going to house-sit. I don't want to be distracted on the Icefall by visions of Fats wasting away in some kennel." Fats was his skinny, hyper border collie. "Only good vibes. Last year, when I got up into the death zone, I hallucinated my grandmother." Exaggerating his Texas drawl: "'Time you *git* back home.' Actually one of the Sherpas looked a whole lot like her. Brightest black eyes. See right through bullshit, which you want in a Sherpa or grandma. I lied a lot when I was little, like practice for being in the closet. So, Delia. Fats loves her. So, she'll be staying here." He said, "Always smart not to leave a house empty," but I knew Billy was curious if I would show that I minded, because Delia was his most recent ex, the lover before me, and thinking *Only good vibes, right*, I said, "Fats will be happy" and kissed Billy on his sunburned forehead.

I gave up on the coffee shop, but when I tried writing in the afternoons in the guest bedroom, sitting up in the twin bed with a legal pad on my knees, he would wander in and start picking up various objects—my traveling alarm clock, my hairbrush—and I would drop the legal pad and hold out my arms. Maybe because he was becoming restless, or was troubled by what looked, in me, like the immobilizing onset of depression, he talked me into going running, and that was how we spent our evenings now, on an oval track whose cinders were the old-school kind, sooty black, gritting under running shoes. On days after a weekend meet, the chalk lines marking the lanes were still visible. The infield was grass, evenly mown, and after running he liked to throw a football there, liked it even more than he ordinarily would have because football figured in the novel he was writing, about two brothers whose only way of connecting with each other was throwing a football back and forth, and he needed the sense impressions of long shadows across summer grass and the grain of the leather to prompt the next morning's writing. When he held a football, his tall, brainy self came together, justi-fied. Pleasantly dangerous with the love of competition, though at the moment all he had to compete with was me. When he cocked his arm back and took a step, tiny grasshoppers showered up. The spiral floated higher, as if the air were tenderly prolong-ing its suspension, and took its time descending. The thump of flight dead-ending against my chest as I ran pleased me. He had trouble accepting that I could throw a spiral, though he might have known my body learned fast. I couldn't throw as far, and he walked backward, taunting for more distance. Taunting I took as a guy-guy thing; my prowess, modest as it was, made me an honorary boy, and was sexy.

One bright evening, as I cocked my arm back, he cried *Throw it, piggy!* Shocked into grace, I sent a real beauty his way, and with long-legged strides he covered the grass and leaped, a show-offy catch tendered as apology before I could call down the field, *What?*, but I was standing there understanding: *piggy* was a thing he called me to himself, that had slipped out. In my need and aimlessness and insatiability I was a pale sow. How deluded I had been, believing I was a genius lover no excess could turn repulsive. The next morning I woke up sick, ashamed that wherever he was in the house he could hear me vomiting, and when I said I wanted a hotel room he told me a tenant had moved out from one of his units and I could have the key.

These studio units, five of them, occupied the shabby one-story stucco box that stood between his house and the street. Flat-roofed cinderblock painted a sullen ocher, this building was a problem factory. Termites, leaks, cavalier electrical wiring. With his tenants he was on amiable terms, an unexpectedly easygoing landlord. The little box I let myself into had a floor of sky blue linoleum; sick as I was, that blue made me glad. The space was bare except for a bed frame and mattress, where I dropped the sheets and towels he'd given me. The hours I spent in the small bathroom were both wretched and luxurious in their privacy; whenever there was a lull in the vomiting, I would lock and unlock the door just to do so. Now he is locked the fuck out. Now I let him back in. Now out forever. After dark, I leaned over the toy kitchen sink and drank from the faucet. It was miraculous to be alone. There was a telephone on the kitchen's cinderblock wall, and as I looked at it, it rang. Thirteen, fourteen, fifteen. I slept in the bare bed and woke scared that my fever sweat had stained the mattress; it was light; that day lasted forever, the thing sickness does to time.

His knocking woke me. He came in all tall and fresh from

his shower, having already worked his habitual four hours. First he made the bed; with the heel of his hand he pushed sweaty hair from my face; I was unashamed, I could have killed him if he didn't make love to me. "I'll check in on you tomorrow," he said. I barely kept myself from saying *Do you love me. Do you love me.* Nausea helped keep me from blurting that out; the strenuousness of repressing nausea carried over into this other, useful repression. "I'm so hungry," I said instead. "Can you bring me a bowl of rice?" In saying it I discovered that the one thing I could bear to think of eating was the bowl of rice he would carry over from his house. I needed something he made for me.

When I woke it was night. Cool air and traffic sounds came through the picture window, and seemed to mean I would be able to live without him. Now and then the phone began to ring and I let it ring on and on. Sometime during that night I went through the cupboards. I sat cross-legged on the floor with a cup of tea and ate stale arrowroot biscuits from the pack the tenant had forgotten, feeling sick again as I ate. He wasn't a man who cooked, or who made things of any kind, really, except books. It didn't matter that I knew this very well, and even understood it; the bowl of rice was now an obsession. It seemed like the only thing I had ever wanted from him, though in another sense all I had done since staring at him that first time was want things from him. In the morning, while it was still dark, he let himself in—I should have guessed there was a master key—with nothing in his hands, and when we were through making love he said, "You're going to bathe, right?" Then I was alone, without a bowl of rice, cross-legged on the kitchen floor with the cup of tea I'd made and the last five arrowroot biscuits, locked deep in hunger, realizing that—because the hunger felt clear and exhilarating, with no undertow of nausea—I was either well, or about to be. I called and made a reservation on a flight to New Mexico that had one seat left. My husband let me cry through that first night back in his arms. You have to *want* to write, but love you can do without wanting: which makes it sound as if it's the simpler thing. He never needed to hear the story.

In the novel he wrote about that time, I wasn't his only lover. House-sitting next door, the narrator's sensible, affectionate ex affords him sexual refuge from the neediness of the younger woman he'd believed he was in love with, whose obsession with him has begun to alarm him. Impulsively, after the first time they slept together, she left her husband for him. How responsible did that make him, for her? He understands, as she doesn't seem to, that there's nothing unerring about desire. At its most compelling, it can lead to a dead end, as has happened in their case. This younger, dark-haired lover keeps *Middlemarch* on her nightstand, and riffling through the book one night while she's sleeping the narrator finds the photograph of the Chinese woman. She lives not very far away, he thinks, and I would have heard if she got married—people can't wait to tell you that kind of thing, about an ex. But, really, how could I have left her? Here the novel takes a comic turn, because now he needs to break up with two women: his house-sitting ex, likely to go okay, and, a more troubling prospect, this young woman inexplicably damaged by their affair. He needs to rouse her from her depression, to talk to her directly, encouragingly, until of her own accord she decides to leave. Tricky to carry off, the passage where, as he holds the picture, the old, sane love revives—the novel's crisis, also the single event I was sure had never happened. I don't mean the novel was true, only that the things in it had happened. The likelier explanation was he'd gone into the guest bedroom while I was out. Far-fetched, his coming into the room while I slept—why would he?—though I could understand why he wanted, thematically, the juxtaposition of sleep and epiphany, and how the scene was tighter for the suspense about whether the dark-haired lover would wake up.

Twelve years later, heading home with two friends from the funeral of our well-loved colleague Howard, who had lived in Berkeley, we stopped in a bookstore. Between the memorial service and the trip out to the cemetery, the funeral had taken most of the day. Afterward we had gone to dinner, and except for the driver we were all a little drunk and, in the wake of grieving funeral stiltedness and the tears we had shed, trying to cheer each other up. Death seemed like another of Howard's contradictions: his rumbling, comedic fatness concealed an exquisite sensibility, gracious, capable of conveying the most delicate epiphanies to his students or soft-shoeing around the lectern, reciting "In Breughel's great picture, The Kermess." If Howard's massiveness was bearish, that of his famous feminist-scholar wife was majestic, accoutered with scarves, shawls, trifocals on beaded chains, a cane she was rumored to have aimed at an unprepared grad student in her Dickinson seminar—"My Soul had stood—a Loaded Gun," David quoted; Alan corrected, "My Life," with the amiable condescension that David's grin said he'd been hoping for, since it made Alan look not so Zen after all. Alan was lanky, mild, exceedingly tall, with an air of baffled inquiry and goodwill I attributed to endless zazen; David sturdy, impatient, his scorn exuberant, his professional vendettas merciless. It was David I told my love affairs to, and when I had the flu it was David who came over, fed Leo his supper, and read aloud. Through the wall I could hear David's merry "showed their terrible claws till Max said 'BE STILL!'" echoed by Leo's "Be still!" That evening after the funeral one of us suggested waiting out rush hour in the bookstore and we wandered through in our black clothes, David to philosophy, Alan to poetry, me to a long table of tumbled sale books on whose other side—I stared—*he* stood with an open book in his hand, looking up before I could turn away, the brilliant dark eyes that had held mine as I came over and over meeting mine now without recognition, just as neutrally looking away, the book in his hand the real object of desire, something falsely enchanted in his downward gaze that convinced me he had been attracted to me not as a familiar person but as a new one, red-haired now, in high heels, in head-to-toe black, a writer with three books to my name, teaching at a university a couple of hours away, single mother to a watchful, emphatic toddler who spoke in complete sentences—though he wasn't going to get to hear about my son, wasn't going to get a word of my story. And in the hiatus of not being recognized there was time for a decision, which was: before he can figure out who he's just seen, before, as some fractional lift of his jaw told me he was about to, he can look up and meet my eyes again and know who I am, before before before before before before before before he can say my name followed by *I don't believe it*, followed by *I always thought I'd see you again*, look away. Get out. Go. And I did, and although behind me where I stood on the street corner the bookstore door opened now and then and let people out, none of them was him. Person after person failed to be him. He hadn't known me, and while it wasn't rational to blame him for this blow to my sense of myself as memorable, as having burned very bright, if not for very long, in his life, I minded that he had somehow retained such power to move me, even if that power was used only, inadvertently, to inflict sadness; and his having this power, while I had none—not the least means of moving him—seemed the newest incarnation of our old inequality as lovers, and this configuration, him dominant, me self-absconding, bypassed my mind and spoke to my body, and made me remember what he had been like, in bed, and just as desire took on a dangerous shine, I saw: how guilelessly I had erased my writing, as if relinquishment was what he had ever asked. If there are two people in bed they are both narrating, but it had seemed otherwise to me: having him, I could not believe another story was needed. How astounded he must have been by my willing losses. My friends came out carrying their bags, and David told me, "This is the first time I've ever seen you leave a bookstore empty-handed, ever," and we pulled our gloves on, telling each other that taking a break had been a good idea, and our heads were clear now, and we could make the drive home. Of course, that was when he came out the door, long-legged, striding fast. Pausing, fingers touched to his lips, then the upright palm flashed at me—a gesture I didn't recognize, for a second, as a blown kiss—before he turned the corner.

"Wasn't that—?" David said.

"Yes."

"Did he just—?"

"When we're in the car, you two," Alan said. "I've got to be at the Zen Center at five."

"The day before the surgery, he told me his biggest fear wasn't that they wouldn't get all the cancer. His biggest fear wasn't of dying, even, though he said that was how his father died when he was only nine, under the anesthetic for an operation that was supposed to be simple, with nobody believing they needed to say goodbye beforehand, and now that he was facing *a simple operation* himself, one nobody dies of, he couldn't help thinking of his father. A premonition. His biggest fear was that he'd be left impotent. Of all the things that can conceivably go wrong with prostate cancer surgery, that was the most terrifying."

"What did you say?" Alan asked from the backseat.

"'Most terrifying'? I'm wondering why it's me, the gay boy, Howard chooses to confide in, about impotence. Because my existence revolves around penises? I'm kind of freaked out, because, you know Howard, his usual decorum, where's that gone? But I want to be staunch for him. I love this man. And he says, 'Not for me. If it came down to living without it, I would mourn, but it wouldn't be the end of the world. For me. Whereas for Martha—'"

"'Most terrifying,'" Alan said. "I'm very sorry he had to make those calculations."

"'—Martha can't live without it.'"

"You were right there," Alan said. "You reassured him?"

"Of course I reassured him." David checked Alan's expression in the rearview mirror. "But it's not something I imagined, that the two of them ever—or still—"

"Or, hmmm, that she could be said—"

"You idiots, he adored her," I said. "That's what he was telling David. Not 'She needs sex more than I do.' But 'This phenomenal woman, light of my life, it's unimaginable that I might never make love to her again.'"

Alan took off his tie, rolled it up, tucked it in his jacket pocket, and then passed his glasses forward to me, saying, "Can you take custody?" I cradled them as cautiously as if they were his eyes. Once he was asleep David said, "That was him, wasn't it?"

We had stood across from each other, not five feet apart, I told David, and he had not recognized me. "After I'd gone he must have stood there thinking *But I know her, I know her from somewhere.* Then he gets it—who I am, and that I'd walked away without a word. Which must have hurt."

"It's generally that way when you save your own skin— somebody gets hurt."

"Even hurt, he blows me a kiss. That makes him seem—"

"Kind of great," David said.

"Wasn't I right? Walking away?"

"Don't misunderstand me," David said. "There's no problem with a little mystery, in the context of a larger, immensely hard-won clarity." He yawned. "I'm not the idiot." He tipped his curly head to indicate the backseat. "He's the idiot. Did I reassure him? Fuck me. When am I ever not reassuring."

Oncoming traffic made an irregular stream of white light, its brilliance intensifying, fusing, then sliding by. I held up Alan's glasses and the lights dilated gorgeously. I said, "You know why we'll never give up cars? Because riding in cars at night is so beautiful, it's telling stories in a cave with the darkness kept out, the dash lights for the embers of the fire."

"You don't have to tell me any stories," David said. "I'm absolutely wide awake."

I didn't sleep long, but when I woke he was in a different mood.

"You know, his novel," David said, "the one about you—is that a good book?"

"If you like his voice it's good."

"On its own, though, is it?"

Mine wasn't exactly a disinterested reading, I said. The style is his style, and like all his work it takes hold of the reader, but unlike his previous books this novel seems rigged in the narrator's favor, and it would have been more compelling if he had made the dark-haired lover—

"You," David said.

—okay, me, but I really am talking about the character now, who is all shattered vulnerability and clinging, the embodiment of squishy need, no more, no less than that. But suppose he had granted her an aliveness the narrator could not entirely assimilate, if she had voiced interpretations conflicting with and even undermining his, if it began to be clear that she was in possession of a rival reality, then the margin of her being that is beyond his ken would imbue the whole with greater emotional veracity, would *test* the narrator's ownership of the story, and cast doubt on the narrator's decision to leave her. If she never gets more than one dimension, then it doesn't matter to the reader that he ditches her. It's not really moving. Whereas if she's alive and the reader is privy to how much about her eludes him, then there is the problem of assessing the loss, and everything gets more interesting, right?

"For her to get more real," David said, "she has to act, right? Give the narrator something to go on?"

"Give him something to go on, yes. But that could come right at the last minute."

"That's a sadder ending," David said. "The way that you tell it."

"I wasn't thinking it was sad," I said. "I was thinking it was—better."

Briar Switch

"Sure you want to go out in that?" he asks from his side of the counter, and in her frustration with his slowness to hand over the keys she says only, "I'm sure." He says, "Because it's really coming down," and she says, "My father is dying," immediately sorry to have marketed as explanation this truth no one should be able to bear, not her, not this stranger whose answer comes after a pause: "I'm sorry." After another pause he says, "Lost my dad last year." How distraught does she appear to his eyes, how likely to end up in a ditch? She discovers the necessary next utterance: "I'm sorry." He says, paging through her paperwork, "Yeah, a year ago." *Mine is going to die tonight, and you're keeping me from getting there*, she thinks and does not say. Ten minutes earlier she stepped from the flow and thumbed her phone awake while disembarking passengers jostled past. She'd stood stock-still, taking in *No messages*, good news with a loophole, since it's unclear, if he does die, how much time would elapse before her brother or sister would remember to call her, and if worst comes to worst—a phrase of her father's—there will be an interval when the last-minute reconciliation she desires no longer has a chance of coming true, though she rushes toward it unknowing. Of all the catastrophes this night can conceivably hold, to fly toward him when he is already dead is the most desolating, and she has no means of ruling it out. The agent says, "Lung cancer," and she wills patience into her response, saying, again, "I'm sorry," then, meaning it, "Lung cancer is terrible," suppressing *What my father has, too,* but maybe he detects their almost-comradeship in the bitterness with which she pronounced *lung cancer,* maybe that semblance of a bond appeases his doubt about her, because what he says next, left thumb anchoring the clipboard while his right fingertips pivot it to face her, is "Please sign by the *X,*" his voice spare, his professional affability chastened by cancer-awe and remembrance of his father, and she likes him for letting sadness show, thinking *Not such a bad delay,* scribbling her never-liked first name and the surname belonging to her father, *not so much time lost,* and if his questions have exceeded the normal agent-customer regimen, he must have felt obliged to rule out the intoxication implied by her haywire demeanor. She finds she's relying tonight on the words and turns of phrase her father favors—or does she always, forgetting the language was his first, and what she owes? *Haywire* is a pet indictment of his, more than once aimed at her, and was it especially intractable to work with, the wire used to bind hay? They stand there ruled by the jolli-ness of Christmas music, between them, easily within her reach, the counter where the document packet waits, and the fob with the keys, and her California driver's license with a ten-years-younger her, the red hair she had then causing people in his position to have to glance from the forty-three-year-old professor to the photo and back again, her credit card with its holograph of a dove whose wings, when the card tips one way, splay open, and when tipped the other, snap shut, an endlessly replicable optical caprice that had fascinated her sister's son on her long-ago last visit when, for fear of seeming an intolerant, starchy aunt, she hadn't stopped his rummaging through her wallet; he'd been set on keeping the card, and her sister had a terrible time getting it back from him, and the credit card's each and every use recalls for her the fluster of her sister's embarrassment and her own realization that she had set the boy up to get into trouble. The agent says, "I used to hide his cigarettes when I was a kid. Stop him smoking, was my plan. Like there aren't a million boxes of Marlboros in the world."

She has no time, and why is it her business to contradict the derision he directs at the futility of hiding those cigarettes—no, immodesty, that's more precisely what he's scorned, the child's narcissism in believing *he* can save the father. But what is *less* deserving of scorn than a child's desire to stave off death? If he could tolerate her saying such a thing aloud, she would say *But that's what I feel, why I need to get there, because I'm the one who can keep him from dying, they don't think so but I'm the strong one, me, it's me he needs,* but no one hearing this would accept these as the truths of a person sane and competent, though they are, she insists on believing they are. She tells the agent, "You were just trying to help." He takes off his glasses and then doesn't know what to polish them on and so puts them back on again and regards her through them (possibly they are both suddenly a little bit aware of his *glasses*) and shakes his head to (she thinks) disavow or apologize for the nearness of tears, and because of those tears she is constrained to try to connect with him again, saying, "I am very sorry for your loss," strange how the imperative for social accord persists in an emergency, she thinks, or does it only persist for women, and he says "Last winter," and then, impressed, "Gosh, this is strange. A year ago today," and she says "No" brightly, credulously, and he says, "That's—I'd forgotten today is the day." She says "My dad is down to hours" and hears how that sounds like a trivial and even heartless confirmation of the coincidence, allowing it to overshadow the individuality of the two deaths. The last thing her supremely private, exactingly rational father would want is for his death to be marveled at publicly, as half of a coincidence. Her father has never held back when offended, and two years ago rebuked some flippant political remark of hers with "You have a smart mouth on you," the resulting lull broken by the clink of knives and forks laid against plates down the length of the Thanksgiving table, nobody willing to transgress against the stare he was directing at her by the assertion of immunity implicit in taking another bite any more than gazelles would have stuck their noses back down to graze after hearing a rustling in nearby grass, and when he said, "It's amazing you ever got anywhere with that smart mouth," their distress—her mother's, her brother's, her sister's and sister's husband's and even the children's—was more readily identifiable as an injury inflicted on people who did not deserve it than her own panic was, both because that panic, clenched, inarticulate, left her ashamed, and because whenever he believed she'd done something wrong some treacherous sliver of self sided with him and accepted his contempt, whereas she didn't believe that the others at the table deserved what he was dishing out. Their quashed enjoyment of what was after all *Thanksgiving* prompted her to resistance—why should they feel afraid at their own table?—and returning his stare she had said, referring, as he had, to her recent hiring by a California university, suddenly hopeful, trusting that if she claimed the achievement with unabashed boldness he would have to concede its worth, "I did get somewhere," and he had said, "And how long before you mess that up," and the silence at the table extended two years, and could have lasted indefinitely, no word from her father (or mother, or sister, or brother), no word from her to anyone at home ever again (because couldn't someone have said *Dad, don't?*—weren't they her family as much as his?), if the hospice worker had not called to tell her that her father had less than twenty-four hours to live. Whose decision was it, to call her at the very end, when, the hospice worker told her, *He's been fighting for a year*? Again the screen of the phone she fishes from her pocket affirms: *No messages.*

The agent turns aside to the computer, clicks in swift bursts, swerves the mouse, replaces the keys on her paperwork with a different set, nods at her to take them. She does, and he says, "Upgraded you."

"What?"

"Best vehicle we've got for snow like this." He says unhappily, "What I should have advised you to take in the first place. So."

But she ought to have known to request their best car for snow; it shouldn't have been up to him to remedy her oversight. "Do you need my card again?"

"No, no. No additional cost. Just, this big guy is gonna get you there safe."

Given his no doubt superior prowess at driving in snow, he's offering to drive, his empathy turning proprietary, and she is about to protest when she gets it. *This big guy* is the vehicle. Embarrassed, she says, "Okay, thanks." When that seems inadequate: "Really, thank you."

"Good news is, the plows are out."

Now that she's holding the keys she risks asking, "Cars are getting through?" Earlier, in answer to one of his questions, she'd told him her destination, the small city her parents retired to.

"You have a shot," he says. "Ever driven in a blizzard?"

"I grew up here." She suppresses an impulse to account for turning up at his counter looking like she's never heard of winter, in the shirt she was wearing when she answered the phone and it was the hospice worker, in the same black suit she'd worn teaching her seminar, ankle boots whose three-inch heels will be tricky in snow, no gloves, too-light raincoat. She says, "I learned to drive here. But it's been a while."

"You've got a full tank of gas," he says. "Say you do get stuck, you'd run the heater for fifteen minutes, get nice and warm, then turn it off, wait till you couldn't stand the cold before starting that engine again, and you'd want to watch the clock all night long, getting out once an hour to clear snow from the tailpipe—remember, once an hour. Highway patrol will reach you soon as they can."

What they're both thinking is, her father will die while she's stuck in the snow, and she takes out her phone, bows her head for privacy, taps twice. *No messages.*

He says, "Hang on just a sec" and rummages under the counter before tearing the wrapping paper from a box and holding out a cap knitted in shambly stripes, olive and turquoise and pink and yellow and purple, saying, "So your ears won't freeze off," and she says, "You knew it was a hat?" and he grimaces and says, "Saw the work in progress," and she says, "But somebody made this for you," and he says, "If I wear it it'll just encourage her," and she dislikes this joke at the expense of the knitter, his coworker presumably, whose not-bad prank, the hat's whimsy a comment on his sturdy blond, blue-eyed humorlessness, just lost its chance. The knitter, whoever she is, isn't going to get to say *Put it on! Oh come on! Put it on!* He must pick up on her reluctance to accept the hat, because what he says next is "Take it for luck." She makes the face you make when someone says a thing wrong enough to make you doubt all the right things they've said up till then, and he says, "I'm sorry, there's no such thing as luck on a night like this, is there. I just mean——." There's a disconcerted tension between them before she commits, pulls on the hat, gives him the goofy smile *he* was supposed to give the *knitter*, and how could she do that, she asks herself, smile when her father is dying, and walks away fast while hidden speakers sing *Angels we have heard on high*—her phone, drawn again from an inside raincoat pocket, maintains *No messages*—and from his readiness to part with the hat, she guesses she's done him a favor, because it suggested the gladness of a person shucking off an entanglement, a gladness whose unwilling witness she has been more than once, the most devastating occasion just last spring, sitting up in a hotel bed as her lover turned toward her from the window with a phone clasped to her ear while saying, promising, really, lightly, naturally promising into the phone *I'll be home tomorrow*, and if her lover had only stayed looking out the window at the lights of the city where neither of them lived, the particular pain of being gladly forsaken would never have been driven through her heart—and what's uncanny, what is really staggering, is the immutability of the shock of loss, and the way no matter who the lover was, however singular, the loss has something in common with previous losses, as if a single never-ending shock runs from beginning to end of her life and she gains access to it only at rare intervals. And when she imagines the grief she will feel at her father's death she imagines it as *another interval* of that shock, which isn't to say *more of the same* because for it to feel "the same" she would have to have adapted to it and that's not possible, there is only living through it without understanding, there is only barely living through it. And already there is the next loss, lying in wait in the next several hours, though he—her father—would hate it if he knew she conceived of the loss of him as *next*, his psyche or character is such that he needs to believe he is *the only*, and she could be mistaken, maybe the rental agent or any person who has gone through the death of a father would warn her not to conjecture from what she's previously lived through, and it comes to her, she can turn around, walk back and ask him *How did you get through this?* and the good agent would grope for an answer, needing some time, maybe, to adapt to these new, higher stakes between them, and she would be almost as comforted by his diligence in seeking the honest answer she needs as she would be by his tendering some useful description of how grief can be borne—only are *use* and *usefulness* irrelevant now, is there any human thing you can hold onto, going to meet grief, or is it saner to walk into it with a bare heart, the sliding glass doors parting and wind booming in, her hair writhing up around the tight knitted cap and slashing across, catching on her chapped lips, the animal in her tuning in to the emergency of zero-degree night. The world takes a giant step closer. All of this is really going to happen. For a stunned instant she can't move, and the doors slide closed again. In the glass-box hush she tells herself *You have to*, and though she's not aware of having moved, the doors slide open again.

2

California girl is what her brother sometimes called her, meaning lightweight and out of touch, no longer adapted to harsh Iowa-caliber reality, and she can't turn out to be what her brother implied she is, a California abandoner, an escaper and eluder of responsibility, the only child *not there* the night her father lies dying, she can't bear that, the parking lot's raw cold ablaze in her chest; it sets her coughing. Her raincoat is gauze, and when she looks down, each button sports a crescent of snow. If only the knitter had knit mittens, too, her hands would be cozy striped paws, not fisted, freezing, in useless pockets. Inside her stupid boots her toes begin to sting. Behind, the low-slung terminal sends out its diligent, snow-defused radiance. If her father is still conscious he has observed that her brother is there and her sister is there and she is not. But they live here. All her sister had to do is drive across town. Her brother lives in a different but nearby small town and would have had to drive for twenty minutes, but what is twenty minutes earlier in the day when the storm had barely begun compared to these wheeling veils, the white sky's swept and shuddering slow-motion dump? She's no longer capable of driving in snow like this, if she ever was. Here comes shame. Let it come. Shame is better than getting herself killed. *Sure you want to go out in this?* Give in, turn back, walk through those sliding doors into warmth, into refuge, choose the chair on the end of a row of chairs, drop your bag, slouch down, cover your eyes, see if you can sleep, but no, to spend the coming hours sleeping in the impersonal haven of the terminal would be the most terrible mistake she's ever made in regard to her father. *No messages* very probably means he is still alive, and if he is conscious and can recognize her, then he will feel forgiven, and it will mean something that she rushed to get to him. Her fucked-up family. As for anger at their withholding news of his cancer, delegating the call to her to the hospice worker, that's going to have to wait. She can see the front door of her parents' duplex as clearly as if she's facing it, and the door is numinous in the way of doors about to open, and she's destined to stand there facing it and waiting for it to open. It seems a minor matter, the distance between where she is now and the actual location in space of that door. Breath pluming, hers the only tracks in the Arctic, halogen lamps blurring and refocusing, car after car, hard-candy colors dimmed, each car a neutral platinum glaze frozen around a core of essential dark privacy. Wonderful, in a way cars rarely are—she never sees cars, really. She's not a person cars matter to, but these do, now, set apart by the storm, they matter like musk oxen would matter, besieged in their fortress bodies, hunkered down to endure, her aliveness called to by theirs, the aliveness of cars which of course does not exist. Still, it is fantastic, the vast field of empty, gallant vehicles. Not too long ago, someone must have shoveled around them and done some scraping of windshields. When she reaches the SUV he chose for her, the big guy, she cuffs snow from its windshield and packs it. The snowball flies soundlessly through falling snow. Isn't that beautiful? Why is it? —something about the opposition, the pure, moving focus of the sphere piercing tall flexing vertical wave after wave of cascading, blown-back snow. The SUV beeps its response, and she hears the thunk of its locks unlatching. Under the dome light whirl the bright particles gusting in behind her. The messenger bag, her only piece of luggage, plops into the backseat, snow fanning out, sparkling across the upholstery. Then comes the chill hospitable order of the new-car interior, the dashboard requiring several minutes' concentration to master—the embarrassment, as if anyone is watching, of not right away grasping how to work stuff like this, or maybe it feels like one's technological prowess is continually being assessed these days and no fumbling with a machine is ever truly forgivable, just as language is an inherently social endeavor and mistakes in figuring out language carry a special, outcast charge of humiliation—and gradually they acquire meaning, the icons below the dials, the knobs precipitating out from inscrutability, wipers, heater, the setting for defogging, the angles of the various mirrors, the rumbling of the big guy that will get her there; then, ludicrous or not, the self-salute to her bravery for being about to drive alone through the falling-snow world that holds her dying father. The massive calm vehicle she controls, which she can make do anything, backing and churning down the broad lane hemmed in by the blind backs of other SUVs, is lovable. She loves this car more than she loves anyone in her family. For this comparison, she apologizes aloud: "Fucked up." A cloud of breath. Does her father know he has only hours left, is he terrified or does he, as her mother has long prayed for him to, believe at last in a life after this, can he still *think*, to what extent is he still *himself*, she wonders, understanding in a distracted way (distracted because she is beginning to comprehend the lag time snow interposes between her steering and the vehicle's response) that she would give anything (now, navigating cautiously between parked monsters) to feel the love that figured in the word *dad* when the car-rental agent pronounced it: love that ought to be in her heart and isn't. Did she love that way as a child? She must have. Everyone does. Was it not just some gift allotted to you, was it finally your *job* to love that way, should she have fought harder against her own hard-heartedness to still be able to love like that, how serious was her crime in not calling for two years?

The big SUV lumbers down the lane between parked vehicles as she tries to get the hang of steering in snow. She can't help it: to think of him is to tinker with consuming narcissistic calculations whose aim is to prove either that he was at fault in their rift, or that she was. She wonders if he would ever under any circumstances have come running to her like this—no. That *no* seems to lift the SUV and swat it through a weightless circle with snow falling all the way around it, shades of gray accreting to suggest a presence looming toward her as in fact a glazed black panel buckles, crunching, and her SUV rebounds, skidding through another destined arc into a second surreal panel flashing and popping with reflections, the accident playing out in fractions of fractions of sliced panic until a fresh fraction conveys the news that her SUV is still riding through a languid circuit terminating in the light-mirroring mass of yet another parked vehicle, which flicks it away. The world comes to a stop.

3

She thinks *I am not hurt*. She looks out through the windshield. No alarms are going off. It is so silent, the widely spaced lights mooning through obliterating snow and the beauty-shock of albino dunes slung and saddled with blue shadow. Either the impacts were too glancing to trigger the air bag or this car has a defective air bag—in which case, it crosses her mind, she can sue the car-rental agency. Or could if she was hurt. She twists against the seat belt to study her wake. The ranks of cars look the same as before, none jolted out of line. But surely that first impact shattered a taillight, or worse. She ought to get out and check; she owes it to the rental agent not to drive away without inspecting the other vehicles, wiping snow from a bumper, a taillight, if she has to, and she'll have to because it's avalanching down, and walking back to the terminal to take responsibility. And then what? Questions. Lines to sign on. Paperwork. Taking how long? Her father will die while she's doing paperwork. She tries to make out the damage she has done but none can be seen, really, not through the falling snow, not unless she gets out and walks back and looks, and once she's done that she'll have to slog back to the terminal, to his counter, and if he's even still there she's going to have to explain, and he may well say he needs to come back out here with her to assess the damage, and then— forms, questions, lines to sign on. She thinks *fuck fuck fuck fuck fuck*. All the while the SUV is idling as smoothly as ever.

4

It continues, the emergency clarity of this falling-snow world, the way the snow *knows about* her dying father and roots for her to get there on time, arrows directing her to the on-ramp, signs that blaze up through falling snow, a conviction of rightness, the highway remembered not from childhood but from adult visits, summers when she had flown out to spend a week, a week turning out to be too long, the burdensomeness of her pres- ence dawning on her father and her mother and on her, too, as well as hatred of herself for not being their irresistible guest, the daughter they would hate to see leave, but—in her mother's telling she was born repellent, sporting a full head of straight black fur, her skin crisscrossed with furious scratches she had inflicted on herself in utero, if her mother's account is to be believed, and if her young mother turned from her with instant loathing there was nothing the nurses could do, they could only bring the baby back again and say *Here's your baby, don't you want to hold her*, and her mother couldn't stand to look and had no feeling for that baby except hatred that she was being thrust at her, and the nurses tried again and the young mother said no again, and at last the nurses slicked the black hair into a Kewpie doll spit curl and tied a bow on it and carried her in and the bow did the trick and her mother took her, and that was the story her mother told her and who is to blame in that story?, if the young mother didn't feel what young mothers ought to feel whose fault is that?, and once when she was eleven she asked where was Daddy for those two or three days when the nurses could not get you to take me, and was told, well, fathers didn't get involved in things like that then, not in those days, it was different, fathers were not expected to, and he was at work, he had to go back to work, and what she'd really wanted to ask was did it bother him that you refused to take me or even look at me, did that concern him, wanting him to have been on her side. If it's any consolation, she can tell herself it could easily be true, he could have wanted to come into the nursery where the bassinets were lined up and lifted her baby self out and held her, if fathers did that then, but fathers didn't, fathers then looked through glass.

Snow falling, her ticking-clock concentration pierced by appreciation of the fact that she's in over her head, not skilled enough for a night like this, *but what can she do except drive.* A motionless mass up ahead casts a beam the wrong way, across her lane, what she thought was her lane. Then a fresh S-curve in the snow terminates in the long, dim, intricate underside of an overturned semi, the trucker stamping his feet while he justifies himself to his cell phone, lifting an arm as she slows, not to halt her but, it turns out, in thanks for her being kind enough to slow to see if she can help, or at least that's how she construes it, his wave and the tilt of his head conveying *Sure, keep driving. You might make it.* Signaling, too: *Good luck.* Or so she interprets it, and how desperate she must be, how fucked and despairing, for that quick sideways tip of his head to mean so much—for her to derive from that stranger's gesture the confidence she needs to continue driving, how ridiculous; yet it changes her mood to have had her striving recognized, her desperation saluted and encouraged, and who cares if it's a stranger who does that for you? *Angels we have heard on high* plays on her mind's radio. *Sweetly singing o'er the*—what? In the cinderblock, abstract-crucifix interior of the Methodist church of her childhood she and her sister share a hymnal, singing *o'er the*—, *o'er the*—. She skips ahead to the line the two sisters can barely sing without giggling: *Shepherds, why this jubilee?* She repeats it until the rhyme arrives: *Why your joyous strains prolong? What the gladsome tidings be*— Skips further to *Come, adore on bended knee,* and she has it whole except for whatever it is the angels are singing o'er, the two sisters in the backseat of the car on the drive home teasing their stoic little brother, *Shepherd, why this jubilee?* until, crushed by their ruthless repetition of the baffling question, he shouts *Because!* After that, a lonely hour with no sign of another vehicle, no one else out in this.

Far down the headlights, snow flings and agitates in an opaque onslaught, but closer, maybe only a yard or so in front of the SUV, there's some kind of boundary where snow detaches itself from the prevailing chaos, seeming almost, fascinatingly, to freeze in a vortex before zipping at her in extreme close focus, detailed down to individual flakes—a trick of vision, thrilling enough that she has to remind herself to look away from the borderline where the snow changes, back out to the farthest reach of the lights nudging into whiteness, the core of the halogens steadily dazzling, probing deeper but never gaining, not giving her much to go on—and it's tedious staring steadily at those few yards of lit world, which might as well be the same yards over and over again, and there it is, *plains. Sweetly singing o'er the plains.* For some reason the acuity of her father's glare two years ago comes back. Her own eyes in the rearview—a fraction of an instant's assessment—are nowhere close to his in intensity. Nonetheless he hated her holding his gaze. *Don't you look at me like that* was a thing he said fairly often. Not from boldness, but out of the need to understand him—*the* unrelenting need of her childhood—she wanted to keep looking right up until she transgressed, to look at him as long as she safely could, but the line was never where she thought it was. When she tilts her head, the bobble on top of the hat adds its mote of weight to the tilt. If she didn't know this highway runs through flat fields, would she still sense, through the fast-falling snow, the vacancy stretching away on every side? How many die of exposure every winter in this county? Not only the homeless, not just drunks, but farmers who go astray between house and barn, whose tracks instantly fill in, according to her father at the dinner table of her childhood, and he was moved almost to tears by a farmer's no longer being able to make out the lights of his house, and none of them knew what to do for him, or how to care more, as it seemed they should, for whoever had fallen asleep in snow.

From the far side of the snowfield that is the median, blades

of light oar intermittently, the snowplow outlandish as a satellite
eking out its transit.

There was a calculation to what the hospice worker had said,
a methodically staged breaking of bad news. She had explained
who she was and that she'd been staying in her parents' house for
two weeks; then the kind of cancer, the multiplicity of tumors
and their aggressiveness, the gamut of treatments her father has
been through; and then that nothing more could be done, medi-
cally, as her father was down to his last twenty-four hours and
the palliative care was straightforward enough to be handled
by the family; and then she had said, "He would want you to
come." *Would* has to mean he didn't definitely say, but he was
not yet, at that point, unable to speak, and he *could* have said *Tell
her to come*, but someone gave the hospice worker her number
and instructed her to call, and that someone, who could only
be her mother, or possibly her sister, but who almost certainly is
not her reticent, laconic brother, is likely to have a realistic grasp
of her father's wishes, and could have been moved to request
that the hospice worker make the call by some pained, inarticulate gesture or even expression of her father's that could be
interpreted as the desire for the absent child to appear. Whoever
this hospice worker is, she's kind. Not detached, as might be
expected of a person who often witnesses death, but speaking
knowledgeably of the dying man's temperament and wishes—
how did she gather all that? When she hadn't responded right
away the hospice worker had said, "I know he wants you to
come." *I* know. How long has it taken for the hospice worker to
become so proprietary? Not long. But it has always been like that
with her father. He just somehow matters to people. He's one of
those individuals who seem, right away, significant, whose good
opinion even strangers solicit, and however it happened he had

sufficiently endeared himself to the hospice worker that she took a moment to regale his daughter with his quirks as a patient, to say *Your father likes this*, about some measure of extra attentiveness taken in his care. What was it? A detail was confided to her and she's forgotten it. But the hospice worker had figured out some preference of her father's, and had gone to the trouble of making sure whatever it was was done the way he wanted, and she's right about that, the hospice worker, nothing gratifies him more than prevailing over customary routines by mischievous insistence on a whim. Still, the possibility exists that the hospice worker was inadvertently misrepresenting her father's wishes in regard to her. This could happen all too easily. Theirs is not a family whose wounds are obvious. As individuals and as a family they're more oblique in their manner, harder to read, than most people are, and on top of that, of course, they dissemble. They want to look like a family that works, because any other kind of family—a family that really could shatter, in which *sister* and *brother* and *daughter* or even *mother*, even *father*, do not name reliable or lifelong presences—is a source of shame, and if that's your family, you keep it to yourself, and all of you, for once in genuine accord, keep it to yourselves.

Somebody's gotten through, not long before. Somebody out in front, whose tracks are not snowed over.

The hospice worker had said, "You need to prepare for his being pretty far gone. It's been a steep slide down for the last ten days. He's lost a lot of weight."

Visible through the roiling snow, a frayed blush—taillights.

What counts as preparation for his being far gone? Where do you start? Do you warn yourself that where you are used to strength there will be frailty?

Veiled rose coalesces into emergency red.

Or that he may not recognize you?

The taillights slew through a long arc that carries them well out into the median, and when it has slid sideways as far as it can go the car spins around, snow jetting from the drift it shears through, spurts flaring as it scrapes deeper into the drift and is locked in place, neither the skidding spin nor its concluding jolt hard enough to have injured anyone inside, she hopes, but probably they're going to spend the night there, and she hopes they have a cell phone and with luck even a blanket and that they know about clearing the tailpipe every hour, the car already fading as she passes, its outline obscured, its headlights like holes torn through to some other, radiant world.

5

Last thing I need you to do, big guy, she coaxes the SUV, *is sidle in close to the curb to be out of the way of the plow.* Her brother's and sister's and sister's husband's snowed-over cars, and a fourth she doesn't recognize, hospice worker's or minister's, occupy the driveway, her parents' duplex, on the left-hand side of the shared facade of ocher brick, untransformed by the fact that her father lies dying within. Her cell tells her *No messages*, and she calls 911 and explains to the dispatcher where she saw the car go off the road into the median an hour ago, and the dispatcher says *Thank you, ma'am*, and she says *Did anyone find them yet?* and the dispatcher says *I don't know about that ma'am, there've been lots of calls tonight as you might imagine*, and as she climbs down into the street, striped hat on and her bag slung over her shoulder, her stupid too-high heels wanting to skid out from under, she remembers her spin in the rental-car lot and brushes snow from the bumper, exposing several long scratches, and when she straightens up she tucks her freezing hands in her armpits and re-members her father scooping snow from the windshield of their station wagon, dropping it into the cupped hands of her five-year-old self, her father saying *Pack it good and tight. Now throw.*

6

Cold that can freeze the tears in your lashes, though there are no tears in her eyes, not then, facing that door. In three previous, widely spaced visits to this place where her parents have lived for the last ten years she conceived an aversion to the doorbell, garishly loud in contrast to the mutedness within the duplex, whose only raised voices are those of talking heads disputing on political programs, *The Situation Room* and *Inside Politics*, her father an obsessive follower of matters political, such programs his particular passion, if *passion* is the word for an interest so re-lentlessly lucid. He was an assistant secretary of agriculture, and once said in her hearing that though he'd never risen as high as he'd hoped to, nonetheless he had his view of the Washing-ton Monument, and when on one long-ago visit to his city, she had stopped by so that the two of them could go for lunch, she had been led from the secretary's antechamber into his office and left there to wait, her dad having been detained elsewhere, and it was like childhood again, like the secret times the child-you gained access to your father's public existence. He was expecting her, of course, yet she felt a sense of trespass at finding herself alone in his true habitat, gazing out of his window because that was the view he gazed on daily, only gradually realizing that the Washington Monument was not visible from that window, and turning to the office's only other window, discovering she had to jam herself against one side, cheekbone to the casing, in order to make out not the whole monument, but only its sharp vertical edge. When she sets her thumb against the button, the gloomy, whimsical notes toll on the other side of the door, and to her surprise they are hard to hear—but now she, at least, has made an overture, and she wants this last minute of her apartness from them to unfold slowly, the snow falling, the tears freezing in her lashes, for finally there are tears. No matter what happened between them she has always been guilty of believing she was responsible for him, and that was puzzling, not only because she was the child and he was the father, but because he was a vigorously self-reliant, hardheaded person, and it is hard to imagine what he might have needed protecting from. There was one story, though, she thinks, blinking her icy lashes, the bell's notes announcing her arrival to her father if he is still conscious and can put two and two together. *I'll never get out of this world alive,* her father used to say, or sing, maybe that was from a song, he had often sung snatches of old bluegrass or hillbilly songs and done a sloppy shuffle in his scuffed leather house slippers, his knees swinging out, then in, a bandy-legged shambolic dance, hands in his pockets, grin widening as he sang *Rolling in my sweet baby's arms*—

Or, what was it, *Gonna lay around that shack*
Till that freight train comes back
—can those be the words?

The story is set in his childhood, in Tennessee, one spring when his mama had done a favor for a friend of hers, a sweetly interfering Baptist lady, driving deep into the mountains, finding the cabin belonging to the elderly bachelor uncle of the

Baptist lady's only after many wrong turns on dirt roads whose
relentless switchbacking began to wear on his mama, as he
could tell by her protestations to the Baptist lady that this was
no trouble, no trouble 'tall. "Winter was bad back in here, Homer
used ever' last stick of kindling," observed the Baptist lady as his
mama parked the Model T on the scrap of cleared ground where
the woodpile once was, overlooking a steep drop at whose base
ran a crick high and fast with snowmelt, an erratically sparkling
strand whose cool resonance lured a mockingbird into trying
water sounds, the boy in the backseat bored, counting the june
bugs pasted to the windshield or picking at his toenails, barefoot
as usual since he was not a boy you could keep shoes on, his
mama in the front seat tending to her own thoughts, an unusual
woman if he could have known it then, an exception to the rule
that women did not drive, and if she didn't seek to ameliorate
the monotony of their long wait for the Baptist lady to finish
with her visit, the relation of adults to children was different
then, formal, the adult under no obligation to try to amuse a
child, no question of the boy's being allowed out to play, either,
since the elderly bachelor uncle was no kin of theirs and good
manners required him and his mama to remain confined in the
car, and the knot at the nape of his mama's sunburned neck was
boring to the boy, as was the set of her broad rounded shoulders
in the floral print of her one nice dress, navy rayon with daisies
detailed down to leaves and stems, and that bothered him, the
messily yanked-up, strewn appearance of the daisies, and maybe
partly due to his aversion to it the print would prove indelible
for him, enduring as long as memory was capable of generating
internal visions (this may be over for him now; she blinks); when
he wanted more to ponder he had bent forward and studied,

through the windshield, the crick glittering a stony near-vertical eighth of a mile below, flashing between toppled boulders, through a litter of sun-starved trees, and he was watching the crick when the car lurched against the caterwauling resistance of the failing hand brake, evergreen branches whisking past as it tipped over the brink and bolted down, jarring rocks free as it went; there was a quaking pause; his mama threw open her door and abandoned the car; whatever the impediment had been, it whiplashed free, sending the car skidding, battering, threatening to topple end over end, door banging, the steering wheel yanked back and forth, stones flying past its windows, the car a viciously shaken tin can, the boy tossed from roof to floor, hearing the shrill *screeeeeeeeeee* of an adamant object raking along the undercarriage as the car reared up and balked, its windshield full of amazed blue sky, stuck with the same dead bugs as ever, the engine ticking and a front wheel revolving, some stick or branch snared in the wheel well issuing a series of decelerating thumps, above that the boil and sluice of trammeled snowmelt. When the boy ducked out the canted door and jumped, clay squelched between his toes. If he'd had a fishing pole he could have cast his line in from here, not that there were any fish in that churn. He squatted to inspect the twilight beneath the car: a stump jammed into the front axle held it in place. He waited, swatting at gnats drawn to his terror-sweat, his mama and the Baptist lady calling his name. Alerted by their agitation other parts of him spoke up—bruises, scrapes—but his voice refused. He had used it up screaming on the way down. From a chink in oil-spattered moss emerged a salamander, arraying its tiny impeccable fingers handhold by handhold as it clambered to the stump's crest and undulated from view. Once it was gone he felt the wreck was over, and getting to his feet he started back up the mountainside, following the zigzag course razed through the woods, the women's cries unceasing till he stepped back out into brightness.

7

A woman she doesn't recognize opens the door and says "You made it" and then "Come in, come in," and then, when she steps inside, "If you've been waiting out there in the cold I'm sorry, your mother had your brother dial down the doorbell so as not to disturb your father when he's resting, there've been a lot of visitors, your pastor's been by twice today, to pray with your mother, in fact the last time he rang the bell we all thought it was you, and of course since then the storm got *much* worse," pausing, reaching to clasp her hands between her own, "Your poor hands! Your poor hands! Cold as ice!" and then, without letting go of her hands, "I'm the one called you," and then, letting go at last, "Well, you best get out of those wet things," and as she bends to unzip her sodden suede ankle boots and set them next to the rabble of boots, adult- and child-sized, on the old towel spread over a layer of newspapers along the entryway's far wall, the faded blue of the towel summoning the backyard clothesline the towel had once been pinned to, rumpling when the breeze off the lake caught it, a much brighter blue then, blue almost as the lake only fifty yards or so from this cottage they stayed in every August, one plywood-walled cubicle for her sister, one for her brother, the farthest bedroom for her parents, no doors to any of the rooms, only frayed floral curtains that could be tugged closed along tight-strung wires, making it possible for her, a thirteen-year-old maddened by her family's infinite shortcomings, stretched sleepless on the couch whose

prickling nap was so saturated with other people's suntan lotion
and cigarette smoke that she could hardly bear contact with it,
to overhear, incredulous, her mother mewing in wrenched, ascending, greedy ecstasy. She unzips her raincoat but hesitates
to shrug it off, unwilling for the hospice worker to continue
playing hostess by taking her coat from her and hanging it up,
but realizes she probably appears forlorn, standing there in her
California girl's coat, and the hat, the foolish hat that she rips
off, static electricity causing her hair to trail after it, and sticks in
a pocket of the raincoat. "I was just about to leave, myself," the
hospice worker says. "Everything that's left to do for him, medi-
cation for the pain, your mother can handle, she's precise, your
mother, she would have made a good nurse, and I was just about
out the door, but I'm so glad I got to meet you," and taking a
down coat the size of a sleeping bag from the closet the hospice worker says, "He's been holding on till you get here," and
peering down, fidgeting the zipper's parts into alignment, she
says, "They do that, they hold until the missing one returns,"
zipping, wrapping a scarf around her throat, nodding at her, *the
missing one*, and she minds the hospice worker's relegating her
inassimilable father to a category, *they*, the dying, but come on,
she tells herself, the hospice worker is making the best of a bad
situation, surely she's picked up on the strain whenever people
refer to her, and even if all they've said is that she is coming
from California, the hospice worker would have noticed the un-
naturalness of tone that attends estrangement in families, and
rather than proceed delicately, as others in her situation might
have, the hospice worker votes for ebullience, radiating welcome, doing everything except throw her arms around her, and
if for her this excess serves to underscore the vulnerability and
shame that shadow her arrival, still, the hospice worker has acted

from kindness, who could do her job except an innately kind, life-force sort of person, and whether she trusts her or not, the generous rejoicing in the hospice worker's voice as she says "You made it in time" causes her to hope.

8

At the other end of the closet is her father's overcoat, and it stops her, his overcoat simply hanging there, not an overcoat she has any special associations with except that by virtue of being his it evokes the first overcoat she knew him in, no cold like the winter cold borne in with her father's overcoat, coldest in its folds, but also, all over, distinctly cold, and as if the cryptic eyes your father turns on you were not mystery enough, this ghostly cold comes as a sly erotic assault, a little squall for your child's senses when that coat shrugs its way down to you, you given the job of hauling it over a hanger, shoulder by father-shaped shoulder, fitting the wire nose into the silk-sutured cave, reading as you always do the secret word hidden within, the word worn by your father, fabled *Menswear* in tapestry script surrounded by a golden lasso, as if everything to do with men, fabulous and wild, needed to be lassoed before it could be contemplated, and the child-you would throw a golden circle around him here, now that he stands smiling down at your struggle with the coat, and only when he turns away do you hold the coat to your nose, and you close your eyes to live completely through the skin of your face caressed by the slippy, male-scented lining of the coat, which has been worn into the ominous, radiant center of the universe, called *work*, that day, that very day, worn into the innermost circle, nearest god, nearest the president, and returned, marvelously intact, an unscathed overcoat that seems, like your dad, an adored visitor whose stay will be brief, whose real life is incalculably distant, rife with unforeseeable demands, calling for him to always be leaving.

9

In the immaculate kitchen, at the rickety table her parents had shipped from Iowa to Washington when her father was appointed assistant secretary of agriculture, and then shipped back on his retirement—(she can summon the sound of her baby spoon ringing against its Formica)—sits her kind, ungainly brother-in-law, hands clasped, explaining death to his two older children, the son and daughter who have inherited his Norwegian fairness and height, his braininess, too, the air of somehow genial uncompromisingness that wins trials for him. The two of them have always liked each other. He is the only one of the adults in this house whose affection she feels sure of, and she hopes that he will glance away from his children and nod, but the explanation he has embarked on absorbs him completely, and holds his two children, whose backs are to her and whose heads don't turn, in thrall. Well-mannered kids, they are too unspontaneous for her taste; she can't love them as she is meant to. But she envies them there with their father, who is doing them the honor of trying to tell them the truth. Do they have any idea how unusual that is? If your father has been honest with you your whole life, how different is the love you feel for him from the love she feels for her father? Is it deeper or merely different in tenor, more trusting? How her brother-in-law mediates between the atheism she suspects him of and the Methodist certainty enforced by the rest of the family, she would be curious to hear. Everyone else must be back in the guest room, and she doesn't want to go any farther into the house unaccompanied. Previous visits, few and far between as they were, had enlightened her about her mother's resistance to her, or possibly to anyone's, crossing uninvited from the impeccable living room and dining room into the equally fastidiously maintained but more private sanctuary of the back hallway leading to the bathroom and the bedroom shared by her mother and father, which has its own bathroom, and the guest room, previously her father's office, where he lies dying. For her mother, boundaries of all kinds are fraught. Her mother must be in the guest bedroom. Her sister and brother must be in the bedroom as well, and her sister's youngest child, a solemn intractable boy of seven or eight, she can't remember exactly. Not too young to be present for his grandfather's death. The strangeness of her family strikes her: the forlorn mutual incomprehension of delicate signals continually misinterpreted, and then these sudden astounding streaks of guileless transparency, as if nothing has ever been kept from any of them, when it has, she protests, when almost everything has been kept from me.

What she needs from him: a last-minute sign that she is loved.

Where she is: the hallway that leads to the bedrooms. The door that is open belongs to the guest bedroom. Another door, nearer, is open as well: the bathroom. From this doorway her brother emerges, his back to her, his head ducked or bowed toward the bundle in his arms, and pity suffuses her before she understands that the long spindly white objects lolling over her brother's arm are her father's shins, that her brother's arm supports her father's knees and those are her father's bare feet hanging in mid-air, jostling with her brother's careful steps, that is what you see when a child is carried, those sleeping feet, and can that really be her father, is he no more than an armful of bones, light enough for her brother to carry the rest of the way down the hall to the guest bedroom, in whose doorway he turns sideways, ensuring clearance for her father's dangling feet, for, tipped up against her brother's other arm, the big gorgeous vigilant head ransacked of every bit of expressive flesh, the sockets of his eyes harsh craters of shadow much too big for the puny bulge of the closed lids. She stands at the other end of the hall from them. For her father to submit to being carried is a blow as terrifying as the annihilation of his male grace and authority. If she turns around and leaves, none of them will ever know she was here. But her brother, in turning sideways in the doorway, has looked down the hall. He has seen her. His grimace means *Give me a minute to get him settled*, or so she interprets it. With her father in his arms her brother disappears, moving toward the bed, she supposes. The door is ajar, or she would be able to see who else is in the room.

She goes down the hall toward the doorway, and knocks on the jamb, watching her brother lay her father down in the twin bed, her brother seeming almost to unfold her father's body, stick by stick, from the bundle it had made in his arms, the big skull with its silvery white swept-back hair tipped upright on two pillows turning toward her knock, eyes staring from the sinkholes of their sockets, lips drawn back from teeth that seem too big for the face, stubbornly recognizable teeth, the idiosyncrasies of the individual teeth, their degree of discoloration, so familiar that in her mind she greets them, she experiences his teeth as a revelation, yes this is her father whose bone-arms with their outsize elbows and wrists thrash at her startled brother, the squalling moan from low in his throat, from, almost, his chest,

Aww awww aaara eeere, disrupted by a violent hard-won jerk of his head, the moan resumed, *Awww aaarragh. Go away*, she hears, *go away*, and backs through the doorway, and listens from the hall as her brother calms him, *Dad, it's okay, Dad, it's all okay*, and she does not know what to do except stand there listening, understanding from some progression in her brother's reassurance that her father has relaxed back into the pillows.

10

Where has her brother-in-law gone, has he taken the kids out to eat, maybe? In the kitchen she makes herself a cup of tea. A stain in the porcelain sink bothers her. She can't have caused that. She only just got here. From under the sink she retrieves her mother's old-fashioned scouring powder and a pair of her gloves—pulling these on makes her feel closer to her mother than she had, seeing her face. She scours until the stain fades and vanishes. She's not an irresponsible person. In the morning she'll call the car rental agency to find out how much damage she did.

On the striped couch in the living room she drinks the cold tea. She feels almost at home on this couch. In an inexplicable break from her chaste aesthetic, her mother had ordered the striped fabric as a daring contrast to the room's pale monochrome. When the reupholstered couch was delivered, its pattern loomed much larger than she had expected, swaggeringly, flamboyantly huge, and her Depression-traumatized mother, who wrings the last minim of use from every frayed and stained and unraveling possession, had resigned herself to wincing toleration of the beast until it wears out. When her daughter strokes

its arm, the striped velvet seems good as new—the couch has a
long way to go.

Other pieces of the story had been confided, when the mood
struck her father. "You know that churchgoing woman took
credit for me being alive," he'd said, amused. "Claimed she got
down on her knees there at the edge of the drop-off and Jesus
heard her." A month after the wreck of the Model T, the Baptist
lady had charmed his mama into laying back in the preacher's
hands and letting the river flow through her hair and over her
closed eyes; after she walked out of that river, her father said, it
wasn't just his mama's sins washed away, but the old, easygoing
life the family had led. Strictness clamped down, no taking the
Lord's name or running around in the woods with neighbor
girls. No dancing. Whippings whenever his mama took a whim,
as she did every washday, her fury blushing her wide cheeks
with a rosiness in other circumstances he'd have found pretty,
wrath pinking her throat and the heavy arms bared for thrusting
into harsh-smelling soapsuds. Out of her four children it was
nearly always he who caught her eye. Impudence, she believed
she read in his face, and in a strong voice she'd call to him to find
a switch in the woods, and when he came back with the switch
she told him to let his pants down and turn around and used it
to administer a series of slashing strokes. Finally one day when
he was told to go find a switch he searched the woods for the
worst he could find, choosing a briar cane whose savage thorns
would dissuade her from ever applying it to his skin. He tested
their tips with his thumb, and grinned. Inconceivable that she
could bring herself to lash him with an instrument so wickedly
equipped to draw blood, and he carried it back to the yard where
his mama straightened from the tub, wiped her hands down her
front, and assessed the briar switch, figuring out at once what

he was counting on—he should have remembered how hard she was to fool. "Made sure I'd never forget that briar switch," he said.

11

Sounds from the kitchen wake her: her sister making a sandwich for her younger son, who sits in a chair drawn up to the table, playing with her mother's salt and pepper shakers, clicking them together in a monotonous yet random rhythm. For all she knows he could be clacking out a Donne sonnet in Morse code: the boy, who falls mute at the least contradiction and can go days without saying a word, is also arrestingly brilliant, and home-schooling him has been her sister's consuming years-long project. Her sister comes out and sits at the other end of the couch and says, "It's just after midnight. I'm glad you got some sleep," and then goes back to the kitchen to sit and watch her boy eat. "Any change in Dad?" she calls to her sister, and her sister says, "Just one time he came awake enough to feel pain, Mom gave him more medicine, and since then he's been peaceful. Mom has been a rock." The hospice worker, after opening the front door, had said much the same: *Your mother's been amazing.* "John took the kids home. I'm going to get this young man home to bed, too, if he will only finish his supper."

Her boy says, "I want to stay."

"You're so tired you can hardly see straight," her sister says—a phrase of their father's.

Her son says, "I want to stay."

From the couch she calls, "He's not going to jump out of the car." In the past her sister has more than once pointed out the bafflement her teasing riddles and non sequiturs inflict on her niece and nephews, and when her sister's boy says, "What car?" she says, "A story your grandfa—", her sister interrupting, "How Grandpa was saved by the stump the runaway car snags on," and with his strict adherence to accuracy her boy says to her, his aunt, "I am not in that story," an assertion his mother confirms, formally, "No, you're not," and sorry to have caused this peculiar trouble she runs her hand over striped velvet, thinking *So he told that story to everyone*, then *Why did I think it was only me*, hearing her sister tell the boy, "This is hard for you, I see that, really hard, and I understand you want to help all you can, but Grandpa can't see or hear any of us anymore. He's not aware anyone is in the room with him, not even you. That part is over, when the sound of our voices gave him some consolation," and she thinks it's extraordinary, the honesty with which the mother talks to son, the depth between them, trust accruing from a million tiny proffers of truth, not an experience, probably, any child of a previous generation of their family has ever had, and who is it whose place she would take if she could, her sister's or the boy's? She wants to be them both. That's what her sister has always seemed to distrust about her, she guesses: the taint of envy in her approach to her sister's children isn't lost on her sister, and down at the primal level where even the faintest, most imaginary threat to a child meets with a parent's hostility, her sister can't help but be angry with her, and to want to screen her son from her—or is she misreading the mother's understandably amped-up solicitude toward the difficult boy, does it really have anything to do with her? After her sister bundles the boy into his snow jacket, she bends to retrieve something from the boots jumbled on the closet floor, then tugs the striped hat down over her boy's ears before asking, in an exhausted voice, "Is this yours? I guess this is yours," and when the boy says nothing his crouching mother says, "Whose else would it be," and the mistake feels right to her, and she watches the mother usher the boy in the charming striped hat out into the night. She thinks that, to most seven-year-olds, the word *consolation* would probably be a mystery.

12

About two in the morning her mother comes out to the couch and calls her name and she wakes and stands up. The two of them hold each other briefly. She says, "How are you, Mom?" Her mother says, "Just fine." Then, "I'm taking a break. Do you want to go in?" "Is it all right?" "Of course it's all right." How does her mother understand what happened when she appeared in the guest-room doorway? She would like to ask, to have her terrible interpretation negated by her mother's superior understanding of her father. From the kitchen table where he has been drinking a cup of coffee, her brother says matter-of-factly, "Go on in. You came all this way." Then, hearing the grudgingness of that, he says with exhausted gentleness, "I know it was bad before. But I know he would want you to try again." In the guest bedroom she is alone with her unconscious father, as slight, under the sheet, as he must have been as a skinny boy in Tennessee. Is she wrong to want to be here? His last exertion on earth was the thrashing meant to drive her away. What would a person who understands love do, if he were her? His lips are parted, his breathing an irregularly timed ruckus. Something should have been done to ease it, it shouldn't have been let get so arduous, should it, his breathing? Before now she has had no idea

of the strenuousness of the act of dying. His lungs will fill, the
hospice worker explained when she asked what the actual cause
of his death would be. "He will drown." But she hadn't understood. Drowning was rivers. It was the sea. Not the body on its
own. Not *within*. Not welling up from *inside*. The untouched
order she associates with the guest room is intact around this
central disturbance, the grappling, stopping and starting hazard
of his breathing. There is no more smell of torment in the room
than if a freshly bathed child rested in this bed, and like that
child's his body is unadorned, neither tubes running into his
nose, nor any intravenous connection, and again, all over again,
but more forcefully, as if she had not fully grasped it before,
it comes to her that what she was told is true, and he really
has sailed beyond help. Apart from the central hollow formed
around the heaviness of his immobile head, the pillowcase is
crisply devoid of creases, his only covering a sheet pulled evenly
across his upper chest, with, under the sheet, his arms arranged
parallel to his distinctly outlined torso, no hand she can reach
for with her own, and she is relieved not to be responsible for
the coldness, the affront to his better self, to consciousness that
may still exist as a strayly glimmering, not yet snuffed-out ghost
in the largely abandoned comb within his skull, of not taking
his hand if it had been lying out in the open, and below the arc
of his rib cage a well, a famished sunkenness, his belly gone, his
hips dwindled to a stark cradle, the close lie of the sheet outlin-
ing the heaped mess of his genitalia, and the torque of the parallel femurs in the shrunken thighs, and the perched eggs of the
kneecaps, and the feet tenting the sheet in peaks. She searches
for proof he is hers. The ear. The lobe ample, the rim a smoothly
continuous curve, the cloistered yellowy, flushed-pink branching and whorls lustrous, the aperture a specific dab of shadow

that absorbed her first words. His browbone protests his gaunt-
ness with the familiar challenging thrust. Laid across the wan
skin, his eyebrows are meticulously themselves. The stitchery of
the lashes of his closed eyes is dearly known. But this has never
been possible before: she can see how he is made. His temple
is a hollow whose bottom shivers across with an arterial quaking. The puzzlework where mandible intersects skull is exposed.
Under the jut of the cleanshaven jaw—the throat, too, shaved
fastidiously close—the central column obtrudes, interrupted by
the cobble of the adam's apple, braced at its base by a wishbone of
tendons straining against the skin. His inhalation snores harshly
and hits bottom with an echoing phlegmy gargle, the contact of
breath and destroyed tissue as liquid as well water echoing to a
dropped stone, followed by the hoarse slow shallow exhalation,
amplified by his slack throat almost to a roar. She bends close
and says, "I'm here. I'm right with you, Daddy." After a long
lapse he takes another breath, *takes*, that's the word, it's never
been truer, the breath grabbed from the air of the world he is
forsaking, dragged in through parched lips incised with minute
cuts, sucked down to the lungs drowning in the still-wide chest.
Then, nothing. Can you die on an in-breath? She leans close
to the face silence has seized, to the parted lips. She holds her
breath with him, but he outlasts her.

About the Author

Elizabeth Tallent is the author of the story collections *Honey, In Constant Flight*, and *Time with Children*, and the novel *Museum Pieces*. Since 1994 she has taught in the Creative Writing program at Stanford University. She lives on the Mendocino coast of California.